ONE DAY YOU'LL LEAVE ME

A NOVEL

BY DEBRA FLORES

For Sam

CHAPTER ONE

My mother died when I was fourteen years old.

It was in the summer of 1985, and it was right out of the blue. There was no adjustment period, no prolonged illness. No time to get used to the idea of being a kid without a mother. One day she just grabbed her keys and walked out of the door, off to buy a pair of shoes or pick up some dry cleaning maybe, I don't know. She didn't tell me. An hour later she was lying in her mangled tiny Ford Escort on the highway, lifeless. Gone forever.

I had to sit on our brown scratchy sofa alone, for forty-five minutes, with two police officers hovering over me until our next-door neighbor could track my father down and bring him home.

"Do you understand what that means? That your mother is dead?" the female officer asked me in a soothing voice, after I took the news stoically and didn't break down into hysterical sobs.

Of course I knew what it meant, I was fourteen years old.

She put her arm around my shoulders and rubbed at my arm. "She might be in shock, poor thing." Her partner nodded his head sympathetically.

Maybe she thinks I'm so out of it I can't even hear her.

My hearing is fine.

My mother's dead. I get it.

I also got that she expected me to cry. If not big heaving

sobs, at least a tear or two. But I just didn't have it in me.

What can I say? I was trained not to cry so I didn't cry.

My mother would have been proud.

When I was seven, a stray cat wandered into our backyard while I was munching on a ham sandwich and reading a picture book on our patio. He looked like he was on his last leg. Scrawny, a large bald patch near his crooked disjointed tail, and a very noticeable limp. I immediately scraped off as much mustard as I could from the ham and fed him every last bit, then ran in the house for more. It probably wasn't a good idea to stuff him the way I did, he immediately threw up, but I couldn't help it. You see a hungry animal, you feed it. And he was hungry.

Of course he stayed, and of course I kept right on feeding him. Within a week or two, my newfound cat friend (who I named Leo) had perked up. Both his bald spot and limp were slowly diminishing, his ribs weren't as visible, and his meow came back. My mother wasn't very happy with the situation, she made a show of being upset about it, but, to my surprise, a couple of cans of cat food started appearing in our pantry each week. Yet still, when, six months later, one of the neighborhood dogs got loose and killed him, instead of sympathy when I broke down crying, what I got was contempt and disdain.

"It was a cat. Do you know how ridiculous you look crying for a stupid cat?"

My mother always said crying was only for deaths. I guess that didn't include deaths of felines you'd grown to love.

It took me a while to learn but eventually I did. Displays of emotion, as far as my mother was concerned, were distasteful and unseemly.

"Quit cackling like that, you sound like a clown." When I laughed a little too loudly for her liking.

"It's a movie, stop that nonsense, or else flip it off if you can't handle it." When I'd had the nerve to yelp at a scary scene.

"Go to your room, we're not going after all. Once you learn to behave correctly, we'll see." When I'd whooped, clapped my hands and jumped up and down at the prospect of visiting Six Flags Over Texas.

By the time I was ten I no longer had to try to contain my emotions, the "correct" way to react now just came naturally to me. The teacher announces we'll be taking a field trip to the zoo next week? You remain in your seat and don't make a sound. You can nod, if you'd like, that's okay, but to act like the untrained monkeys around you? Stomping and cheering and shrieking? Unacceptable. I was starting to see my mother's point of view.

My father wasn't much help. He was away on business most of the time. Or that's what I was told anyway. It wasn't until I was nearly eleven that I began to realize dentists don't actually make out of town house calls. What was he supposed to be doing? Filling cavities in a kitchen? Extracting wisdom teeth while his patient watches *Family Ties* on the living room TV? It was a year after that that I realized what it meant.

If my mother had a problem with it, that he was home only a few days out of the month, she hid it well. Then again, she had to didn't she? Unless she wanted to be a hypocrite and actually display some sort of emotion. But really, I don't think she cared. When I think about it I can't recall there ever being any sort of tension in the house whenever he was there. I never sat, shoulders scrunched up, at the breakfast table, ready to duck at any moment in case pots and pans started flying across the room. No, she would cook the eggs, cook the bacon, then slide some on to my plate, some on my father's, and then leave the kitchen. Leave me to sit there with my silent father as he drank a cup of coffee beside me.

Maybe she'd gotten so good at hiding her emotions she

just didn't have them anymore.

I never got to that point.

But she'd done her damage.

And it went beyond that.

Because affection requires emotion doesn't it? Therefore, affection, along with crying, complaining, laughing, pouting, all of it, was out.

As a kid, I remember being jealous all the time. Of my friends. Not because they had better clothes than I did, or the newest and coolest toys. That they got cable the year it came out. I had all the material things I needed, or wanted, most of the time. No, I was always jealous of my friend's mothers. It was so bad I used to fantasize about getting hurt somehow while at someone else's house. Nothing too extreme. A scraped knee or a twisted ankle. But I would have been okay with a broken bone too. Just to have someone fuss over me. Even if just for ten minutes.

"Are you telling me your mother never, not once, hugged you? Ever? As in never? That's impossible."

"That's what I'm saying."

No one ever believed me. They thought I was exaggerating.

And she wasn't even content to make my life miserable when she was alive, she kept right on at it after she was gone.

If she hadn't chosen to get behind the wheel after drinking half a bottle of vodka, I wouldn't have had to be sent off to live with relatives who were essentially strangers to me. My father made a half-hearted attempt at being a single father for a few months before deciding to make a clean break from his old life. I visited him and his new wife and baby twice, in Hawaii, before I turned eighteen. Then there were phone calls, then letters. Then nothing. I haven't heard from him in three years. I don't even know where he lives these days.

For four years I hopped around from relative to relative. An uncle in Austin. A cousin in New Mexico. My aunt Jane in Alabama. My grandparents, also in Alabama.

That was a treat. My grandfather, who didn't see eye to eye with my mother (big surprise there), was an ex-cop who'd been kicked off the force. I was never told why he'd been fired but I could take an educated guess. He was a big man who liked to punch things. Mostly people. I couldn't understand how my mother could have grown to be such an emotionless woman when her father was nothing but a raging ball of emotions.

Years later, when I was twenty and having had plenty of time to reflect on just what a sad and apathetic woman my mother was and how it had affected me, my aunt tried to give me one of those she-wasn't-always-like-that sob stories.

Something about her father not allowing her to marry her high school sweetheart or something to that effect, I didn't pay much attention. It wasn't my fault she was a teenager back in the stone ages, back when your parents could dictate who you would or wouldn't marry. And anyway, what difference did it make who she married? As if that excused her behavior.

"You need to cut her some slack," my aunt Jane had said. "She did the best she could. She made sure you were fed and clothed didn't she? You didn't freeze to death did you?"

"They do the same for inmates on death row. That doesn't make prison guards great parents to the inmates does it?"

"You call me, when you figure it out. After you've hit a few bumps in the road and life smacks you upside the head. Because it will. You think it has already," she said, and laughed, sending a cloud of putrid cigarette smoke in the air, "but just you wait and see. One day you'll wish she was your biggest problem."

It took me twenty-four years to finally understand what she meant.

CHAPTER TWO

San Antonio, Texas 2010

When I walked into the cafeteria that day, Friday July 9th, 2010, I was thinking about presents and the fact that I hadn't bought one for the party I would be attending the following day.

I'd put it off and now it was too late. I could have ordered nearly anything I wanted to online and had it delivered straight to my door in two day's time. Now I was going to have to go to an actual brick and mortar store after work. Like it's 1987.

How barbaric.

The television, mounted on the wall just beside the entrance, was on, as always. I only glanced at it as my assistant James and I, walked past it. The news. Same old, same old. Politics, crime, weather. Right now one of our senators, something something Yates was speaking into a bank of microphones while standing outdoors on the steps of some important building or other. Her white hair was being whipped around her head by the wind as she leaned far over the podium in front of her and jabbed her finger at the camera accusingly.

"She must have had men crawling all over her when she was younger," I'd told my friend Janice a few years back.

"Yeah, I can imagine. For an older woman, hell for any woman, she's striking. And that screw-you-I'm-in-charge-here attitude doesn't hurt either. Very alluring."

I couldn't disagree with her on the striking part, but I'd have to take her word for it on the attitude. Politics wasn't my thing.

"...over six hundred thousand missing persons cases in the U.S. alone. What we need..."

That's all I caught her saying as we passed by before we were out of hearing range only five feet away. The volume was set on low, as always, and the closed captioning was on, as always. In case anyone was interested. No one ever was.

Who needs TV when you have a smartphone?

By the time we made it to the back of the large room, to one of only two empty tables left, the TV and thoughts of presents and parties, had left my mind completely.

"Walter wants those spreadsheets on his desk by the end of the day," James said, looking at his phone one last time before setting it on the table along with the pile of folders he'd carried in with him.

"Well then Walter's going to be disappointed." James nodded with a grin. He didn't like Walter any more than I did.

Usually, if I don't skip lunch entirely, I'll have something at my desk, a chicken sandwich or veggie wrap delivered from one of the nearby restaurants, or I'll have James bring something up from this same cafeteria. But that's rare, having him fetch me lunch. It didn't sit well with me, it felt too close to the old female secretary having to make the coffee scenario for my liking. It didn't matter that the roles were reversed, it still bothered me.

But today, because I was hungry enough that skipping lunch wasn't an option and I wanted something a little more substantial than a few vegetables stuffed into a wafer thin tortilla, I accompanied James downstairs.

He didn't remark on it, but I knew he must have thought it was strange. We hadn't, in the three years he'd been with the company, ever had lunch together even though we got along well. We talked about things other than business, but not much, and never too personal. How's your daughter adapting to high school? Have you tried the new restaurant at The Quarry? This heat is unbearable isn't it?

And today was no different. As soon as we sat to eat, folders splayed out between our two trays, we began discussing the upcoming advertising campaign. Or tried to. We didn't have to shout to one another but it still took some concentration to hear each other over the usual generic busy cafeteria noises. The clunking sound of ice being dispensed into paper cups at the soda fountain. The clanging of pots and pans coming from the kitchen. The hum of several conversations taking place all at once and all around us. The sound of forks and knives scraping and clanking against ceramic plates. Someone dropped an empty tray on the hard-tiled floor, cursed mildly, then picked it up and chucked it, noisily, on to the return counter. The cash register was beeping away, the cash drawer opening and closing.

So it should have been impossible really. To hear anything from the front half of the room, much less the TV. Even if it were turned up beyond the first one or two bars on the volume graph. My back was to it. There were at least nine or ten tables between it and where I was sitting, each nearly full with people eating and chatting away.

And yet, halfway through the lunch hour, as I sat, one hand holding a fork, the other rifling through a small stack of papers James had just slid in front of me, I heard it.

"All I need are the contracts, which should be deliv-"

"Shh," I said, cutting James off and raising a finger in the air.

Music. I heard four beats before I snapped my head to the

side.

I closed my eyes, trying to isolate the sound, trying to filter out all the laughter, a ringtone from someone's phone, the shouts for more bread coming from the kitchen seeming to echo and reverberate around the room as if it were an empty cavern.

A few beats more and then the music was accompanied by a voice. It was a girl's voice, or a woman's, I couldn't be sure. The fork I'd been holding rattled as it landed on the plate in front of me.

"Karen?"

"Shh!"

I caught the first few words of the lyrics before I opened my eyes and twisted in my seat to face the TV. I tried, in vain, to catch the rest of the words, but it was useless. Everyone seemed to have raised their voices up a notch all at once. On the TV only a single white note showed up on the screen in a small black box, no closed captioned lyrics.

Why is everyone shouting? Why now?

I stood and made it halfway across the room, my eyes never leaving the screen, before I had to stop and lean against a wall. The music was still there, I could hear the rhythm of it, but the girl's words were drowned out by the voiceover.

As far as I could tell, it was a commercial for an Alzheimer's drug. A rapid series of different scenes of a couple through various stages of their life. Young, on the beach, pants rolled up and frolicking in the surf while holding hands. A wedding scene followed by a scene of an infant in a crib being watched over while it slept. A living room was next, the now middle-aged couple with their three children plus a dog on a couch. And on and on until it cuts to an elderly couple with pained expressions on their faces as they sit in a doctor's office. The scenes play again, through the eyes of the old man, but this time the faces of his wife and children are blurred and distorted. The implication being that he's lost his memories of them.

There wasn't anything special about it, it was pretty formulaic, still, when it was over, and the music faded away, my throat felt constricted, and my eyes had begun to sting.

Getting teary-eyed over a commercial? And at work? I had half a second to feel like a fool before I felt a hand on my back.

"Karen? What's going on? Are you okay?"

I turned my head to the side and saw the bottom half of a black skirt, legs, black heels. One of my hands was still braced against the wall, the other one was on my knee. When did I hunch over?

"Yes...yeah, I'm fine."

"You sure?"

When I straightened up I found Margaret, who works in accounting (I think), staring at me, her hand still resting on my back. The noise level all around me seemed to have gone down appreciatively and when I turned to my side I could see why. At least half of the people in the room had come to a halt to stare at me as well. Some of them with forks halfway to their mouths. Embarrassing.

"Yes, I'm okay," I said, nodding, even managing to give her a weak smile.

"Cafeteria food? Looked like you were going to be sick there for a second," she said, with a smile of her own, but a nervous one. Like she was worried she might have to step back quickly in order to avoid getting splatter on her shoes.

"What?"

"You were clutching at your stomach."

Was I?

"Oh. Yeah, maybe."

"Are you sure you're okay? You look a little pale."

"Is everything okay?" James asked from behind the two of us.

Lord, if my mother were here right now. *"Get it together and stop acting like an idiot."* She always did hate spectacles.

"Yes, James, everything's fine."

Several more people were now looking away from their plates and their phones, to see what all the fuss was about. Now that I was gathering a crowd.

I straightened up even more, feeling the blood rush to my face. I didn't know if it was anger at the thought of my mother or just embarrassment that did it, but at least it would help my color.

"Yes, Margaret, I'm sure, but thank you for your concern. I haven't eaten much this week, you know, work. Must have just gotten a little light-headed." Which was partly the truth. I'd eaten just fine.

Satisfied I wasn't going to faint, vomit, or clutch at my heart and collapse, Margaret patted my back one last time, smiled again, and then started making her way back to her table. I followed James back to ours.

I could feel him watching me from the corner of his eye all the way back so I did my best to walk as steady as I could even though my legs felt both stiff and rubbery at the same time. Even though my heart was still racing, and the thin film of sweat that had popped up at the top of my spine was now turning ice cold.

I must have done a decent enough job. Everyone who'd still been eyeing me warily went back to their salads and sandwiches or their phones and conversations. James sat but continued to watch me as I took the seat opposite him again.

"I'm fine, James. You can relax. Why don't we get back to it?" My voice had lost its quiver, gained back some of its usual assertiveness. He nodded, unfurrowed his eyebrows, picked up his burger and took a bite, then started to rummage through the files in front of him again.

"And I'm sorry," I said, clearing my throat and picking up my fork, not that I was in the slightest bit hungry anymore, it was just for show. "I didn't mean to cut you off like that."

He chewed and shook his head. No problem.

I stabbed a spear of broccoli, tapped it on the plate, then set the fork down.

"So as I wa-"

"Did you hear-"

He looked up, smiled, then gestured with his hand, you first.

"Did you hear the song on that commercial just now?"

Another shake of his head. Another bite of his burger.

"None of it? Are you sure?"

He swallowed then answered. "Yes, I can't hear the TV now, even if I tried. It's too low."

"It had a peculiar beat, an old sounding beat, like a song from the fifties or sixties."

He put his burger down and wiped at his mouth with a napkin.

"One day you'll leave me."

"Excuse me?"

"Those are the first few words I caught, the first words of the song. Does that ring any bells? One day you'll leave me? Do you know of any old songs that start with those lyrics?"

"Again, I'm sorry but you're asking the wrong guy. I'm not much of a music person and when I did listen to music, back in my teenage years, it was all Metallica and Iron Maiden."

"There was something about that song," I said, turning my head to look at the TV again, as if it could jog my memory somehow. The news was back on, there was now a picture of a young kid with dark curly hair on the screen with the caption BOY MYSTERIOUSLY VANISHES FROM HOME underneath it.

"Something you want to use for a campaign?" James asked, as I turned back to him.

"No, nothing like that, I just...I had an odd feeling, when I heard it. It sounded strangely familiar. Like there was a memory attached to it...but there can't be, I know I've never heard it before. At least I don't think I ever have."

"Like musical déjà vu?"

"Yes," I said, "exactly. It was exactly like that except it was so..." I tapped the middle of my chest, my sternum, unable to express in words, even to myself, how hearing an unfamiliar piece of music had affected me.

"Okay, uh, why don't I just look it up?" He tilted his head down and reached for his phone but he kept his eyes on me. The way you do when you're in the company of an unstable person, unsure of what they'll do from one moment to the next. I was just sitting there, I wasn't pacing back and forth, mumbling to myself and pulling at my hair with both hands, but there must have been something in my expression, the look on my face, that concerned him. And, admittedly, it wouldn't take much. I keep my emotions in check, especially at work, and since James and I never socialized outside of work, he's only ever seen the straight-faced, no-nonsense side of me. This little display of emotion, coupled with what just happened, must seem like a mini mental breakdown to him.

"No James, it's okay, finish your meal. It's not important, and it's not work related. Not your job."

"I don't mind," he said. It was something to do. If he could find the song, give me a title, maybe I'd snap my fingers and say 'Of course, there it is, I *have* heard it before, mystery solved.' and we could go back to discussing meetings and contracts.

"James, please, finish your lunch, I've already interrupted you enough. I won't even remember the song by the end of the day." I even believed that. "We'll discuss the contracts later."

He went back to polishing off his burger and fries agreeably enough while I pushed the food around my still nearly full plate with my fork, repeating those same five words over and over again in my head. After a minute I pushed the plate away from me entirely, off to the side, the smell was making me queasy. I tried to trick my brain by clearing it of everything, then thinking of the music first, the beginning beats to the song, and then, just as if it were actually playing, the words. I thought if I did that, the next one or two lines would just roll out naturally. That is, if I *had* ever heard the song and they were lodged in my brain somewhere. But no, nothing.

By the time James had finished eating I was no closer to figuring it out.

He stood, took both of our trays back to the kitchen area, then returned.

"Who's that man at that table over there?" he asked, as he sat once again.

"Hm?"

"That man, sitting two tables down from us."

I looked up at him, forcing myself to refocus. After ten minutes of staring off into nothing while drumming my fingers on the tabletop, thinking, everything had gone fuzzy.

He had his head turned partway to his right so I followed his gaze.

"No idea, why?"

"I've never seen him before."

I took another quick glance at the man he was referring to. "Neither have I but he looks young, probably a new hire. Judging by the suit, the look, I'd say he's in sales."

And trying to make a good impression, I thought.

The majority of the people in the room were wearing business attire, myself and James included, but not all. This building was mainly corporate offices but we did have a retail store on the first floor that sold our line of athletic clothing and shoes which meant among the suits and ties, the blazers and high heels, there were also a few younger people, in their late teens or mid-twenties, both male and female, dressed in jeans, t-shirts, and sneakers. Not a look I particularly cared for. Call me old fashioned or stodgy, but I believed, no matter where you worked, no matter what job you performed, you should at least attempt to appear professional. But what could you do? Even the CFO, who was sitting at the table directly across from us, had shed his suit jacket and loosened his tie.

However, the man James had pointed out, sitting ramrod straight in his chair, alone, a cup of steaming coffee sitting in front of him, was dressed and groomed immaculately. A crisp dark grey suit, obviously expensive and well-tailored, fit him perfectly. He looked tall, he was slim, his hair was so perfectly cut, the part on the side so razor sharp it almost looked fake. Like a Ken doll.

"He doesn't look right," James said. He'd turned back to face me but his eyes darted back to his right once or twice.

It was true he did stand out somewhat. He was the only one in the room sitting alone, the only one not talking, and the only one who seemed not to be moving at all. His cup of coffee sat on the table in front of him untouched, his hands rested motionless on his lap. If he had been staring straight ahead you could have mistaken him for a mannequin. But he wasn't, his head, the only part of him, it seemed, that wasn't in perfect alignment with the rest of his body, was tilted slightly to his right and down, the expression on his very handsome smooth face looked pensive, and even a little mournful.

"Right how? He looks...troubled, to me. Maybe his day isn't going quite as he hoped. As I said, he looks young, doesn't even look like he needs to shave every day. Might be his first corporate job. Perfectly normal to be a little freaked out."

"No. No, it's not just that. Although his pretty looks are a little off-putting aren't they?" James asked, turning down the corners of his mouth. "Almost makes him look like he's made out of plastic. But that's not what's bothering me. He wasn't here when we walked in. And I didn't see him come in after us."

Anybody else and I would have waved my hand through the air dismissively. You're being silly. But this was James.

The first day he and I met he knocked on my office door, came in, introduced himself, curtly, shook my hand and then refused to sit down when I offered him a seat in front of my desk. Said he preferred to stand, thank you. He was older than I was, thirty-nine to my thirty-five at the time, and he was a man, working for a woman. I took it as a power play.

I'd seen plenty of them over the years, men who oh so subtlety suggest you should take the lunch orders since women have superior memories and handwriting, a dig disguised as a compliment. Or 'Would you mind making the coffee? Not because you're a woman, of course, it's just that all of us guys are too stupid to operate the machine.' with a wink to the other men in the room the second you turned your back. If you complained, you weren't tough enough for the big bad corporate world. If you made a big deal out of being referred to as hon or sweetheart, if that bothered you so much, your little feminine soft heart couldn't handle that, how the hell were you going to handle negotiations with people who weren't even on your side?

So yes, even though things of that nature had happened before, it still pissed me off, James refusing to sit and instead standing off to the side, looming over my desk. But I had only dug my fingernails into the palm of my hand and let it go. Let him think that, as the man, he was in control. He'd learn soon enough.

And as it turned out, my restraint saved me quite a bit of embarrassment. He couldn't care less that I was a woman. He refused to sit down because that would mean being in a vulnerable position. His back to the door.

He'd served two tours in Afghanistan and the last one had cost him his leg. He never sat with his back to any door. He scanned every room, every rooftop, every parking lot, every window, everyone, wherever he went, whoever he was with. He'd once spotted a man standing on the roof of the twelve-story building next to ours from my window within three seconds of entering the door. He pointed him out to me, or tried to, I couldn't see a thing. He gave me exact coordinates. Fifth window from the right, next to the antenna. Still nothing. It wasn't until the figure moved that I finally spotted him. James worked out that the man was wearing blue overalls and was working on the antenna, so not a sniper, and relaxed.

"How did you see that? He was perfectly still."

"That chair is perfectly still," he said, pointing at the chair he'd refused to sit in that day, "but you can still see it can't you?"

Not a great analogy, but to him, probably perfectly clear.

So I didn't *not* believe him, that the man who was still sitting without any movement hadn't been in the room when we walked in, I'm sure he wasn't. James doesn't miss those sorts of things, but to say he hadn't seen him come in after us, well...

"Are you trying to say he just popped up out of thin air?"

"No, of course not. It's just disconcerting, that's all. I don't know how I missed it, him entering the room without my being aware of it."

Maybe he came in during my little freak out, I thought, but I wanted that whole embarrassing situation to fade from his mind as quickly as possible so I said nothing.

"Should we be concerned? Do you think he's dangerous?" I asked. (Ah, the wonderful post-9/11 days, where everyone is suspect.) But, in my defense, he looked more than just disconcerted when he turned to look at the man once again. Not fearful, I wouldn't say that, it was more the way you'd look if you were seeing something that doesn't quite make sense. Something that messes with your equilibrium. Like a very convincing and disorientating optical illusion. Or staring into a mirror that's directly facing another mirror. Like staring off into eternity.

"No," he said, finally. "No, I don't think he's dangerous. There's just something a little off about him."

I glanced over at the man just one more time, quickly, before putting him out of my mind. I trusted James's intuition wholeheartedly. If he said he wasn't dangerous, I believed him.

But perhaps I should have paid attention to the "there's something off about him" bit a little more closely than I did.

CHAPTER THREE

For the next hour, after returning to my office, I tried to get back to work. But how could I? That song. That song wouldn't leave my mind. No matter how many times I tried to shake it out, to concentrate on the memo I was composing, it would last for all of five minutes before I found myself staring off into space or at the corner of my laptop instead of the screen, my hands splayed out on the keyboard, unmoving, as the music played on a loop in my head like an old damaged 45 vinyl record that keeps skipping back to the beginning. Four beats, those five words, then back again, complete with the hissing and crackling sounds hipsters swear make music sound better.

It was useless. Until I found out what the hell the song was and why it was boring a hole in my head, I wasn't going to get anything done, so I gave in and pulled up YouTube on the screen in front of me.

I typed in the words "one day you'll leave me" and the name of the drug, Novmentis, into the search bar and hit enter.

I thought I was going to have to do a little more digging than that. Right at the top of the page, there it was. The thumbnail was a picture of the old white-haired man from the commercial with a distressed look on his face. It was so easy I almost felt disappointed. As if I had been robbed of that feeling of triumph when you finally find something that's hard to locate or solve a problem you have to work hard at for hours to figure out.

I was just about to click on it when I noticed the picture beneath it.

A black and white one of a young woman, her lips parted slightly as she, presumably, sings into a small microphone. The title to that video was "One Day You'll Leave Me - Judy Paige, 1964". Without thinking about it, I clicked that thumbnail instead.

After a second or two of a blank screen, the black and white image of what looks like a stage in a large cavernous room appears and then a girl, or a woman, emerges from somewhere off to the side, walking towards the camera and a microphone stand. It's apparent she's nervous. As she walks she looks down to the ground for a moment, then back up, she swallows, licks her lips, she scans the room, or stadium, first to her left, then to her right. Just before she reaches the stand, and the music starts up, she seems to spot someone in the unseen audience in front of her and locks eyes with them. She smiles at whoever it is and gives them a little wave before she takes the microphone in her hand.

For the next two minutes and twenty-two seconds I couldn't be sure if I even breathed.

That feeling of familiarity hit me again, except this time it's a hundred times stronger.

I have to have heard it before. Had to. 1964. Maybe my father or mother used to play it in the house when I was a young child and I've just forgotten? That didn't seem very likely though, there was very little, if any, music played in that house. Perhaps it was used in the soundtrack of a movie? That seemed feasible. Background music you don't necessarily pay attention to but it still enters your subconscious mind. I must have watched that movie, heard the song, at some point in my life when something big was going on, some important event in my life and my brain connected the song to that particular memory?

Yes, I was grasping.

I had to.

Because there was no other explanation for what I was feeling.

The first thing that struck me, as she began to sing, was how extraordinarily beautiful this Judy Paige was. Painfully beautiful, in fact. The most striking of her features were her eyes. A green so pale and clear that they looked translucent, like water. The kind of eyes that, if you were to see them in a modern picture, you'd automatically think Photoshop. Cynical, I know, but hey, we live in cynical times.

I wondered how old she was. She looked young but I had no way of gauging exactly how young. It's difficult, trying to determine the age of people in images from the past isn't it?

My father once showed me pictures of his mother, my grandmother, and asked me how old I thought she was at the time they were taken. I looked at the picture, at my grandmother sitting alongside her sisters and brothers with her frumpy dress, thick stockings, and bulky old lady shoes. I looked at her unsmiling face underneath her odd over-sized drooping hat and was confident when I said she was forty. Maybe late thirties. My father had chuckled and told me she was fourteen. I didn't believe it, not until I saw the year 1926 written on the back of the photo and did the math. I remember feeling sad about that. How a teenager, a young teenager at that, could look so morose. To me she looked as if she'd seen seventy years of hardship and was asking whoever it was behind the camera to put her out of her misery, quickly. My father assured me that that wasn't the case, it's just the clothes, he'd said, the style, and people didn't smile for family portraits back then. It still made me sad.

This was a little like that, only not to that extreme. It was 1964, not 1926, but still, the makeup, the hair, the outfit, all outdated and old-fashioned, made it hard to judge. What she was wearing, a knee length skirt, low heels, and a long sleeved form-fitting jacket that covered everything but the very top of her neck, wouldn't have looked out of place on a sixty-year-old woman sitting on a pew at church. Even the color of the outfit, pale yellow, was subdued and tame. Her hair, brushed back at the forehead and curled outwards and upwards at the ends, reminded me of pictures I'd seen of Jackie Kennedy before her husband's assassination. Hard to imagine a pop singer on stage these days wearing something a First Lady might wear to an inauguration, but there it was.

Not that the clothes, the makeup, or the hair looked horrible, they didn't, they were just way more conservative than my 21st century brain was used to seeing on someone so young.

And none of that really mattered anyway.

Because above her beauty, above her charming smile and dimples, above those amazing eyes, was her performance. You couldn't look away from it. *I* couldn't look away from it.

If she had been nervous at the prospect of singing live before an audience, in front of the camera, and I believe she was, the moment she began to sing, that nervousness vanished. I can't say she had an extraordinary voice, it sounded young and untrained. It was unpolished. But my God, did she make up for it with her conviction. She had a young voice but it was powerful. She didn't have today's technology to help her out there, auto-tune and amplifiers, or whatever it is singers use these days, only a comically small microphone with an actual cord that disappeared behind a curtain behind her. The band, playing somewhere off camera, was loud, and the crowd in front of her, which you couldn't hear when she started to sing, began to cheer halfway through the song, even louder than the band played. And yet, even then, her voice soared above it all.

I could see why the audience was going crazy. I could feel it. It was the pure joy she exuded as she sang, it was infectious. The song wasn't an upbeat one, it was rather sad, a ballad about losing someone you love, and probably not meant to be delivered in such a joyful way but she made it work somehow. I knew that no matter what had happened before in her life, for those two minutes and twenty-two seconds, she was happy, probably happier than she'd ever been. This is what she was meant to do.

The song ends, the music stops, and the audience, still unseen, erupts in a roar as she graciously bows and waves and thanks everyone, twice.

I sat there for at least five minutes afterward, motionless, just staring at the now still screen, stunned at what I'd just seen. And there were two very powerful but competing thoughts running through my head the entire time. One, that I wanted to, no, *needed* to, watch the video again, immediately. And two, that I never wanted to see it again, ever.

There was a quick rap at the door and then James poked his head into the office.

"I have those contracts if-" He stopped midway when he finally looked up at me and not the paperwork in his hands.

"What's up? What's the matter?"

"I have to go."

I closed the laptop and grabbed my purse from the bottom drawer of my desk.

"Did something-"

"James, please, I'll be in early Monday if anything else needs doing before the meeting but right now I'm leaving."

"Yes, ma'am."

I'm never going to live this down.

First that ridiculous scene in the cafeteria, and now this?

At least four people had seen me storming out of there. Only James had seen me actually crying but the rest had to have seen the after effects, the red eyes, or the...no, please don't tell me I smeared my mascara. I checked the rear view mirror. No. Good. That would have been a disaster. Still, storming out of the office early? I don't storm out of places, I'm not a stormer. And I don't leave early. That alone is going to raise questions. If anything, I always stayed late. There was always something else to do. One more report to look over, one more memo to write.

If he thought I was having a slight meltdown earlier, I could just imagine what James was thinking right about now. A full-fledged nervous breakdown. It's the only explanation. I was crying. In public. At work.

There has to be some logical explanation, I thought, as I left the ramp and merged onto the busy highway. Could I blame it on stress? Didn't seem likely. The upcoming campaign? Nope. I was good at what I did, I never stressed about work. I had a great career, no kids to worry about, financially secure, no health problems, no relationship falling apart. Single, yes, but I wasn't bummed about that. Not really. I had friends, I dated from time to time. I was happy with my life. I was. Wasn't I?

Of course I was.

Then what? Why would watching a video of a singer who I'd never even heard of before cause me to break down like that? And why would it make me feel, while watching it and afterward, both happy and sad at the same time? And not just sad, sad doesn't cause you to act the way I did. Sad is the last day of summer. Or when you go to the fridge for that Reese's Peanut Butter Cup you remember stashing in the freezer the week before and realizing you ate it two days ago. That's sad. This was not. This was an aching emptiness. An almost gut-wrenching feeling of loss and sorrow. And how does that make sense?

A car blared its horn behind me. I was driving too slow. Whoever it was lost patience before I could pick up my speed and changed lanes, then zoomed past me on my right. When I turned to watch them pass, the billboard hovering above the side of the highway caught my attention. It was one of those changing digital ones, that, when I turned to look at it, was a black and white image of a young woman holding a naked pudgy baby in her arms. I caught it right before it changed. It was too quick for me to make out what it was the woman and her baby were hawking before it switched over to a color picture. A close-up of another woman, only her blue eyes and part of her nose visible, who was wearing rimless glasses. The words TWO PAIR ONLY $99! in bright red letters blinked on and off to her left.

Seeing that, the image changing from greyscale to color, triggered something else in my mind, something else that didn't make any sense.

The video I'd seen was in black and white.

Why would I think her eyes were green? How could I know she was wearing yellow.

CHAPTER FOUR

But I had to check didn't I? I just had to go and check.

Ten minutes after arriving home, just long enough to kick off my heels, pull off my skirt, and change into something more comfortable, I was sitting on my couch, laptop in front of me.

I pulled up the same video, just to make sure it really was in black and white. Again, grasping, but you never know. Maybe my mind was playing tricks on me. I'd read 1964 in the title and I just assumed it would be in black and white and therefore *saw* black and white.

No dice. No color anywhere.

I played it again. And again. And then four more times.

After the seventh time seeing her nervously walk out on stage, swallow, wave to someone she knew, and then begin again, singing that now familiar song, I opened up another tab. This time I did an image search.

Several of the pictures that popped up on my screen were, like the video, in black and white, but not all. I clicked on what looked like a publicity photo, a headshot, in color, and the photo enlarged, taking up almost half the screen.

Crystal clear green eyes.

Coincidence. That's all. Only coincidence. There are only so many colors eyes can be. Brown was off the table, they were too light. What was left after brown? Green, blue, maybe hazel. I had an over thirty-three percent chance of guessing the correct color. A one in three shot, that's hardly noteworthy. So I dismissed it.

I closed that tab down and went to her Wikipedia page instead because I was curious. What had become of her? Why had she not gone on to become a household name? She was obviously talented and the crowd loved her, surely that one concert or show couldn't be the only thing she'd ever done, could it?

No, as it turned out, it wasn't.

Once upon a time she was one of the most famous singers in the country.

Her name was Judith Lynne Paige, stage name Judy Paige, born May 10, 1945. I thought the name Judith fit better than Judy. Judy sounded too cutesy for her grown up conservative look but maybe that was a sixties thing. Johnny, Connie, Patsy, Bobby, Chubby. Made sense.

Just underneath her date of birth, was her date of death. October 18, 1991.

Dead. She's dead.

I pressed the tips of my index fingers to the corners of my eyes, willing myself to keep it together. My mother's voice was ringing in my head again. *The one time you should have cried you didn't. You don't cry when I die, but you're about to cry over the death of a woman you didn't even know and who died almost twenty years ago? Can you not see how ridiculous you look? A grown woman, crying over the death of a stranger. Asinine.*

That helped. Feeling anger helped. It kept the tears from falling.

I inhaled deeply a couple of times, called my mother a few names under my breath, then continued reading.

It was a small plane crash. A sudden burst of bad weather on an otherwise clear day. Only forty-six years old. So damned young. Too young. If she'd lived she'd still only be sixty-five right now. Even that was too young to die.

I was surprised to see she'd been born and lived all of her life not too far from here. A town right on the southern edge of Dallas by the name of Leyfant. Never heard of it. Why hadn't she moved to New York? Or Los Angeles? Isn't that where famous people migrate to?

Underneath that information was a listing for her spouse, or partner.

"No way." I said it aloud, to the empty room. "No way."

Sharon Sauer. (1981-1991; Paige's death)

She was gay.

Why does that matter? It's 2010, who the hell cares if you're gay or not, we've moved past that, legal gay marriage is a thing now. Not in all states, no, but it's only a matter of time. I give it another few years and even Texas will jump on board. It matters because she was gay in the mid sixties. I grew up gay in the eighties and that was hell enough, I could only imagine what kind of experience she had not only being gay during that time but famous on top of it all. That must have been a special kind of hell. Although, I thought, maybe she was one of those women who don't figure out they're gay until much later, ala Meredith Baxter? Which is a mystery to me, I knew when I was five, knew it instinctively, but hey, if they say it happens, it happens. Who am I to question it?

If I'd been curious to find information on her before stumbling on to this little piece of data, it had now tripled in intensity.

And that's how it began.

This obsession that would take over my life. An obsession that shouldn't have happened at all. I don't know how that music cut through the noise of the cafeteria, how I heard it. But somehow it did, it had. Would I have heard it eventually? At home watching TV at a louder volume maybe? Perhaps. Perhaps not. I don't know.

Many, many, years later I will still wonder about it.
What if I hadn't?
But why ponder questions we'll never have answers to?
The fact is, I did hear it.
And this is what happened because I did.

I didn't eat, I didn't drink, I didn't move from my couch for hours. I read, I looked at pictures, I watched more videos.

The show I'd seen at the office is what shot Judy Paige into stardom. She hadn't even been scheduled to perform that day but one of the acts became unavailable on short notice so she took the spot. Unknown, not signed to a record label, just filler, basically. But when nearly all of the teenagers who'd been at that concert suddenly started calling radio stations asking if they could please play "One Day You'll Leave Me", the record companies took notice and within two weeks she had been signed to a record deal. A record was made and sent to nearly a hundred of the top radio stations across the U.S. and her song jumped to number one on the billboard charts five weeks later. She went, from total obscurity, to selling out records in a very short time. In a matter of four or five weeks. Unheard of today.

For almost three years she was the "it" girl. Several hits in the top ten, though she never again hit number one. (Music critics opined that had it not been for The Beatles, she would have had at least four or five number ones, but hey, The Beatles were The Beatles.) And there was at least one nonprofessional critic who thought the same. A comment on YouTube from someone who sounded a bit unhinged. THOSE FUCKING ASSWIPE BEATLES SCREWED HER OUT OF A LONGER CAREER! Lord, that was forty years ago, calm it down.

She made several appearances on shows like Ed Sullivan, American Bandstand, Hullabaloo, Mike Douglas. She toured Australia, England, Italy, France. She appeared in movies but only to sing. A weird quirky thing they used to do back then, I guess. Hey, I know! Why don't we have a scene where someone just spontaneously breaks out into song on the beach! That happens, doesn't it?

She was on top of the world. Teenage boys all across the globe had crushes on her, girls emulated her style, her hair, sang to her songs in front of mirrors holding hairbrushes in their hands at pajama parties. Her music blasted out of car windows, dorm rooms, dance halls, proms, birthday parties, you name it.

And then, after three or four years, it stopped. As quickly as she rose to fame, that's how quickly everything collapsed. Times, and the music along with it, were changing rapidly. The Vietnam War was intensifying, protest songs were becoming popular, the British invasion was taking over, Nancy Sinatra was singing about walking all over someone with nothing but a glittery shirt, panties, and boots on. An outfit that certainly wouldn't be worn by a sixty-year-old woman to church. And the hippies. The hippies were starting to emerge. Janis Joplin and Jimi Hendrix. Rock groups like The Doors and even Pink Floyd started up. No, sweet girls in grandmother approved Sunday outfits singing about boys you meet in the hallways of your high school were becoming a thing of the past.

I hunted down every video I could find of her, which, to my surprise, were very few and far between. Most were in black and white, later ones in color, but nearly all of very poor quality. Fuzzy and grainy with time stamps splashed across the middle of the screen. I searched other video hosting sites and found one or two not posted to YouTube but still of no better quality. I read every article I could find on her, and again was frustrated with how little there was. She was once the biggest selling recording artist in the country and I could now find more information on some random guy who filmed a double rainbow than I could of her. How is that fair?

I did luck out and found nearly twelve teen magazine articles some die-hard fan had scanned and uploaded to his site. Not very informative, these were articles written in the sixties for her teenage fans, but amusing. "Judy Paige Talks Make-Up!" "Vote For Your Favorite Judy Hair-Do!" "Judy Goes Shopping" And what I found even more amusing was that in nearly every one of the articles, they mention her weight. As in "The 5'4", 108 pound singing sensation Judy Paige was out on the town..." Was that a thing back then? Citing a woman's weight? When did it stop? And also, there was something screwy about the numbers. Because she was petite, she was definitely slim, but 108 pounds? No. Clearly someone was lying. I know because at 5'4" myself and at 120 pounds, I'm considered thin. At 108 I'd look emaciated. Did she lie? Or was it the writers? Maybe this was the low tech version of Photoshop and airbrushing? Just tell the public you're thinner and the power of suggestion will make you appear thinner. For the first time since I began my investigations, I laughed. And also found myself wishing I could speak to her, to find out if it was her idea to lie or the reporter's.

After reading teen magazines published almost twenty years before I'd become a teen myself, I finally had to call it quits. It was three in the morning. I was sitting in a dark room, I had to use the bathroom, and I had a headache caused by either hunger or staring at a computer screen for eleven straight hours that wasn't going to get any better on its own. Still, headache or no headache, hunger or no hunger, my brain screaming for sleep, I didn't want to quit. I felt compelled to search one more website, one more article no matter how small and insignificant, no matter that it was all just the same information repeated over and over, I felt a need to keep digging. So I did.

I clicked on one last link, hidden in the text of the page I was on that referenced that same show, without much hope.

I'd already read all there was to read about it. That was the show that gave her her big break. The one that was captured on video and the one that I'd watched now ten or twelve times. I figured it would take me right back to the video. Which I would watch again, gladly. But what popped up were three pictures, pictures I hadn't seen before on someone's personal blog. The entry was titled "Do You Remember Your First Concert?". Underneath the title was a block of text and then the three pictures. One of them was of a young man in a jacket, tie, and short shiny hair. He held a guitar in his hands and one of his feet above the ground as if the photographer had caught him mid-tap. Another was of three young black women all in matching pretty pink dresses and beehive hairdos, crowded around a microphone stand, singing, their mouths open, all three of their hands in front of them, presumably snapping their fingers.

The third was of Judy Paige, on stage, from a different angle to the video, this was taken by someone in the crowd maybe, who must have been sitting way over to the left of her. It was a full body shot. And it was in color. The first color picture I'd seen of her on that day, maybe the only color picture of her on that day that existed.

I closed my laptop without even bothering to power it off.

I had a fairly good chance of guessing her eye color. But I couldn't explain how I'd guessed, how I'd known, that her outfit was, indeed, yellow.

CHAPTER FIVE

The sound of the doorbell woke me only five hours later. Followed by pounding on the door, then more ringing, and more pounding.

"Okay," I mumbled to myself. Getting up off the couch was an ordeal, maybe hunching over a laptop for eleven hours wasn't the greatest of ideas. Nor was sleeping on the couch.

Ring, ring, ring.

"Yes?" I asked, opening my front door with one hand, my other hand rubbing at the small of my back.

The tall pudgy guy standing before me looked, there's no other way to put it, slovenly. Large loose black concert t-shirt, red shiny shorts that went down well past his chubby knees, and clunky dirty sneakers without socks. Not that I should be judging anyone on their looks at the moment. My own hair was a scraggly mess, I was still wearing the wrinkled silk shirt I'd worn to work the previous day, and even though I couldn't see them, I'm sure my eyes were puffy and red, I could feel it. They felt gritty.

The guy took me in, head to foot, then shook his head. Had three or four too many martinis last night didjya? But he went on with his spiel anyway.

"Hey, me and my buddy," he said, pointing with his thumb behind him, "are cutting lawns, wanted to know if you need yours cut." At the curb in front of my house was a large shiny grey pick-up truck with another guy, this one not pudgy, just plain fat, sitting in the passenger seat puffing away at a vaping device. The white billowing clouds he was aiming out of the window were being pushed in my direction by the breeze and I could tell by the slight scent that he was puffing on something fruit flavored. Watermelon? Mango? The debate was still out on whether vaping was safer than cigarettes or not but I could tell you definitively, that the smell was better, by a mile.

"Not at the moment," I answered, rubbing at my eyes, "but eventually, yes. Do you have a card, or a website, so I can check rates, make an appointment?" Now that my eyes had adjusted to the brightness of the morning I could see that the young man in front of me couldn't be past his teens, eighteen at most. My lawn was cut every week during the summer at the same time and by the same company I'd been using for years but if I could help out a neighborhood kid who was starting up a business, I was more than happy to.

"Nah, nothing like that yet, we're just going around asking people. So should I come back in a few days then?" he asked, looking antsy to leave now that he wasn't going to be put to work immediately.

"I don't know, what are your rates?"

"Ninety dollars."

Next door, Mr. Peters, wearing his usual Bermuda shorts and flip-flops, was eyeing the stranger at my door while he unraveled his garden hose.

"And that's for..."

A heavy sigh. "Cutting the lawn."

"Yes, I understand that, but does that include trimming and..."

"No, that's just for cutting."

"Uh huh." Ninety dollars. Ten dollars more than what I was used to paying, but again, I thought it was worth it. "And I'm assuming that's for the front and the back?"

"No, just the front. The back," he said, and looked past my shoulder, as if he could see through walls and into my back yard, "is another ninety. If it's the same size."

"You do realize that's over twice what I pay the company that does it now and they do trimming and…"

"Whatever," he said, and turned to walk away. Nice.

Halfway down my walkway he addressed Mr. Peters. "What about you pops? You need your lawn cut?"

Mr. Peters waved him away with a flick of his hand. He twisted the outdoor spigot and water gushed from the hose.

"Fucking old people," I heard the budding entrepreneur mumble to his friend before he hopped in behind the wheel of his truck and they drove away.

"Great customer service," I shouted to Mr. Peters, and chuckled. I thought it was funny.

"What's that?" he yelled, cupping his hand to his ear.

"I…nothing," I shouted back.

"What?"

He's not that old. Can't be past his early sixties. Surely you don't start losing your hearing that early do you? I tried to smooth down both the back of my hair and my shirt as best I could before making my way across my lawn toward him. It's worth a shot, can't hurt to ask.

"Good morning Mr. Peters."

"Good morning Ms. Stephens, not watering today?"

I had to stop and think why he'd be asking me that for a second. Over his shoulder, down the street was another one of my neighbors out watering his lawn and two houses down from that another, a woman, was watering hers. The water restrictions, that's it. Watering only by hand, only on certain days, and only at certain times of the day. What's next, breathing only every three minutes? Conserve oxygen?

"No sir, I think my lawn will survive."

"Once I'm done here, I'll do yours." He said it cordially enough, but I could hear an undertone of "silly women, think green grass just grows on its own" in his voice. Mr. Peters was what you'd call a bit ornery. Not mean, he wasn't mean, just one of those people who think society, culture, kids, music, grocery and gas prices, and, well, just about everything has been going down the crapper since the mid-seventies.

"That's not necessary Mr. Peters, it's fine."

He dismissed that with another flick of his hand just as he'd done with the kid.

"I'm doing mine, won't take much longer to do yours." I could do without the gruff dismissive tone, but I decided it was best just to let it go.

"Mr. Peters, do you know who Judy Paige was?"

It was like flipping a switch.

"Judy Paige?" he asked. Someone should have been here to film it. It could have sold millions of those youth-in-a-bottle snake oil serums. His back straightened, his chest puffed out, his knitted eyebrows smoothed out and lifted, the crease that normally existed between them was gone, and his smile, which I rarely saw, was so genuine it made me smile back at him. I wouldn't have been surprised to see hair start growing out of the top of his shiny pink balding head.

"I haven't heard that name in decades! Why do you ask?"

"No particular reason, I just heard her song on a commercial and it drew my interest." And now I want to know every single little thing about her. But I'm not insane. Really, I'm not.

"Is that right? A commercial for what?"

"An Alzheimer's drug, I don't remember the name." I did, but that wasn't the important thing here, was it?

"Was it Aricept?" he asked, his shoulders beginning to droop once more.

"No, no I don't think so."

"Cognex?"

"Mr. Peters." I may have raised my voice a little but at least I stopped myself from clapping my hands in front of his face. "Judy Paige?"

"Oh yes, yes," he said, and his shoulders perked right back up, "oh my, I had the biggest crush on her when I was, oh, twelve years old? Heck, every boy in my school had a crush on her. It was the eyes. Clearest green I've ever seen. You know we all fantasized about asking her out?" He threw his head back and laughed, which turned into a coughing fit. I leaned back an inch or two, until the hacking and flying spittle stopped.

"Ah, the innocent dreams of adolescent boys huh? Not that any of us stood a chance in hell. She was a young lady at the time, we were all scrawny school kids with freckles and crew cuts."

"And," I added, "she was, well, she wasn't interested in..."

He waited for me to continue with a puzzled look on his face.

"Nothing," I said, waving my hand, "please, go on." He didn't know. No need to break the man's heart. He'd probably seen the same pictures I'd seen. Judy out on the town with more than just a couple of men. Actors and singers. Her arms wrapped around their waists, theirs around her shoulders, both smiling brilliant smiles. It really must have been one of those late awakenings for her. Unless. It was all for show? Hey, look at me, boy crazy, just like all the rest of them. I imagine it would have been career suicide to say otherwise.

"I had it so bad I used to sneak my sister's teen magazines out of her room so I could see if there were any pictures of Judy in them. Waded through pages of silly stuff like how to sleep comfortably with rollers in your hair, how to talk to boys, and how to politely but firmly dissuade them from getting fresh by trying to hold your hand in a dark movie theater."

He burst out laughing again but this time, thankfully, he skipped the hacking.

"You know," he said, he lowered his voice and tucked his chin to his chest as if he'd reverted back to his twelve-year-old self, complete with flushing skin. "They once had a sort of contest, where you could vote for what kind of hairstyle Judy should go with next. One of those silly things from the past. You'd snip out a little section of the page with your choice and send it in to the magazine."

"Yes! I saw that very article!" Why I was excited about this, I don't know. Maybe because it felt like time travel - here I was talking to a man that had read something, held something in his hand almost fifty years ago that I'd read just the previous day. I somehow felt connected to that time, to her.

"Alright," he said, perplexed at my reaction. "Well, I couldn't say anything, it wasn't boy's business, of course, but oh was I mad at my sister for voting for short hair. I swore if Judy cut her hair I would never talk to her again."

"So what happened?" I asked, although I already knew, she never had short hair.

"She went with the long hair," he said, with a satisfactory smile and a wiggle of his bushy grey eyebrows.

"Lucky you."

"Oh yeah, yeah." He looked down to the ground and switched the hose from one hand to the other, there was a puddle forming at our feet.

"Did it last long? Your crush?"

"What?" Mr. Peters looked back up as if from a daze. "Oh yeah, it did. A couple of years at least, but then the Judy Paige hysteria died down, she sort of just faded away. It's a shame. As for me, I mourned for a bit, then Grace Slick came along and I forgot all about Judy. Which was a mistake," he said. "Shoulda stuck with Judy, she stayed a wholesome girl-next-door beauty. Grace Slick was part of the hippie movement. We all know how that ended. Shoulda stuck with Judy. But by that time I was nearing sixteen, hormones, and all that. Started listening to that earbleed music, can't hear a damned thing now. Nope," he said again, shaking his head mournfully. "Shoulda stuck with Judy."

He slipped back into a haze for a second and his grip on the water hose loosened. It went from watering the grass to watering my foot.

"Oh, sorry, sorry about that."

"No problem, Mr. Peters, it's just a flip-flop," I said, shaking my foot and sending water droplets flying.

"You know, I should look her up, on that computer thing. See what she's up to these days."

Not much. She's a little bit dead.

"Maybe that's not a good idea, she'd be much older now, wouldn't she? Not the young lady you remember. I think you should keep that memory instead."

He turned his mouth down and tilted his head. "Eh."

After a few more minutes of conversation, of my trying to steer him onto another topic, I thanked him for sharing his memories and for the offer to water my lawn and left him to it. Hopefully I'd veered him off the subject enough that by the time he turned off the water and wound up the hose he'd have forgotten all about Judy and his long ago crush.

I walked back to my door and into my house both happy to have learned a little more about this woman but also deeply envious of Mr. Peters. He was there to witness it, to hear her songs on the radio for the first time when they were new and fresh. What that must have been like, I could only imagine.

Inside, I managed to shower, change, and eat a banana before my laptop called me back.

I'd spent eleven hours the day before watching the same seven or eight videos over and over again. I had listened to songs that were so obscure Mr. Peters probably hadn't even heard them. Unreleased songs, bits of jingles she'd done for commercials, covers she'd done of famous songs. Anything and everything, but only up to a certain time period.

I had an aversion to reading anything or watching any videos of her past a certain time. And it wasn't just a vague feeling of uncomfortableness, of not wanting to see her past her prime, I literally averted my eyes from pictures of her past a certain age when they popped up alongside the black and white ones taken at the start of her career. It wasn't even that hard, because there seemed to be a gap of time in which there were very few pictures taken of her, or fewer, I should say. There weren't that many to begin with. So that it seemed as if she jumped from her mid-twenties straight into her late thirties or early forties. But that probably wasn't just me, I think anyone would feel for the woman. On top of the world one minute and then within a space of a few years, reduced to singing her old songs over and over again at small venues and oldie's shows. That couldn't have been a good feeling.

But I was running out of options. I'd read everything there was to read, I'd seen every video, seen every picture. Of her youth, that was.

The newer articles, the newer pictures and videos were all I had left if I really wanted to learn more about her.

So I forced myself to look, to read, to watch.

But I really wish I hadn't.

Because what I found just gutted me.

CHAPTER SIX

Something bad happened to her. Something devastating. Had to have.

The first video I clicked on was of an interview. Just her and a local small time reporter. No thrills, no frills, this was a couple of years after she'd had a hit on the radio. It wasn't even on YouTube, I had to scrounge around for it on a website that looked old and defunct. It didn't even look complete, as if the designer took a break midway through designing it and then just decided to hell with it. But the video at least had a description to it. Along with the date. November 1970.

It's a quick two minute long interview in what looks like a small nightclub. There's people milling around in the background, not paying her any mind. It's a small town on the edge of Illinois, and not even they're impressed with her. But even though clearly this was a huge step down from what she once used to do she seemed happy to do it. She's just as beautiful as ever, maybe even more so. Older, yes, from the nineteen year old superstar she once was but still only twenty-five, and still with those same crystal clear eyes and vibrant smile. She'd updated her hair, the sixties makeup was gone, and Mr. Peters was right, she hadn't gone the hippie route. She was wearing a tasteful blue and yellow sweater. If she were wearing bellbottoms, I couldn't tell, the video only shows her from the waist up. But that was enough for me to see that she looked content. Even with her career already pretty much over she doesn't seem at all down about it. She isn't morose, she doesn't look put out, that she's being interviewed by a man who looks old enough to be her grandfather and, by his own admission, did not care for pop music and had never heard any of her songs. Instead she smiles warmly at him while she answers his dull questions, she smiles at the camera, she even makes him laugh at the end of the clip. As if this new low-key life, out of the spotlight, is something she has embraced, and is even enjoying.

The next video I found was filmed only two years later.

I had to watch it in increments. It was too painful to watch all in one go.

It was one of those old variety shows. Magic acts, a juggler or two, someone spinning plates on sticks, that was considered entertainment, apparently, once upon a time. A comedian. And her.

My first thought, after I instinctively covered my mouth with my hand and tears sprang to my eyes, was that she was ill. She must have been battling an aggressive form of cancer. It's the only thing I could think of, the only illness that would cause such a dramatic change in her appearance. She was skeletal. When, years before, those articles had cited her as weighing 108 pounds I knew that couldn't be correct, that was too thin, but now, what I was seeing, was far beyond that. She didn't even weigh a hundred pounds, maybe not even ninety. At 5'4", that's probably not even very survivable. Her eyes were glazed over and dull, her smile was gone. She sang, she sang that same moving song again but so flatly she could have been singing the words to a recipe for bland food. There was no strength in her voice, none of the passion she had as a nineteen or twenty year old. The audience felt it as much as I did, the applause when she finished was lukewarm at best. She looked as if she wanted to be anywhere but under those lights and in front of that camera. But she managed to get through it, she sang her song, looking haunted and lost.

Immediately I tried to find out what happened in her life because obviously something had. Something life-changing. I was sure I'd find out she did indeed have a debilitating disease or that maybe she really was despondent about her career not being what it once was and had turned to alcohol or drugs. On second thought, no, not alcohol, not even alcoholism could change you in the way she was changed. Not that fast. Drugs though, hard addictive drugs could do it. It didn't seem like something she'd do but videos don't lie. She was in a bad way. A very bad way.

Of course I didn't have any luck. Fifty thousand videos, pictures, coffee mugs, and t-shirts of a grumpy looking cat but nothing about her. I couldn't find a thing. Either she didn't make it public, what it was she was dealing with, or there was no longer anyone around who cared. It was heartbreaking. Everyone had moved on, like Mr. Peters said. Seduced by edgier music and women starting to show some skin on stage.

I found three more videos that were just as painful to watch as the first. It was difficult to believe it was the same person. What could possibly have happened to her in such a short amount of time to change her so drastically? Whatever it was, it took years of her life. From what I could gather, from the information I could piece together, from the scant videos and pictures of her during the time, she suffered for nearly nine years before she seemed to recover. Starting in the early eighties, she gained the weight back plus a couple of extra pounds, her hair thickened back up, the shine in her eyes reappeared along with her smile. And her voice. That amazing powerful voice had regained its strength. She became a songwriter, writing for other musicians or for television and movies. She was never very successful, but, to me, she seemed happy. And while she did write songs for herself, she mostly still sang those few songs that had been hits way back in her heyday, because that's what the audience always wanted to hear.

The last video I clicked on, I knew, was it. I'd come to the end of the line. Her very last performance. I didn't want to watch it but I'm glad I did. It was one of those reunion type shows. You know the ones, several bands who are now decades past their prime, singing songs you played on your boombox when you were twelve, now grey-haired and prancing around the stage, dancing the way old people dance at weddings. It's sort of charming, but also kind of sad and embarrassing. A little cringey.

Again, I had to force myself to watch. Watch her sing a song she'd probably sung a thousand times by then, surely she must be sick of it. I know I would have been. Whether she was or not, I don't know, it didn't seem like it, but I wasn't in her head, so I can't say. Maybe it was just the performer in her. Grin and bear it.

At nineteen what made her performance amazing was her powerful voice and her ability to connect with the audience, to transfer to them the joy and excitement she felt of being onstage and being in the moment. My life and your life, she seemed to be saying to each teenager in the audience that day, is just beginning, the future is ours.

At forty-six, her voice, if it was possible, was even more powerful, but in a different way. She was older. She had decades of experience behind her. Experiences her nineteen-year-old self hadn't been through yet. The song, which is about heartbreak, about losing someone you love and being frightened you'll never be that happy again, is something her nineteen-year-old self knew nothing about. She had yet to experience profound heartbreak and loss. At forty-six, she had. She definitely had. Because she brought the house down.

The audience, a mixture of old and young, but mostly older, were all seated sedately at the beginning of the song.

They weren't disrespectful, they'd bought tickets after all, they wanted to be there obviously, but looking at them before the music started, I had the impression they were all a little disappointed. As if they were expecting their teen idols to come on stage as actual teenagers once again, not people like them, people who had aged, a little thicker around the middle, larger foreheads due to receding hairlines, people who now took the same medications for sore joints and heartburn as they did. But by the middle of Judy's song, several audience members had risen to their feet, and by the end of it, all the seats were empty. People were stomping and clapping and whistling. There were even a few wiping at their eyes.

I didn't know which version I liked better.

Sadly, only two months after that performance, she would be dead. At forty-six.

My doorbell went off again, and again, I had to rub at the small of my back as I made my way to the door. Somehow it had gone from eight in the morning, it had only been an hour hadn't it? Since I was out talking to Mr. Peters? According to my watch, no. It was now four in the afternoon.

"Why haven't you answered - whoa. Are you okay?"

Janice, one of my oldest friends, was standing on my doormat, looking exquisite as always, in a baby blue sundress with matching nail color and immaculate hair making me look like a frump in my capri pants and tank top.

"Yeah?" I said, making it into a question.

"You sure? You're not being held hostage? Blink twice for yes...or, you know, just walk out," she said, leaning over, trying to peer into the entranceway beyond my shoulder to make sure there wasn't actually a deranged escape convict lurking somewhere behind me.

"I'm fine. What's up? What are you doing here?"

"Really?"

"What?"

She raised her hands in front of her. "Megan and Rachel's party? We're supposed to be there about," she checked her watch, "now?"

"Oh wow, oh my God, it completely slipped my mind."

"You? Something slipped your mind?"

"Yeah. It did."

"What's going on?" she asked, turning her head to see what I was looking at. Which was nothing, my eyes had just wandered above her shoulder to the street, not focusing on anything. "You look like you're doped up, and are you going to let me bake out here in the sun or can I come in?"

I focused back on her.

"Yes, of course, come in."

"Seriously," she said, following me down the foyer to the couch and my laptop. "Are you okay? You don't look like...yourself."

A polite way of telling me I looked like hell. "I'm fine, I've just been up all night, working." I closed my laptop before she could take a look at the screen, which was a freeze-frame of Judy on stage, in black and white. I'd been re-watching that same video again when the doorbell rang. The first one I'd seen the day before but what seemed like months ago.

"Since when do you work on the weekends?"

"Since they sprang a large project on me late in the week."

"And you let them get away with that?" she asked, with disbelief all over her face.

"I'm not that much of a hardass, jeez," I answered, before we plopped ourselves down on the couch.

"No," she agreed, "you're not, I just don't buy it, that's all. You never bring work home with you and now you've been up all night with it and you forget about the party? And, sorry, but uh...this," she said, pointing at me from head to foot, "this is not you, this crumpled bum look. I don't think I've ever seen you look like this, and definitely never in the middle of the day."

"Well. Maybe I'm in love."

She laughed.

Rude.

"Sure honey, sure you are," she said, and patted my knee condescendingly.

"Hey! I can't fall in love?"

"You absolutely can...but not like this. You don't do this," she said, now pointing directly at my hair and wagging her finger while she did it.

"What are you..." I patted my hair. "Oh. That bad?"

"Nah, I've seen worse. Not on you, but I've seen worse. But come on, chop-chop, get up, go get dressed, put a comb through that, I'll wait."

"Oh, no. No, I'm not going," I said immediately, feeling anxious at the thought of being stuck at a party making smalltalk for hours, not being able to re-watch the videos I'd watched now dozens of times each. Not being able to continue digging for information on this woman I didn't even know existed two days ago. "I'd make you late. And I still have a lot to do."

"Okay," she said, crossing her arms across her chest. "Stop. Tell me what's really going on. This isn't about work. It's not about being in love. You look like you haven't slept at all and your hands are shaking. Have you eaten?"

I raised my hands off my lap to look at them. A slight tremble. I immediately clasped them together and set them back on my lap.

"Not since breakfast," I admitted. And only a banana. That I did not admit to.

"So are you going to tell me or do I have to drag it out of you?"

You'll have to drag it out of me, I thought. How could I explain something I didn't understand myself? And how could I try to without sounding deranged? But I was going to have to take a stab at it, I knew that. Janice wasn't going to let it go. She wasn't a nosy person, but she was a person who cared deeply about her friends. If she thought something was bothering me, she'd sit on that couch for hours, for days if need be, until I fessed up.

"Fine. But you have to promise to keep the judgment down to a reasonable level."

She dropped her eyes to the laptop on the coffee table and then back up at me with a half amused, half nervous look.

"This doesn't have anything to do with porn does it? If so, I'm out."

"No, it's about as far away from porn as you can get."

She didn't look convinced.

"No judgment," I reiterated.

"Go on," she said, waving a finger in the air.

"Okay, at the risk of sounding like a nutball, do you know who Judy Paige was?"

"No. Should I?"

No surprise.

For the next ten minutes I gave her a condensed version of the past twenty-seven or so hours. From my hearing the commercial, how I felt compelled to seek it out, how I'd hardly moved from this couch because I felt as if I had to piece together this woman's story and the more I tried the more frustrated I was growing with the lack of information.

Janice listened, no raised eyebrows, no smirks or snorts, and interrupted me only once or twice.

"So she was gay in the sixties? When she was famous?"

"I don't know, no one ever asked her. I don't think anyone cared."

And once more. "The woman she was with when she passed away, is she still alive? What was her name?"

"I don't know. That's not really important."

Of course I knew but just as I had an aversion to watching the videos of Judy as an older woman, I had an aversion to thinking about the woman she'd spent the last ten years of her life with. To put it plainly, I was jealous of her. But I kept that to myself as well.

Once it was all said and done, instead of looking at me as if I'd gone off the deep end, Janice only smiled.

"You're obsessed."

"Why are you smiling at that? It's not healthy."

"Of course it is, maybe not obsessing over a dead woman, that's probably not a great idea, but still, I think it's healthy for you. A little. Maybe it's a mini-breakthrough."

Janice knew all about my mother and how it was difficult for me, to show, or even feel strong emotions. She knew I didn't do obsessions. I never have. Even as a teenager when obsessions are the norm. I had had a couple of crushes on female celebrities back then. Michelle Pfeiffer was one. I remember thinking I had it bad back then. But what it boiled down to was watching Grease 2 whenever it came out on cable and checking the TV Guide to see if any of her other movies were going to be on. I watched Scarface two or three times, but I didn't care for the movie and my desire to see Michelle wasn't strong enough to override that. So it was a tepid obsession at most.

And later, as an adult, I never did seem to get the whole all-consuming start-of-relationship giddiness that others felt. Janice and I had had this conversation years before when I explained to her that the woman I had started seeing a few weeks before was starting to irk me a bit.

I'd met the woman, her name was Carol, at a party. We talked mostly to each other the entire night, at least four hours, but when the party ended she asked if I wanted to go get a drink somewhere else. I had turned her down. I had work the following morning.

"So you weren't really interested in her?" Janice asked.

"Yes, I was, I am. I told her we could see each other over the weekend."

"You didn't feel compelled to say the hell with getting enough sleep, I want to spend more time with this woman, now."

"But I was going to spend more time with her, over the weekend."

Janice shook her head and allowed me to go on.

"Well, we saw each other on Saturday and again on Sunday and she asked if I'd take the next two days off, she wanted to drive south, to the beach, spend a couple of days lounging around."

"And you said no."

"Well, yeah, you don't just take off of work to lounge around on a beach. We're not hobos."

"You've never felt like ten minutes is too long to spend away from someone? At the beginning of a relationship, you've never stood staring out of a front window for twenty minutes waiting, impatient for their car to pull up into your driveway?"

I thought about it for a second.

"No."

"Wow."

"Is that the way you felt when you and Melissa first started dating?"

"Oh yeah. I had it bad. I almost lost my job. I showed up late for two weeks straight, I called in sick three Mondays in a row, I went to see her on my lunch break a couple of times and then just didn't go back until the following day. Melissa actually quit her job two days after we met. She wasn't happy there anyway, and she was looking around for another position before we met, but our meeting and wanting to spend time with me made her just up and quit after two days. I'm that irresistible, I guess."

"That's ridiculous, I'm not going to quit my job because I met someone. The bank that holds my mortgage doesn't give a damn if I'm falling in love, the grocery store isn't going to let me have free food because I can't keep my hands off of a woman. And anyway, isn't it better to have like a slow-simmering sort of affection for someone? You have this big ball of overpowering emotion and it just burns out doesn't it? That can't last."

"Oh yeah, because that's what someone wants to hear, I have a slow-burning affection for you. Like a sooty dying fire."

"I don't think I like your attitude."

She grinned, then continued.

"Okay, okay, you're right, that level of passion doesn't last but it gets taken over by something else. It's what I felt for Melissa, in the beginning, and now what I feel for her is something different, but we've been together now for eight years, and I know I want to spend the rest of my life with her. Still."

I sighed. "I guess I just don't have it in me, to muster up that kind of enthusiasm. I really think my mother screwed me on this. I thought I had overcome it, I fought against it, but yeah, maybe her being such a...you know, chastising me for showing any emotions at all, maybe that has something to do with it."

"Maybe," Janice said. "Or maybe you just haven't met the right person? Maybe you do have it in you and..."

"I'm thirty-four, I think that ship has sailed. That seems more like a twenty-something thing to do."

"No. I refuse to believe that. I know you. I know you feel deeply about things, about people. Even if you have a hard time showing it. It'll happen."

But it hadn't happened. Ever. It's probably why none of my relationships ever seemed to work out. Women always seemed to think I wasn't fully committed to the relationship, that I could take it or leave it, and it wouldn't bother me either way, that I didn't really care for them. It wasn't true, I was, I did. I wouldn't go out with someone if I didn't like them. In one or two cases, I loved the person. Maybe not as passionately as they might have liked, but I thought I did. I was saddened when they decided, and it was always they who decided, that it was time to move on.

But I did start to question it myself, when we would break up and I didn't do what I think most people do these days. I didn't check their online activity. Check to see if they were dating someone else, I didn't check to see if they'd posted pictures of themselves, arms around another woman, if they were at parties having a good time while I wallowed in misery at home. Because I didn't wallow in misery. I was fine. It didn't work out, time to move on. Maybe I was just broken.

"So show me," Janice was saying to me now. "I need to see who she is, this woman that has you obsessing over her. Must be something special."

So I did. I opened my laptop, clicked replay on the video that was already on the screen. The video I didn't even need to see anymore to tell you exactly what would happen. Every gesture, every smile, every point of the finger to the audience.

"Wow," Janice said, nodding her head once the video ended, looking genuinely impressed. "I can see why she caught your attention. She's very expressive isn't she? I don't know if it's her eyes, her smile, or the way she sings that's most captivating."

"All of it."

She turned back to the computer. "I wonder what it was like for her. It couldn't have been easy, being gay then."

"Yes! Exactly. She came out to the public in '80 or '81. That was pretty damned brave don't you think? It wasn't the sixties, but still, you remember what it was like. It was horrible back then but she did it."

"What? Are you sure? I've never heard of her, never heard anyone mention her, you'd think we'd know wouldn't you? The more role models the better?"

I shrugged my shoulders. "We didn't have internet back then, how would we know? The media didn't care, her career had long since been over. And even if they did, I think they would have covered it up. She was a wholesome dimple-cheeked cute pop singer that all the boys had crushes on, it wouldn't have fit with the image of what people thought lesbians were supposed to be at the time. We were sick, perverted, twisted. Take your pick. If Judy Paige was gay, then hell, anyone could be gay. The school librarian could have been dating the typewriting teacher. They couldn't have that."

"That's a shame."

"It is. And maybe that's why I'm obsessed. I want to know her story. I want to know what it was like for her back then. Was she lonely? How did she meet women? She was in the spotlight, it's not like she could sneak out to a gay bar, if there were any back then. She looks happy, in these videos, but maybe she was just good at hiding it, the loneliness, the unhappiness? It's heartbreaking to think she had to smile for the camera when she might have been miserable the whole time. I hope not, I hope she was happy."

Then, as much as I didn't want to, I showed Janice the video that had shocked me. How she seemed to have changed overnight and not for the better.

"Is that the same person? Are you sure? The video is pretty grainy."

"It's her."

"Oh, that's much better," she said, when she clicked, on her own, a video from the time of her coming out. "Hey didn't you say, let me see." She stopped the clip and clicked over to the Wikipedia page. "Seems like whatever she was going through, she met this woman, see? The dates? She met this woman, this Sharon woman, and she came out of it. She fell in love. That's sweet."

That hadn't even occurred to me. And I didn't want to hear it.

I made a show of checking my watch. "You should get going, I'm making you really late. I'm sorry."

"No, it's okay, but yeah, I should get going. Melissa ought to be getting there pretty soon."

"Why is she showing up separately?"

"Her mother."

"Oh. Right."

"Yeah. Mel drove her to her doctor's appointment, and the two of us in the same car? After twelve years, the woman still has a problem with her daughter in a relationship with another woman. I swear she's still living in the sixties. Can you imagine? That poor girl," she said, pointing at an early picture of Judy on the screen, "had to live in a world filled with that attitude."

"Yeah, I know."

"Okay," she said, standing up and smoothing down her dress, "look, research your little heart out, but you have to eat. Right now."

"I will."

"No, now. Come on," she said, dragging me up off the couch by my hand, "let me see you, I'm not leaving until you head to the kitchen, walk with me."

At least she hadn't told me I was crazy. But that's because I hadn't told her everything.

I'd made it seem as if my primary interest in the whole thing was learning her story. Simple curiosity. I hadn't mentioned the jealousy or the eerie coincidences. How I'd guessed, correctly, the color of her eyes and her outfit. Or about this aching emptiness I still felt.

And how, the more I learned, the stronger that feeling was growing.

CHAPTER SEVEN

I thought it would burn itself out. Another day of watching the same videos over and over again. Reading the material I'd combed through before and learning nothing new. Surely I would get tired of it, give it up, the compulsion to keep digging would pass. But, if anything it just got worse. Until I did something I have never done in my life. Skipped work without an actual valid excuse.

"What do you mean you won't be coming in to the office for the week?" Walter, not my boss, I'd already cleared it with her, just a colleague who was working on the campaign with me, so it was really more of a courtesy that I was telling him at all.

"Exactly what it sounds like. I won't be in until next week."

"That's impossible. We have a meeting tomorrow afternoon, to discuss the upcoming campaign and the financial repo-"

"Walter, you don't understand, I'm not asking permission. I'm merely informing you that I'll be taking the week off."

There was a long pause and if I listened closely enough, I might have been able to hear his jaw muscles working over the line. "I see."

"If there's anything you want, if you feel the need to get in contact with me, don't. You can go through James. If he thinks it's important enough, he'll get a hold of me."

"It's your funeral."

"Yes it is."

"This is not go-"

I hung up on him and pocketed my phone.

That was Sunday evening, today was Thursday morning, and I was driving down the highway. First time I'd been more than ten feet from my front door in five days. I didn't know what, if anything, I'd accomplish by making this trip. What had convinced me to pack a bag and hop in my car was that I didn't have anywhere else to go. I'd exhausted all the resources I had. What I needed was to look at actual proof that I'd never be able to satisfy my curiosity and be done with it.

I know that's not actually true. There was one more thing I could do. Sharon Sauer. The woman she'd spent the last decade of her life with. She was still alive. I'd done research on her, as much as it bothered me to do so. There wasn't much to find, she was now seventy years old, she wasn't posting selfies on Instagram every ten minutes, but she did have a Facebook page that I figured someone, maybe a family member, nagged her into creating. It looked as if she created it, then left it there to gather dust.

But from it, through her friends, or the people connected to her page, I found she'd moved on after Judy's death, pretty damned quickly I might add, and had now been in a relationship with another woman for nearly nineteen years. What the hell Sharon? Did you even mourn or did you pick up your current girlfriend at the funeral? I didn't look any further. I didn't look for pictures. I didn't need to know any more about her. I just needed to know that she was there and if I got desperate enough, I could seek her out. Maybe get some questions answered but that would be my very last resort. She bugged me. There it is. I was acting as if she was my ex's new girlfriend. Behavior I always thought of as juvenile and silly before.

What I needed, before I went knocking on doors and bringing back painful memories for what was probably a sweet and kind old woman, was to try one last thing.

To visit Judy's grave.

Why? Who knows. Why not? There was nothing else I could do. People go to celebrity's graves all the time. It's not weird. I'm going with that.

I found her final resting place easily even though it was no Graceland. It was in an ordinary cemetery in the ordinary town of Leyfant with Dallas only a few miles away. There was nothing to mark the spot as anything special. If you were there to visit someone else's grave you'd pass her headstone by without a second glance. It was plain. Her name, date of birth, date of death. No mention that she was anything other than someone who'd lived once and was now just gone. I liked it. It was tasteful.

But if I thought coming here would help me in any way, I knew fifteen feet away, as I approached her grave, that I had been wrong. All it did was make me feel worse. I'd found nearly every scrap of information I possibly could on her already, there was nothing more, and now there never would be. Coming here only hammered that fact home.

There were a few other people in this part of the cemetery, but not many. An elderly couple and a teenage girl were huddled around a black headstone a little ways off to my right. The man and woman were dressed in their Sunday best, the girl had on flip-flops, skinny jeans and a too-large t-shirt. The graphic on the back of it was a giant hand with its middle finger extended. She had her phone out, tapping away at it, while her grandmother held a handkerchief to her mouth and wiped at her eyes. To my left, a man in a suit was standing at a grave six over from Judy's, his hands clasped behind his back, his head lowered as if in prayer. And underneath a tree, some thirty feet in front of Judy's headstone, was another man seated on a bench with an umbrella on his lap, the cool wind was rustling his shaggy hair.

I didn't cry when my mother died. I never cried when I visited her grave. I paid my respects, I left flowers, but I never cried. I cried now. Once I was standing directly in front of the headstone. And with my mother not here to chastise me "You don't know this woman, never even met her, what possible reason could you have to cry? People are looking at you, you're making a spectacle of yourself", I let it out. If that's what I needed, to cry, to let go of this inexplicable grief, so be it.

"I'm sorry for your loss."

After the worst of the crying subsided, a good five minutes later, a shiny black shoe appeared next to my own. Almost touching it. I took a step to my right, away from it, and only just glanced at the person who'd invaded my personal space. It was the man I'd seen standing with his head bowed, maybe praying.

"I never met her," I said. He said nothing.

After a full minute I was becoming annoyed when he didn't step away. Who does that? Even though I'd told him I'd never met her, clearly I wanted to be left alone, this was a cemetery after all, not a nightclub.

"If you don't mind, I'd-"

"She was quite something wasn't she?" he said. Quietly. Contemplatively. He said it without turning his head, his eyes remained on the stone.

"You know who she was?" I asked, turning to him. He looked young. Twenties. Mid-twenties maybe. He stood the same way he'd been standing earlier, hands clasped behind his back, head bowed.

"You could say that."

Even though I wanted to be alone, I couldn't help it, talking about her.

"You were a fan of her music? I don't mean to be assumptive but you look rather young. I didn't even know who she was until just recently."

"No," he said, "not a fan, as such. I just knew who she was."

Then how did he know, or why did he say she was "quite something"? Isn't that something a fan would say? Or someone who knew her personally? Which was impossible, he was too young. Unless he was a relative? Knew her when he was a young child before she died? I couldn't be that lucky could I?

I turned to look at him more closely. Try to see if there was any resemblance at all. There was. But not to Judy Paige.

"Are you following me?"

"Following?" he asked, finally turning his head away from the grave to look at me. "No. I don't follow people."

"You were in the cafeteria, at Celecur headquarters. Last Friday. That was you wasn't it? You were sitting at a table with a cup of coffee in front of you."

"Yes."

"And now you just happen to be at the same cemetery as I am, in the same area, four hours away?"

"No, it didn't just happen."

"Uh huh." I waited for him to elaborate, to tell me what that meant exactly but he didn't seem to think any further explanation was needed.

"So...you are following me? Is this...I leave early, then I don't show up to work this week, is that it? Someone thinks I'm off interviewing for another job? Giving away corporate secrets? Did Walter put you up to this?"

"I've already answered your first question. I don't follow people. As for the other questions, no, this has nothing to do with employment or interviews or this Walter person."

"Then what...you know, I don't even care. I'm not in the mood. I'm leaving. I'll be coming back, once you're gone. If I see you again, I'll just call the police and let them sort it out."

He remained perfectly at ease. The mention of police didn't seem to bother him at all. He stood just as he had the entire time, facing the headstone, hands laced together behind him, his head turned toward me, his face just as serene.

I turned around and started walking away.

"Would you like to meet her?"

"What?" I asked, stopping and turning around.

"I asked if you'd like to meet her. Judith."

I shook my head and turned again, ready to walk away for good. But again, I stopped, and I turned back. I don't know why I would engage a lunatic, but I did.

"Did you happen to notice you're standing on her grave?"

"I noticed. But the question still remains. Or actually, no, it doesn't, I know the answer. I know you would. I know why you're here."

"Sure you do, good-bye."

"You're here because you can't get her out of your head. From the moment you heard that song it's been haunting you. So much so that you haven't been able to think about anything else."

I took a couple of steps back in his direction but still kept a good distance between us even though he didn't seem threatening. He hadn't moved the entire time.

"Okay what's this about? Who are you?"

"You can call me Mr...Smith, if you need a name. And this is about you. I'm offering you a chance, an opportunity. To do something very few people get to do. The chance to go back. 1964 is it? The year that video was made?"

"I see. So you hacked into my computer and took a look at my search history. Congratulations, you've managed to accomplish something thousands of thirteen-year-olds can do.

Is this a modern version of the medium scam? You ferret out information on a vulnerable person, someone who can't get over the death of a loved one maybe, and you offer to contact this deceased person, ease a grieving parent's mind? Let me guess, you have a time machine but it's got a busted tire? All you need is a couple of thousand dollars for repairs and then I'll be on my way? Is that how it works?"

A purely rhetorical question, of course. By the time he spoke again I was already ten feet away, making my way towards my car.

"Why do you suppose no one else saw that ball move?"

For the third time, I froze where I was, only this time it was out of fear, not out of curiosity. This was something far more invasive than just a peek into my online activity. And also impossible.

"Impossible for me to know about that, correct? You never told anyone about it, never wrote it down, it's not on a hard drive, not on a computer anyway, nothing I can hack into, is it?"

When I turned back this time, he'd turned towards me, his back to the headstone.

"Just. All up here," he said, tapping at his temple with two slender fingers. "Are you willing to listen now?"

I didn't think I had a choice. I was too shaken up to speak, or to move.

"What you saw that day, was a...glitch, you might say. That term isn't incredibly accurate but it's as close as I can get, and I believe that's the word people use to describe such things. Although it's very rare that anyone actually sees a glitch. Though plenty of people claim to. Some people are just lying, a large percentage of them actually. Others so desperately want there to be such things that they convince themselves they've seen something extraordinary. And in other cases, someone honestly believes they've seen something out of the ordinary but they haven't. Optical

68

illusions, tricky perspective, odd lighting conditions, that sort of thing. But you, Karen, what you saw, was the real thing."

I remained quiet for a long while, letting what he'd just said sink in. He didn't seem to mind, didn't feel the need to jump in and fill the silence.

"No. It wasn't," I said, after what seemed like ten minutes but was probably only thirty seconds or so. "I was nine. Kids see weird things. It happens all the time."

"You don't believe that, otherwise you'd have forgotten about it a long time ago. You don't obsess about it, but every few years that memory comes back to you doesn't it? Why? Playing ball is hardly a momentous event, why would that memory stick with you for twenty-nine years?"

I didn't have an answer to that. It's a question I'd asked myself plenty of times on many different occasions.

It was summertime, I remember that, and it was a clear sunny day. No rain. No fog. Nothing but bright blue skies. Nothing, in other words, to obstruct my view. Although sometimes I've tried to make excuses. It might have been the sun was in my eyes, it blinded me. But that was just that, an excuse. It had been early morning, nine-ish. And we'd been facing west, not east. The "we" were seven kids from the neighborhood, playing with one of those rubber balls kids used to play four-square with, in the backyard of a friend who lived down the block from me. Because this was 1980 and without money to play video games with at the arcade, a ball would have to suffice. I don't remember every detail of what happened, who it was that got a little too enthusiastic and kicked the ball into the tree, or who exactly it was that climbed up into the tree to retrieve it, but I do remember clearly, that the six of us who remained on the grass were all staring at the same exact thing. A red ball stuck on one of the outer branches of a tree. That's when I saw something that would baffle me for decades.

The ball moved.

And when I say moved, I don't mean the wind picked it up and it jumped to another branch. I mean it was in one spot one second and in another the next. As if I were watching a segment of film that had been spliced together with missing footage between the splices. The footage of a ball being moved from one spot to the next, so that all I saw was a ball disappear and reappear instantly a couple of feet to the left of where it had been.

Yes, it's absurd. Which is why, when I saw it, I immediately turned to my right, and then to my left. I was expecting what anybody would expect when something inexplicable happens, I was expecting an explosion of "What the hell was that? Did you see that? WHAT THE FUCK!?" but what I got was nothing. All of the kids, two on my right, three on my left, didn't react at all. They went on staring at the ball, waiting for whoever it was that climbed the tree to get to it so we could resume our game. I checked again and again, hoping to see someone at least turn their head, as I had, maybe with a look of confusion on their face, but still I got nothing.

I know what I saw, I was sure of it. And when the boy who'd climbed the tree changed course, I was even more sure of it. He'd been heading in one direction, up the trunk and out onto one of the thick branches, but when the ball moved, he changed course. He turned to his right where the ball moved to. He'd seen it in one place and now he was seeing it in another. He just didn't find anything odd about it, apparently.

I only half-heartedly played for another few minutes before I made an excuse about having to get home to do some chores and left. I never said anything about it to anyone, who'd believe me? A couple of the kids there that day were older by a year or two, I didn't want them to think I was acting like a baby. They might not banish me from the group but I was pretty sure there'd be a lot of teasing and ridiculing going around so I kept my mouth shut about it.

I thought about it for days but eventually, as these things do, it faded and became just a memory. But a vivid one that would come back to me every once in a while. It was a hallucination, I would think when it did. Had I eaten that day? It was summertime after all. Back then, kids woke up, they pulled on a pair of shorts and shoes, they grabbed a bowl of cereal, and they were out the door until the sun went down. Maybe I hadn't eaten. Maybe I was dehydrated. Maybe the sun was in my eyes. But if so, like this Mr. Smith, or whatever his real name was, said, why keep remembering it? Why hadn't it gone the way of birthday and Christmas presents? I'd gotten a few good ones, I'm sure, over the years, things I'd probably begged for and was excited to get and I can't remember a single one. Why was that memory so vivid, when others had faded and eventually perished?

"You never forgot about it," Mr. Smith said, "because you know you saw something special and you've been trying to figure it out all these years." He paused. Maybe for effect, maybe not.

"I can save you the trouble. You never will. But," he said, raising one finger in the air, "having seen what you saw, it should make what I'm proposing a little easier to believe shouldn't it?"

No. Not at all, I thought.

"Yes, it does. Because it's made you wonder, and question, from time to time, if all of this," he said, as he both raised his arms to his side, palms up, and tilted his head back to look at the darkening sky, "is really all that it seems."

I reflexively looked up too. Dark clouds were rolling in, but nothing unusual about that. Nothing out of the ordinary. A black bird flew overhead, but that's about it. Green computer code didn't suddenly appear splashed across the vast grey. I'd never seen the movie, you know which one, but it's become so synonymous with the sort of scenario this man was obviously hinting at that it's impossible not for it to come to mind.

"You've never talked to anyone about it, wouldn't want anyone to think you're crazy." He lowered his arms and tilted his head back down. "And, I know, it's nothing you've seriously believed or spent much time on. Just a passing thought once in a while, an interesting thought experiment."

"Even though," he said, raising that finger in the air again, "there are several highly respected and reputable physicists out there who have suggested this entire universe might be nothing more than a sort of simulation. And those are just the ones who will admit it."

He doesn't look real, I thought. I mean, of course, he looked real. He looked as real as the girl across the way still completely absorbed in her phone and the man with the umbrella still sitting on the bench, looking right at us. He was looking this way but he didn't have an alarmed expression on his face as if I were here talking to empty air. What I actually meant is that he looks perfect. I'd noticed it in the cafeteria, his hair looking fake because it was just a little too neat, not one strand out of place. The demarcation between hair and skin too sharp, too even. And his face, so symmetrical and so smooth, he wasn't just handsome, he was beautiful. The word ageless popped into my head.

Like staring off into eternity.

"So you're suggesting this is all a...simulation?" I asked with a smirk.

"I'm not suggesting anything. But let's say it is. Hypothetically. Would that sudden knowledge make a difference? If I told you it was, would that stop you from feeling pain? Or love? Would it stop you from having to eat, sleep, or breathe?"

"I don't know. Would it?"

"No. You'd go on just as you always have. You'd have to wouldn't you? Because even if it were and you knew it was, there's no way of breaking out of it, it's not The Truman Show, you couldn't reach some hypothetical edge and bust your way out into another world."

He lost me at The Truman Show.

"Okay, well that's all very interesting but I'm leaving now."

"I realize how it must sound, I'm only using the simple term of simulation and referencing a movie because that's all I can do. You don't have the language for me to explain it to you properly."

"Is that so? I'm not smart enough is it?"

"No, you're not."

What is it with men and pushing buttons? You're cute honey, but really, the men are talking, you wouldn't understand.

I knew he was talking nonsense but now I was getting angry and I couldn't help wanting to hear what he thought I was too stupid to comprehend.

"Try me."

"Impossible."

"Try."

He nodded. "Are you familiar with quantum mechanics? String theory? The double-slit experiment? Spooky action at a distance? Quantum entanglement? Dark energy and matter?"

"Actually yes, I am." First strike.

"And you understand them all, fully?"

Okay, maybe not a complete strike.

"No. I can't say that I understand them fully, physics wasn't my major in college, but not even physicists understand them fully. So that can't be held against me."

"But they understand them better than you do, surely."

"Yes, of course they do, it's their field of study."

"Fair enough. But tell me, when you say you're familiar with all of these concepts, what does that mean exactly? That you've watched a few videos? Animated explanations of interference patterns and delayed choice and quantum eraser variations presented to you by a talking cartoon rabbit? Or do you understand the actual math behind them?"

"Almost impossible to grasp for a layperson isn't it?" he asked when I didn't answer. "What about two plus two? Three minus one?"

"What? Look, I don't have to-," I stopped myself, took a breath, and took a moment to watch the man under the tree rise from the bench and start to walk away. "I don't appreciate being condescended to."

"I'm sure you don't, but I wasn't being condescending. I'm only trying to explain something to you in a way that you might understand."

"Yes, okay? Yes, I understand simple arithmetic. Can you just get on with this?"

"I'm trying. So you would agree that the level of difficulty between simple arithmetic and advanced theoretical physics is vast, correct? So vast that even if I stood here and explained the principles to you for hours, even days, you wouldn't be able to grasp them."

"I think we've already established that."

"Good. Now what I'm trying to tell you is that to me, the math on which these theories are based, is as simple as arithmetic is to you. And what you are asking me to explain is as complex to me as quantum mechanics is to you. Do you understand?"

"Like trying to explain algebra to an ant."

"That's a little over the top, but yes, I think you get the idea. You don't have the language for it. But you shouldn't feel bad about it, there isn't a physicist alive who has it either. They don't even know what dark energy is yet."

"And you do?"

"Two plus two."

There was a flash of lightning far off in the distance followed by a low rumble of thunder. I turned to watch the girl in her skinny jeans and her grandparents start to slowly make their way back to the graveled path and their car. It was going to start raining soon.

"Why don't you have a seat? So we can discuss what's next."

When I turned back Mr. Smith was already seated on a bench that hadn't been there before, only two feet away from me, slightly angled towards Judy Paige's headstone. Underneath the tree, the bench was gone.

"How..."

"Does it matter?"

Solid wood, I felt when I reached out, tentatively, to touch it. I was half expecting my hand to pass right through it, as if it were a hologram or made out of smoke.

"Please, sit."

I sat, powerlessly, as if in a trance.

"We can sit here for days and I can attempt to explain to you the hows and whys and whatever other questions you may have which I'm sure number in the hundreds but what would be the point? You wouldn't understand and you still wouldn't believe me, that you can go back. Would you?"

"No one would. No one sane, anyway."

"Are you sure? You say you're familiar with the double-slit experiment. The experiment that seems to show particles can retroactively change their behavior. Isn't that time travel?"

"The operative word there is seems."

He tipped his perfectly sculpted head left and right as if weighing the validity of what I'd just said.

"Well, to the scientists of today, yes. But I understand your skepticism. Human beings learn by experience. You've only ever experienced time in one direction. It's all you've ever known. It's all anyone, or most everyone here, has ever known. Why would you believe anything different? But this is getting us nowhere isn't it? A lot of talking in circles. The only way you're going to believe me is to experience it."

The guy was a loony, but a convincing loony, I had to give him that.

"You came here for answers. About her." He pointed a finger in front of him, directly to the headstone. "I'm offering you an opportunity to get them."

"I...you know, this is just...way out there. You can't really expect me to believe..."

"It's going to start raining soon," he said, nodding up towards the sky. "You should go before it does."

"Go?"

"Yes, back, it won't be raining there."

"Back to...?"

"1964."

I'm sure I made several facial expressions, derision, incredulity, outright mockery, before speaking again.

"Okay, I go back to 1964, I meet Judy Paige, I choke on clouds of cigarette smoke, I get my answers. But I come back right? You won't leave me stranded in the land of beehive hairdos?"

"Oh yes, you'll have to come back."

A single drop of water landed on my bare arm.

"Here it comes. Look, Mr. Smith, neat trick with the bench and all, but I think I should get going."

"What do you have to lose? If I'm lying, nothing happens correct? You get in your car and you drive away, live the rest of your life as if you never met me. But what if I'm not lying? Are you willing to give up a chance of a lifetime?"

He was right, I had to give him that. Even if he was delusional, I didn't have anything to lose, except for a minute or two before he was exposed as being a complete and maybe unstable fraud.

"Okay, you're right. Nothing to lose. Beam me up then. Do you have a magic wand? Or do you sprinkle pink sparkly dust over my head? If you tell me I have to drink some sort of disgusting concoction, deal's off."

He was not amused.

"I need a serious answer. Yes. Or no."

Whatever you say.

"Yes, the serious answer is I'd love to meet her, but come on, you can't really expect me to bel-"

CHAPTER EIGHT

It was almost, but not quite, instantaneous.

For two seconds, maybe three, I was in complete darkness, yet what seemed like a thousand images flashed through my mind in that small space of time. And voices, dozens of voices, one on top of the other. It was nearly impossible to distinguish one picture from another, any one voice, what was being said, what the images were supposed to mean. Only a few stuck. A swing set. Waves rolling in on a beach. A soft lullaby. A red car. A black typewriter.

I wasn't aware that I'd shut my eyes, but I must have, because now they opened.

The first feeling that hit me, naturally, was disorientation. Just seconds before I'd been outdoors, sitting on a bench in a cemetery under a darkening sky and now I was indoors, in a brightly lit unfamiliar room lying on a stranger's bed, wearing a nightgown.

What. The. Hell.

The disorientation didn't leave me but it was temporarily overridden by another sensation: fear.

Instinctively, I threw the thin cover off of me, stood up, and backed myself against the wall behind me and stood perfectly still.

This can't be happening. This can't actually be happening.

It's a hallucination, I thought. He injected me with a drug, a very powerful fast-acting hallucinogenic maybe. Or a dream. He conked me on the head and now I'm in a coma.

But I dismissed those ideas pretty quickly. People having hallucinations don't realize they're hallucinating do they? And a coma dream, I imagined, would be like everyday ordinary dreams. Not very detailed. Dreams are vague and slippery. Fragmented. What was surrounding me looked and felt as real and as solid as everything I'd ever known to be real.

The only other option is that he did it. He actually did it.

Because clearly I was no longer in the year 2010. There were no lights on in the room but it was brightly lit because the sun was out in full force. No dark clouds here. And I was standing in what looked like a bedroom you'd see on an early episode of Bewitched, except in color. Orange curtains and rug, green walls, a sharp edged white dresser with a hideous star shaped mirror above it. A fan whirred away as it sat on the sill of an open window to my right. It did nothing to cool the room down, only circulated the warm sticky air coming in from the outside. Who lives in Texas without central air? No one, unless you like sleeping in a pool of sweat. That is unless central air doesn't exist. Then you have no choice.

Okay, that's all fine and good, but why am I wearing a nightgown? And why would he plop me down in someone's house?

"Hello?" I called out. Out of fear or nerves or just sheer incredulity, my voice came out sounding high pitched and thin.

This is not good. Not good at all.

I could feel my shoulders tensing up as I stood there listening for footsteps, waiting for someone to burst through the open door demanding to know what the hell I was doing in their house. Maybe aiming a shotgun right at me. Hey, 1964 or not, this is Texas after all. At least I think it is.

There was no answer, the house was completely silent.

No one is here. You live alone.

"Hello? Mr. Smith? Are you there?"

Nothing.

I started to make my way to the door, slowly, feeling the carpet beneath my bare feet. Scratchy and rough, and as real as anything I'd ever felt before. I stopped just to the side of the door jamb, peering down the hallway, listening again, for any sign of movement. Creaking floorboards, breathing, a gurgling coffee maker perhaps. Still nothing. The only sounds were the fan and, somewhere behind it, another motor of some sort, coming from outside.

Before I ventured out into the hall I turned back to look around the bedroom I was about to leave. Something seemed off about it. Now that my fear was somewhat subsiding, now that I didn't seem to be in any immediate danger, I was able to notice that something about the house felt peculiar. I couldn't put my finger on it, what it was. It had to be something very subtle. Like the angles and lines were maybe askew by a centimeter or two, not enough to make the house look distorted, but my brain still registered it. Weird. But hey, they didn't have laser levels back then. Or, I guess not back then, it's now, back then is now. Laser levels don't exist. Uneven walls? As if that mattered right now.

"Hello? Anyone here?"

There was still no answer as I made my way down the short hall. The first door on my right was a small bathroom. Pink tub, toilet, and sink, lime green tiles. Eesh. The next door on my left was a small bedroom, smaller than the one I'd just left.

Single bed, stripped, no linen, and no personal effects. The scent of Pine-Sol. There were a few cardboard boxes stacked in a corner. A few books and magazines in a neat little pile at the foot of the bed. Obviously no one actually used this as a place to sleep.

You live alone.

That voice, or thought, again. But I don't live here.

The hallway ended in a living room with a small kitchen off to the left. And if I was uncertain whether I was supposed to be in the past or not before I was pretty certain I was now. At least I knew that was what was intended. The TV sitting in front of an uncomfortable looking low-backed sofa left no doubt. The damned thing was made out of wood. Last Christmas. A present. It looked like it weighed a ton yet it stood on four spindly looking legs. If I wasn't so freaked out I might have laughed. I thought of the television set we had when I was a kid. It was made of wood too, one of those heavy as hell consoles that sat on the floor, and although there was no remote, it did at least have push buttons. This TV had one big clunky knob and three smaller ones.

Beside the sofa, sitting on an end table, was an avocado green lamp with a white cloth-like lampshade.

I bought that lamp, two months ago. At Wegman's? No, Wellman's.

An image of a store on the corner of a busy intersection flashed through my head, complete with the retro looking pink and brown sign that sat above the door to the entrance.

A beige rotary phone sat on a dainty wooden table by the entrance to the kitchen.

I mouthed, silently, a number that came to me right out of the blue.

What's going on? Is this some sort of backstory? Information being fed to me to help me fit in, so no one gets suspicious that I don't belong here?

"Mr. Smith? Hello?"

My eyes darted around the room. I turned to look behind me, back down the hallway, at the two doors, at the bedroom at the back of the house. Even up at the ceiling. Expecting him to emerge from somewhere or even just talk to me as a disembodied voice emanating from the walls. And why not? I've just been transported to the past, what's a little more kookiness gonna hurt?

"Are you going to answer me? You can't just leave me here without an explanation can you? I don't know what I'm supposed to do!"

I was once again met with silence. Inside the house that is. Outside I could hear birds, what sounded like a car passing slowly down a street, and that motor again. This time it was louder, without the noise of the fan covering it up, and now it was coming from behind the front door.

Okay. Think.

Let's say I am in the past.

I really have no other option right now.

So first thing's first. I have to find out where I am. Second, I have to find out when I am. Third, I have to find out how the hell I'm supposed to go about finding Judy Paige.

It hit me then, that I was most likely in a world where she was alive. Somewhere out there, she was a living breathing person that I could actually talk to. If I could get past security that is. You can't just walk up to a famous singer, I imagined, even in these supposedly gentler times.

This is just getting easier and easier.

The paper. I get the paper delivered.

I stumbled on my way to the front door. What is with this screwy depth perception? Are the floors uneven too? I was certainly not standing in the most luxurious of houses, it was tiny, the entire thing could probably fit in my living room back home, so yeah, it might very well be that it was just shoddy construction. And I didn't have time to worry about floors and walls, I didn't know how long I had. Hours? A day? Two? Instead of being so sarcastic and snotty I should have asked a lot more questions. But I hadn't believed anything was actually going to happen did I? And I certainly didn't think it was going to happen so quickly.

Lesson learned. Don't be snotty, and ask anyway.

I automatically grabbed a housecoat from the rack by the

door and put it on. The picture of an attractive woman, late thirties, immediately flashed in my head. Brown hair, hazel eyes, pleasant warm smile. I could even smell the flowery scent of her perfume.

Is this hers? Am I wearing her nightgown? Is she the one who lives here? And where is she?

"Mr. Smi-" Oh forget it.

Everything I knew about the past, before the late seventies, when I experienced it myself, I'd learned, naturally, from books, movies, and TV shows. Because, as Mr. Smith said, we only ever experience time in one direction. Once today turned into yesterday, that's it, there's no going back. Time is a one-way street. Or so I thought. So all I'd ever seen of this time period were black and white photos and films. Or else aged colored images. Pictures that had an odd orangey tint to them and out of focus footage that made everything seem drab and dull and, I always thought, depressing. As if the past was murky and colorless. As if the very sky hadn't actually turned blue until I was born.

I was wrong.

The second I opened the door I was bombarded with colors. Brighter even, it seemed, than the world I had left not more than fifteen minutes before.

Maybe because the sky then had been overcast and gloomy and the sky here was bright blue and clear that made such a contrast but I wasn't so sure.

Across the street, in front of the house directly across from this one, was a flowerbed bursting with pinks and reds and yellows. Every lawn was covered in grass so green it looked like AstroTurf. An ochre colored tank of a car rolled by, a metallic teal one was sitting in a driveway three doors down, another orange one right next door. And sitting in the driveway of this house was a beautiful maroon one. That's the car from the picture, in my head, before I opened my eyes.

My car. 1962 Dodge Dart Convertible.

There were two women headed in this direction, strolling down the sidewalk, talking companionably. Both looked to be in their late twenties and both wore colorful sleeveless dresses and low heels. One of them, the one in the bright blue form-fitting dress, had longer hair, past her shoulders and wore a wide white headband. The other, in a dress that was either coral or salmon, depending on what they called it these days, had chosen a dress with a flared skirt. Her hair was short, at the nape of her neck, that is. Up top it was piled high in a tall beehive. She wore a ribbon just above her bangs. Both of them had purses dangling from their slim arms, and, I could see, even from this distance, that the both of them wore that very distinctive sixties style makeup. Jet black eyeliner on the edge of their eyelids that extended past the corners of their eyes. And long, obviously fake eyelashes.

I smiled at what I was seeing but I wasn't nearly as awed by the whole scene as I thought I should be. Maybe it was because I'd spent the past week pouring through websites that had image after image of women in the same outfits, the same hair and makeup. I'd immersed myself in this exact time period day and night now for what seemed like months. The clothing, the cars, the music. It was still amazing to see it, don't get me wrong, but by this time maybe I was just desensitized to it? When I couldn't find any more videos of Judy, I'd allowed myself to click on videos suggested to me by whatever algorithms YouTube uses. Videos of other sixties musicians, which led to sixties TV commercials, and then TV shows and eventually even silent 8mm home movies of families living in neighborhoods just like this one, hell I could have watched a film of this exact neighborhood for all it looked familiar to me. Now I wish I hadn't. I felt let down at not being completely awestruck at what should have been a mind-blowing experience.

The two women both nodded their heads at the boy in

my yard while he pushed a lawn mower over the grass as they passed, and he nodded back.

A story. I need a story. What am I doing in this person's house? House-sitting? Will that work?

"Good morning Ms. Bryant," the boy called out before I could think of anything else. The lawn mower shuddered to a stop and he waved his hand over his head as I walked out on to the porch. Ms. Bryant?

"Good morning...George." His name is George. He's fifteen, but he looks twelve. It must be his thin frame. And that he's dressed like Opie. Jeans rolled up at the cuffs and Chuck Taylor sneakers. His hair was so short and neat it looked as if he'd just stepped out of a barber's chair.

Before I could even make it three steps he saw what I was looking at and jumped into action.

"I'll get it!"

He wiped the back of his hand across his brow before walking over and retrieving the paper that had landed at the edge of the grass.

"Thank you," I said, as he handed it to me. "It's warm out here, would you like some lemonade?" Did I have lemonade? Yes, I did. Do I pay him? Do I have money? No. I don't pay him. His father, George Sr., has him cut my lawn because I'm a single woman and I couldn't be expected to cut it on my own could I? It's a neighborly thing.

I had to smile, thinking of the pudgy kid with the attitude and his vaping friend who wanted an exorbitant amount of money to cut my lawn just days before.

"No thank you, my ma doesn't allow me to have too many sugary drinks and I've already had a Coke. Besides, I'm almost done. Already finished the back."

"Ah, I see, well if you change your mind, or if you want a glass of water, just come on in."

He smiled in response and went back to his lawn mower.

The paper turned out to be the Leyfant Express, good,

that's good, and the headline read SCRANTON ENTERS GOP RACE TO COMBAT GOLDWATER. Goldwater I knew, but only vaguely. I knew he had something to do with politics, obviously, but I couldn't tell you in what capacity. Scranton was a complete mystery to me, and unimportant. The date was June 13, 1964.

But that's two weeks before the concert.

I wanted to meet her to get answers. To get her story. How am I supposed to do that when she doesn't even have a story yet? Right now she's an ordinary everyday nineteen-year-old girl in a sea of ordinary everyday nineteen-year-olds. How am I supposed to find a person who isn't famous? Out of habit I looked around me. No iPhone in sight.

I have a rotary phone. And a phone book. That's about it on the technology front. Why didn't I commit her parents' names to memory? How many Paiges was I going to have to call? Jesus, how does anyone do anything here?

I was just about to walk back into the house to get to it, start dialing away, when the lawn mower shut down again and George called out behind me.

"Oh, Ms. Bryant? I almost forgot," he said, pulling something out from the back pocket of his jeans, "ma said to tell you thank you, for letting her borrow it."

What he handed me was a small ornate silver mirror, the kind with a handle. What I saw in it sent me running back into the house, rotary phones and phone books forgotten.

CHAPTER NINE

Strangely enough, after the initial shock, of seeing a complete stranger staring back at me from the mirror, first from the handheld one and now the larger bathroom one, I accepted it without much fuss.

"Although a warning would have been nice!" I yelled up at the ceiling.

But okay. Okay. I can deal with this. And at least things were starting to make a bit more sense.

It was only my consciousness, complete with all my memories intact, that had made the trip across the years. This information being fed to me was actually memories. This person's memories. The woman staring back at me. Ms. Bryant.

But why? Is it just impossible to send an actual physical body back in time? Maybe. Or is it that I would have stood out too much with my phone and Fitbit? And does that mean...no...could it? It must. Did this poor woman just suddenly find herself sitting on a bench in a cemetery fifty years in the future? In another century? Not only that, but this woman, or girl really, couldn't be more than a couple of years older than a teenager (please don't be a teenager). So if what I think happened actually happened, she'd find herself not only lost in the future, but almost twenty years older.

God. How awful.

At least I knew, more or less, what to expect in the sixties, but there'd be absolutely no frame of reference for someone traveling to the future. What would she make of it? Smartphones. Personal computers. Ear gauging and tattoos. The President. Hopefully she's a civil rights supporter. If not, that's going to be one tough pill to swallow.

If it were a movie it might be humorous. Confused person from the past having to find their way through an advanced world full of mind-boggling technology. Having to live in a completely different culture than they were used to, where interracial marriage and homosexuality were not only no longer illegal but were considered pretty ho-hum as far as scandals went.

But this wasn't a movie. She was a real person, not a fictional character. She had neighbors. Most likely family and friends. A boy named George cut her lawn and called her Ms. Bryant. She read. She shopped for lamps. She slept in a warm room with the fan on. She wore a nightgown to bed.

She had a higher voice. It wasn't fright. She was taller than I was. It wasn't uneven floors. It was the difference in height that had disorientated me. It wasn't much, two inches at most, but it had been enough for me to notice. She probably weighed as much as I did but at two inches taller she appeared thinner. She was also pretty, the way young girls usually are, soft features, full lips, smooth untouched skin. Bright eyes.

The only feature that looked like mine. Her eyes. Not because of the shape or color, although they were brown like mine, only a touch lighter, but no, it was something else. I couldn't tell what it was, but there was something there that I recognized. That corny "the eyes are the windows to the soul" line came to me. Was that it? I still held on to what made me, me. My sense of self. My consciousness. My memories. If that was my soul, then perhaps the line is true, sappy as it is.

I stood there, looking back at myself, or her, for several minutes. This is bizarre. Time travel? That's old hat. But this.

I looked at my hands, the scar I used to have was gone. A small round patch of shiny skin just above my right wrist thanks to my grandfather and his errant cigarette when he'd had one too many whiskeys one evening. In its place was a tiny birthmark I'd never had.

I reached up, patted my soft cheeks, my jaw, down to my neck, then to my ears and earrings. Simple single pearls on each ear. As soon as I touched them a scene formed in my mind. A cake glowing with candles. Streamers. A scratchy 45 playing on a record player. Laughter and conversation all around me. An older plump woman wearing a pink and green dress with white wavy hair and thick black cat's eyes glasses handing me a small blue gift-wrapped box.

All of a sudden I felt wrong about what was happening. If I had access to her memories, as vague as they were, this was an intrusion, a flagrant invasion of privacy. It doesn't get any more intrusive than this.

"Okay, that's it." I left the mirror, left the bathroom, and walked back into the living room.

"Mr. Smith? Answer me! I don't want this anymore. This isn't right!"

Outside, the lawnmower shut off and didn't turn back on. George, it seems, had finished mowing Ms. Bryant's lawn. Only he hadn't had he? He thought he had but Ms. Bryant didn't live here at the moment. He also believed he'd just spoken to her minutes ago and he hadn't done that either. This charade had now affected two unsuspecting innocent people and was going to end up affecting a lot more by the time it was all said and done. And all for what? So I could satisfy some sort of curiosity?

"I'm done! You hear me? Mr. Smith? You can't do this to people. I can't do this to people. It's not...right."

Nothing.

"Damnit."

What's my name?

Evelyn.

Evelyn. Jeez, even the name sounded pure and innocent.

"I know you can hear me. I'm not taking part in this any more."

I sat myself down on the sofa, crossed my arms across my chest, and waited. As if taking that stance meant I'd be taken more seriously.

A few more cars passed by outside. I heard a couple of voices, kids, shouting to one another. George, I think. Done with his chores, now off to do whatever it is fifteen-year-old boys and their friends do on a Saturday morning in 1964.

Ahead of me, sitting on top of the yellow kitchen counter was a small box of Frosted Flakes. Tony the Tiger on the front, no different than in 2010, but this Tony had a tiny nose and a funky looking football shaped head.

It really is 1964. I haven't even been born yet. That's freaky. And even freakier? My mother's alive and she's younger than I am right now. She's twelve years old at the moment. And happy. According to my aunt.

"She was a cheerleader, if you can believe that."

No, I couldn't. I couldn't even form a half hazy image in my mind of her jumping and kicking her legs out like a lunatic (that's surely what she would have called such behavior), of waving pom-poms in the air and cheering. Cheering? No way. Shouting. Not ever.

Still, my aunt insists she was once a girl who loved to dance, to laugh, to play. My aunt told me all this in an attempt to make me feel for her I suppose. But it hadn't worked. Even now, thinking about it, knowing that she was out there somewhere, that if I wanted to, I could actually see my mother again, and not as the hateful bitter person she'd become but as a fun-loving young girl, I still had no desire to do so. Even if I had all the time in the world, which I probably didn't, and even if she lived in the house across the street and not over six hundred miles away in Alabama, I still wouldn't.

That's not true.

Okay. Yes. If I was being completely honest, yes, I would. If she lived across the street, I would. She had been cold and distant and unaffectionate but she had had her moments. Not many. But a few. Unless I was remembering incorrectly. I was only five when she'd picked me up from school that day, from kindergarten. When I'd been sick. I remember being really cold, then burning hot at moments, but mostly freezing throughout the day. My skin had gone all red and blotchy. My legs hurt, my arms, my whole body had ached. And all I had wanted to do was lie down and sleep but the teacher hadn't let me. I only remember fragments. My mother touching my head. Then her own face going a bright red as she yelled at the teacher. A panicked look on her face when she'd rushed me to the school nurse and couldn't find her. A phone, I think. More shouting. And then finally my father's car and the backseat where finally, I got to lie down. I think, I can't be sure, my mother had my head on her lap as she used a magazine to fan me with as she brushed away the hair sticking to my hot damp forehead. That's all I remember, I must have dozed off. I woke in the hospital a day or two later. But those memories, beyond waking up in a cold room with a nurse hovering over me, are gone.

She'd had her moments.

What are you doing thinking about your mother?

She's out there. You're wasting time.

You have one chance. Do you really want to go back without meeting her?

After almost thirty minutes of sitting there with no indication whatsoever that anything was going to happen besides time moving on one second at a time, I gave up.

It would seem I'm stuck here for the time being. It's not like I can drive to the train station and buy a ticket back to

2010 can I? Maybe once I do what I came here to do that'll be mission complete and soon after I'll find myself back in the world of YouTube and Netflix and watching nearly anything you want nearly any time you want and Evelyn will be back here, where you watch whatever three networks decide you'll watch and at what time you'll watch it. Hell, for all I know, she might not even want to come back.

Still, I decided from here on out, I wouldn't dig. I'd try my best to access only the memories I needed to in order to accomplish what I needed to accomplish. I'm sorry I interrupted your life Evelyn. I didn't mean to, I didn't know about any of it. But it'll be over soon. Maybe even by the end of the day, I thought, because I just remembered something important.

It almost never failed, whenever Judy was on a talk show or interviewed for an article in the paper or a magazine, the interviewer always asked the same tired question again and again. Tell us how you went from total obscurity to having the number one record in the country practically overnight. Every damned time. Didn't matter if she was twenty-two or forty-two, they all asked the same question. Personally, I would have told them to move on, ask me what I'm doing now, not what happened decades earlier, but she never did. She was unceasingly polite and answered the question as completely, as cordially, the fifteenth time as she had the first. If she ever felt annoyed, if she ever felt like screaming "Everyone knows that story by now! I've been recounting it since I was twenty!" at the top of her lungs, you'd never know it. In fact, just months before her death, at the age of forty-six, she'd been asked again, to retell the story. The interviewer, a young guy who looked bored, why was he interviewing some old sixties one hit wonder who no one even remembered? (Completely wrong about the one hit wonder, it was just that that first song was so famous everyone forgot about all of her other hits.) Even so, even with the evident disinterest, she answered the question as politely, if not as enthusiastically, as she had the first time.

So I knew the story well.

Two weeks prior to that now famous concert, she always joked, she'd been at a teen dance club and since she knew the drummer of the band playing that night, she'd been allowed to sing one song. And was practically booed off stage.

She had named the place, not every time, but at least a few. It was the name of a planet. Mercury? No. I found myself once again scanning the coffee table for an iPhone that wouldn't be invented for another four decades, thinking I'd just pull up the video and check. Darn.

Mars? No, Saturn. That was it. The name of the place was the Saturn and Sun Hall. Bingo.

I found the number in the phonebook and dialed it. I had to shake my head at the ridiculous amount of time it took. One digit, turn, click-click-click, as the dial returned, another number, a seven, click-click-click-click-click-click-click, then back again. I shook my head, but I smiled as I did it. I thought it was quaint, but then again, what the hell do people do when their house is on fire? Was 911 a thing already? Probably not. Maybe dial the operator? But the zero was the last digit after nine, that's still a long time to have to wait. I guess I'd just have to hope I didn't have an emergency any time soon.

No one picked up, but I didn't really expect anyone to. It was only just past ten in the morning, the local teens wouldn't start putting on their dancing shoes until five, right? Dance until the wee hours of nine p.m. and in bed by ten. Because in my mind, that's what sixties teens did.

As much as I wanted to hop in that shiny red car and go explore this colorful innocent world, I knew it wasn't a good idea. I didn't know what I was dealing with. Any number of things could happen. Suppose I got in a car wreck. What then? Even if it wasn't severe, even if someone didn't lose their life, it could be bad enough that someone would end up in the hospital. Surely that would alter the future in ways I couldn't even imagine. And what if it was me that ended up in a hospital? I'd miss meeting Judy, and there would be no way I'd be able to find and meet her after today. And even if I were careful, even if I just walked down a few blocks, to a store, suppose I'm browsing the funny looking detergent boxes in the local grocery store and at just that moment, I blocked someone's view. A boy who would have spotted a girl down the aisle. A girl he was instantly smitten with. A girl he nervously followed until he got the nerve up to talk to, to ask if she'd like to go out for a soda sometime before she left with her mother. A girl he'd end up marrying and having a family with. That would definitely alter the future. And it would just take a split second to do it.

No, safer to sit here and wait it out. I skimmed through the paper. I chuckled at the "For the Ladies" section. "Molasses Bars are Perfect for Ladies Lunches" complete with a recipe. Two entire articles on how best to roll your hair. One for wet hair, one for dry hair. An advertisement for a donut making machine that women could buy, make dozens of donuts at a go with, sell, and make money by working right out of their own kitchen! So these work from home schemes aren't just a modern thing.

I tried to watch television but the reception was horrible, even using the fine-tune dial, moving the rabbit ears of the antenna every single position they could possibly be moved in, and fiddling with the horizontal hold, I was only able to get one channel in clearly and it was airing a soap opera. Pass. I've never been a soap opera person. In any era.

I dialed the club again. And once again there was no answer.

By noontime I was in the bedroom closet, figuring out

what I was going to wear. The decor of the small house was hideous, there was no getting around that, but the clothes. Wow. Say what you will about some of the horrible hairdos of the day but the clothes were, I had to admit, amazing. This Evelyn girl had taste. The closet was comically small compared to what I was used to but it was packed with dozens of dresses, blouses, and skirts of the brightest colors I'd ever seen. Oranges and greens and yellows and blues. There were bold geometric designs and softer flower ones, paisleys and polka dots. The colorful ones looked as if they ended above the knees but there were also a few, subtler in color and design that ended well below the knees. And shoes. A lot of shoes. Flats, heels. Sling-backs, pumps. In just about every color imaginable. But not one pair of sneakers.

There was no answer at the end of the line at one p.m. Or at two.

By three, after sitting outside for an hour, in the backyard, on the very first step of the three leading down into the just-mowed grass (trying to keep out of sight of the neighbors), I was beginning to panic. She never specified the date. What if it was Friday? She said two weeks, but that didn't mean anything. She wouldn't have said thirteen days, who does that? I went back in and redialed the number I'd already committed to memory. Nothing.

I thought about my hair. Which, coincidentally, was almost exactly the same as it had been in 2010. An above the shoulder bob parted on the side, darker shade of brown but other than that, nearly identical. Huh. Who knew I'd been walking around with 1964 hair in 2010. I browsed through a couple of fashion magazines I found in the extra bedroom and saw that yeah, while a lot of women had hair like Judy's (which I learned was called "a flip"), and some what looked like weird alien heads because of the tall beehive hairdos popular these days, there were quite a few who did go for the more natural look. That's one hurdle, thankfully, I wouldn't have to jump.

I took a shower and washed my hair. I had to, thanks to my foolish decision to sit outside, in Texas, smack dab in the middle of summer. Then again, the temperature inside wasn't much cooler, so I guess no harm no foul. After searching the bathroom and the dresser in the bedroom for a good ten minutes I finally realized the convenience of fast drying hair lay somewhere in the future. I wasn't going to find a blow dryer, much less a ceramic coated flat iron anywhere, so I improvised by turning the bedroom box fan on high and brushing my hair straight in front of it until it dried. And the result wasn't too shabby.

On my way back to the living room the phone began to ring.

CHAPTER TEN

I let it ring. Make as small a ripple as you can while you're here. It's for the best. But when it rang ten times and then, a minute later, it began to ring again, I had no choice but to answer. Suppose whoever was on the other end of the line got worried and came over?

"Hello?"

"What took you so long?" A young sounding female voice barked at me.

"I was...in the bathroom. Sorry."

"Oh. Okay, well, I'm ready. I'll be waiting for you out on the porch."

"Waiting for me?" Who is this? Why would she be waiting for me?

"Yes. On the porch. Like you asked. Ralph?"

Does she think my name is Ralph?

"I think you might have the wrong number."

"You're a gas Evelyn. A real gas," she said, without any humor. "What's wrong with you? You sound funny."

Fran. Frannie. The movies. Viva Las Vegas.

"We're supposed to go to the movie show."

There was no answer. Instead I heard a muffled male voice somewhere in the background.

Ralph. Frannie's brother and a boy I didn't want to see.

"What did you say?"

"Nothing Fran. Listen, I don't think I can go after all. I'm really sorry but...I'm not feeling very well." I sniffed for effect. "I think I might have caught a cold."

"A cold? In summer?"

What, summer colds don't exist in the sixties?

"Yes, I woke up with the sniffles and it seems to be getting worse."

"Is that all? The sniffles? You're going to stay in on a Saturday night because of a few sniffles? You sound like my granny."

Wow. Thanks. I placed the back of my hand against my forehead as if she could see me before saying "No, I think I might have a fever as well. I might even be contagious. I really should just stay home."

"But...so I have to stay in on a Saturday night just because you might sneeze on me? We were supposed to go eat too, you promised, and I'm hungry!"

Boy, whoever this Frannie was, she sure was obnoxious.

"I'm really sorry Fran. Why don't you tag along with Ralph?"

"If you're not going, he's not interested," she said, disappointment dripping from every syllable. "And without you picking me up I'll be stuck in watching Hootenanny on television with my folks."

I had to stifle my laughter at the word Hootenanny but it worked in my favor, it must have sounded like a stifled cough.

"Hm. Well, maybe you should stay in if you're that ill."

"I think so."

"Oh, alright." She didn't sound like it was alright, she sounded like she wanted to punch me right over the phone. "Rain check?"

"You bet."

There was a clunking sound as if the phone might have been dropped or banged against a wall followed by that same muffled male voice.

"Give it...no...leave it off Ralph!"

After a second or two Frannie apparently gained control of the phone once again.

"Okay Evie, Ralph's getting on my last nerve. I'm going to go wrangle his neck."

She was gone without even a goodbye.

Why the heck was I friends with her? She sounds horrible.

Then it occurred to me that she might know about the club. When they were open, was there a dance tonight? What time? I thought of calling her back, the phone number was right there in my head, but that wouldn't be a great idea. For one, I'm sick, why would I care if there was a dance tonight? And also, if by chance she called someone else, someone else with a car, so she didn't have to stay in eating a TV dinner and sitting on the couch with her parents tonight I shouldn't put the thought in her head. She just might fancy dancing tonight instead of a picture show. If she showed up and I was there instead of bundled up in bed things could get ugly.

I dialed the number to the club again but I had long since stopped smiling while I did it. It had ceased to be quaint. More like a pain in the ass.

"Saturn and Sun."

"Hello. Is this the Saturn and Sun?"

"That's what I just said, hon." I couldn't tell whether or not I should be upset at being called hon, it was difficult to say if I was speaking to a woman or a man. Could have been a man with a slightly effeminate voice or a woman who had a hoarse voice and smoked two packs of unfiltered cigarettes a day.

"Right. Um. Will there be a dance there tonight?"

"Of course there is. There's one every Saturday night."

"May I ask what time the doors open?"

"Eight o'clock."

"And do you need a picture ID to get in?"

"A picture what? Look, sweetheart, I've got things to do,

if this is a prank-"

"No si- um. No, not a prank. I'm from out of state, I apologize. Is there a cover ch-...an admission?"

"A dollar. But let me save you the trouble, you don't sound like a teenager and if you're over twenty, out of towner or not, you aren't getting in."

"Understood. Thank you for your help."

"Good-bye then."

"Good-bye."

I'm twenty.

But just to make sure, I found my purse right where I always put it, in the bottom cabinet under the small kitchen counter.

Picture ID. Funny. What my driver's license was, was a postcard sized piece of thick paper without a picture and no lamination. Fill in the blank with all the important information written in plain blue ballpoint pen ink, by hand. Date, name, address, a signature line for the issuing clerk or patrolman (mine was signed by a D. Wallace), a checkmark indicating I'd paid three dollars, my date of birth, which was April 11, 1944, and the line next to "Race" was filled with w-f. White female. That's all folks. Height? Who cares. Eye color? No matter. Signature? Who needs it? Stamped across this very important information, in red, were the words "Licensed Operator In Front Seat". So not allowed to drive from the back seat then. Got it.

But to be fair, there was a license number (or "receipt no." to be exact) that wasn't handwritten, it was printed, so at least they were taking something seriously.

By six o'clock I was standing in front of the full length mirror hung on the back of the closet door. Not bad. Not bad at all. I'd chosen a purple and green paisley designed sleeveless dress with yellow accents that ended just above the knees and matching yellow low heeled shoes. I hadn't worn this much color since I was a child and now I didn't know why. How did this ever go out of fashion? In just a few short years this fun feminine dress and these delicate shoes were going to be replaced by dingy bell-bottom jeans and clunky Frankenstein-style platform shoes. What an absolute tragedy.

I felt uncomfortable, almost itchy, sitting behind the wheel of a car and starting the ignition without the pressure of a seatbelt strap holding me in place. My very first car, a beat up 1983 dung-colored Honda Civic had been a stick shift and I had hated it then, but I was glad for it now. And even though it had been at least fifteen years since I'd driven a car with a manual transmission, it came back to me in a flash.

Driving down the road, Chapel of Love on the radio, a powder blue convertible with the top down pulled up next to me for a few seconds before it sped up and passed me by. It was filled with six young girls, on their radio Mary Wells was singing My Guy. Rumbling down the road at at least forty miles an hour and not a single strand of hair being whipped around. The amount of hair spray in that car alone, wow. Regardless, helmet heads or not, that perfect scene with the perfect soundtrack filled my heart with joy. It was the picture of innocence. Of youth. Of a world full of promise. Every single one of them had a smile on their face as they all tried shouting over one another. No cell phones, no worrying about likes and followers, no snapping pictures to show off to anonymous people on the internet, while ignoring the real friends right in front of them. They were living in the moment.

Was this world, this time, any better, any safer than the one I'd come from? Probably not. It looked like it, it really did, but it probably wasn't. After all, right at this very moment somewhere in the country, I'm not sure where, Charles Manson was only a few years away from being released from prison and starting up his "family". So many innocent girls would be lost. Girls just like the ones in that car. I hope they have fun tonight. And I hope none of them ever feels the need to wander too far from here.

A few blocks down the road I stopped at the Texaco where a teenage boy wearing grey overalls filled my tank with gas and cleaned my windshield while I went inside to buy a Coke and a map. All total, gas included, I paid with two one-dollar bills and got thirty-five cents back in change.

I almost made it out of the door without any strange looks. Almost. When I nearly ripped the skin off my palm trying to twist the cap off of my Coke bottle. The clerk, a tall thin man with a long sharp nose eyed me funnily then pointed his bony finger at the bottle opener mounted on the edge of the door.

After that it was smooth sailing.

Sort of.

I pulled out from in front of the gas pump and off to the side so I could take my time reading my map. Easy enough, I'd grown up reading actual paper maps. The club, from the looks of it, was on the north side of Dallas. Clear across town from where I was coming from. Good thing I'd left an hour early.

Also, I'd been to Dallas several times, I thought, as I pulled back out into the street and turned in the direction of the highway. But, it was evident, after ten minutes and entering Dallas proper, the Dallas of the mid-20th century and the Dallas of the 21st century are two different animals altogether. Landmark buildings that I'd known, were not there, not built yet, and buildings I'd never seen before were standing where I'd known there to be open air. The skyline was different and there was evidently a huge construction project taking place on a major part of the highway system. And on top if it all, in my head I was thinking if this was it, if

I were here for one night, I wanted to take it all in. I wanted to read every billboard sign. I wanted to look at every colorful car. I turned to look at all the women, most of them in skirts or a dress and heels, and all the men, nearly all in ties and slacks, walking around. In front of stores, walking leisurely down sidewalks, making their way from their cars to the front door of restaurants or movie theaters. I wanted to see the planes flying overhead.

So instead of smooth sailing, I got lost.

Three stops to ask for directions later, I pulled into the packed parking lot of the Saturn and Sun at 8:34 p.m..

The moment I saw it, that plain square wooden building which looked more like a utilitarian no-nonsense schoolhouse than a club, my heart began racing and my hands slipped on the wheel, nearly causing me to clip one of the parked cars.

She's in there. She's alive and she's somewhere in there only forty feet away. Until this moment it had all still seemed unreal. I was going through the motions but in the back of my head was the thought that it was all just a dream. Yeah, I'll get close but at the last second, I'll wake up. That's the way it always works.

But I parked in the first spot I saw, and I didn't wake up.

I turned off the car, I jumped out, and my feet hit the ground and I was still there.

I walked, hurriedly, to the front doors whispering to myself under my breath, don't wake up, don't wake up. I didn't notice anyone around me. I didn't notice that the sun was already halfway past the horizon. And I didn't notice the person eyeing me from the window just off to my right.

"Aren't you forgetting something?" I recognized the scratchy voice.

"Excuse me?"

"Admission?" A woman, it was a woman after all, of about forty or fifty, hard to tell with her squinting through the smoke curling up from the cigarette she held in her right hand, asked me from her place behind a window. No bullet proof glass separated us. Just a plain open window and behind it, a counter with a grey metal cash box sitting on top of it.

"Oh yes, sorry. I'll be right back." In my haste to get inside I'd forgotten my purse. I'm losing time. Think.

Once I got back, I handed her my dollar.

"You're the out of towner aren't you?" she asked, the dollar clutched in her puffy hand. The other hand holding a fresh cigarette. The pungent smoke kept rising in thick ribbons and seemed to be getting sucked into the mound of shiny black hair piled high on top of her head like it was a sponge. I had to keep myself from grimacing. I could only imagine what it smelled like, her hair. A mixture of smoke and ten cans of hairspray. And sweat. Bleh. It was a hot night.

"Yes," I said.

"How old are you?"

"Twenty."

She eyed me for a second and I realized my mistake. If she asks for proof, for my driver's license, she'll see I'm not from out of state at all. Stupid.

"You don't look twenty."

Oh no.

This close, I was this close! So close I could hear music and the stomping of shoes on the floor behind her.

Why did I lie? But, then again, so what? I lied about being from out of town, she can't keep me from going in because I lied can she?

"You sounded older on the phone, but you look younger."

I put on my best exasperated look. "I left my driver's license back in-"

"Ah," she said, waving her hand dismissively through the air, ashes dropping down onto the counter in front of her, "go on. It's a teen club. You look younger than twenty but not that young, go on, have fun."

"Thank you."

Before I entered, I stopped to take a deep breath, trying to calm my nerves. One shot, you've got one shot at this. I noticed two signs in front of me, taped at eye level, one next to the other, on the door. One read PARENTS WHO COME CHECK IN ON THEIR CHILDREN MUST BE ACCOMPANIED BY A MEMBER OF THE OPPOSITE SEX. Hm. Not as innocent a time as I thought. And the other read WEAR WHAT YOU LIKE, BUT SLOBS WILL BE TURNED AWAY.

My laughter calmed me down before I took a hold of the handle and opened up the door.

The dance was already in full swing. The band, all the way towards the back of the room was mostly hidden by all the people already out on the parquet dance floor. I could only see the tops of three of their heads but I could hear them just fine. At the moment they were well into a fast song I didn't recognize but everyone else did judging by the enthusiastic clapping, stomping of feet and twirling. I breathed a sigh of relief. Not as bad as I thought it was going to be. When I read the word children I thought I was going to be in the equivalent of a junior high sock hop. Thirteen and fourteen year old kids. That would have made me uncomfortable. But nearly everyone I saw had to be at least sixteen, and most looked seventeen and older. The boys, like George my neighbor, had short haircuts, neatly parted and shiny. They wore slacks and bow ties. Some wore suit jackets even though the room was warm and there was no sign of any air conditioning, only a large industrial looking fan whirling away in the corner of the room, off to my right. The girls, most of them, were dressed in the bright colors, short dresses, and low-heeled shoes that I'd seen in my closet - but not all. Some were dressed more conservatively, with longer skirts and blouses buttoned up to their necks and ribbons in their hair, but none wore pants. And there wasn't a pair of jeans or sneakers in sight. Because slobs weren't allowed.

I stood just inside the door scanning the dancers, scanning the few kids off to the side sitting in chairs, looking for her. The lights were dim, but it wasn't dark. Was that to discourage any funny business? Necking in a dark corner maybe? Sneaking sips from a flask?

The music grew in intensity, until it ended in a crescendo.

The dancers all came to a stop en masse and clapped. Some whistled, some whooped. Most of them wiped at their moist foreheads.

"Okay, this next number," a young voice boomed from weirdly shaped speakers I could see mounted to two or three pillars throughout the room, "is called-"

The rest was lost. I didn't hear what the next song was called, nor did I care.

The kids, waiting to get back to what they'd come here to do, were still long enough and parted in just a way that I could see between them.

Sitting towards the back, alone, her eyes fixed on the band, was Judy.

I'd know her face anywhere.

I'd come here to get answers. To what questions? I don't know exactly, just...answers.

I'd come here, ultimately, to see if in getting those answers I'd be able to rid myself of this inexplicable feeling of sorrow and loss I'd had since the moment I'd heard that song.

I didn't even need to talk to her to know.

That feeling was gone. In an instant. The moment I saw her face.

But it was replaced with something else.

An even stronger feeling.

A feeling so strong, to me, that there was no question about it.

I belonged here.

And I was never going back.

CHAPTER ELEVEN

The music started up again, this time it was a slow number with a melancholy beat. I heard a few moans from the crowd, but only a few. One or two couples left the dance floor, looking down towards their feet bashfully. But they were replaced by one or two more. I skirted around to my right, between the dance floor and the now slowly swaying teenagers with their arms wrapped around each other, and the small set of wooden bleachers set up further to the rear of the hall that Judy was sitting on. At the very far end.

What now?

All the time I'd wasted sitting around waiting for someone to pick up the phone and I hadn't bothered to think up what I was going to say to her. What could I say to her? Hi there, I just traveled back in time from the year 2010, how about this weather huh? Sure is hot.

In order to gather my thoughts, try to come up with a realistic and non-creepy way of approaching her, I took a seat on the opposite side of the bleachers from where she sat. Sitting between me and her were two girls in pastel-colored dresses who sat shoulder to shoulder, and, closer to me, a boy wearing a short sleeved lime-colored shirt and a heck of a lot of aftershave. He looked as nervous as I felt. He was awfully fidgety. His left leg was jumping up and down as he tapped his foot on the floor repeatedly and he kept rubbing both palms up and down his lap, as if trying to dry the sweat off of them. What's up with him? Too much Coke? After another few swipes of his hands on his slacks he blew out a puff of air, and rose to his feet. He turned to his right and walked towards the pair of girls who looked towards him with obvious hope in their eyes. One of them had clasped her hands together and held them just underneath her chin. You didn't have to be a mind reader to know what she was thinking. "Let it be me. Oh, please, please, please." But he didn't even glance their way as he passed them by. He was heading straight for Judy.

Oh boy.

He stopped in front of her, held out his slightly trembling and sweaty hand, and spoke a few words that I couldn't hear.

She raised her head to look at him, the tips of her light brown hair only slightly bobbing as she did.

Don't do it. Don't do it, Judy, just dance with him. It's only a dance.

But she did it.

She smiled, pleasantly, said a few words, pointed her finger in the direction of the band, but shook her head, no.

Oooh. That's gotta hurt.

But he took it graciously. Or as graciously as he could, anyway. He nodded his head, turned, stuffed both hands into the pockets of his pants, then walked as quickly as his skinny legs would carry him past the snubbed girls and then me, his eyes trained on his oxford shoes the entire time. I watched as he headed towards the refreshment table set up near the front. There were a dozen or so soda bottles and two large trays of cookies and lemon bars set on top of it. Off to drown his sorrows in caffeine and sugar, poor thing.

My heart went out to him. How could it not? This wasn't a typed out "no" on a computer screen or phone. He'd had to face that rejection head on. You had to respect him for that. Part of me wanted to go after him, try to soften the blow. To tell him that it had nothing at all to do with him. He was just barking up the wrong gay tree.

But the other part of me told me to quit wasting time.

When I turned back, Judy had also risen to her feet and was walking away.

Before I could jump up to follow her it dawned on me she was only heading towards a pair of doors that read "Boys" and "Girls" on them at the very back of the room, behind the band.

Okay, calm down. Unless she planned on climbing out of a window for some reason, she'll be back.

A minute passed before she reemerged, dabbing at the skin just beneath her bottom lip, as if wiping away lipstick, and then pinching a strand of hair off of her forehead. She did not walk back to the bleachers, instead she stood behind the band, her hands held together in front of her, waiting.

She's so pretty, I thought. And so, so, young.

And I wished that I could have just five minutes of seeing her the way everyone else could. Just a cute nineteen-year-old girl in a cute turquoise dress with the rest of her long life ahead of her. A wonderful life that was just now about to begin. The kind of thought, the kind of picture, that makes old people smile.

But I couldn't see that. Because while I saw the girl, I also saw the woman. At twenty-six, at thirty-six, and finally, at forty-six. She'd never reach forty-seven. I knew that she would have some good years, great years even. But I also knew that something was coming for her, something bad. And even when she made it out of the other side of whatever that bad thing was, she wouldn't have long to enjoy it. The girl I was looking at had only twenty-seven years of life ahead of her. That's it. That's all she gets.

We're not meant to know the future. We're just not.

When the song ended the singer thanked the cheering crowd then turned in Judy's direction and held his hand out towards the microphone stand in an "it's all yours" gesture. And I understood what was about to happen.

Jeez, I've been here all of ten minutes and I'm about to witness yet another awkward heartbreaking moment.

Oh, it was horrible. I stunk up the place.

That, or some variation of it, is how she always described what I was about to experience.

Even if I had no way of knowing that this wasn't going to be the performance of a lifetime, I would have been able to tell that something wasn't right. The singer didn't even bother to make an introduction before stepping off the stage (which was a fancy name for a platform barely eight inches off the ground), and as he did, both he and the guy holding a guitar gave the drummer meaningful looks. Thanks a lot, Jimbo. The drummer, in turn, looked apologetic. Sorry guys, I promised my pop. None of them even acknowledged her. No thumbs up, no "Good luck", no "Knock 'em dead" or whatever phrase is popular at the moment, something with "groovy" in it probably.

Judy shook her arms and hands out, climbed on stage, and started fumbling with the stand, trying to lower it. It nearly got away from her but she pulled it back by the cord before it could topple over and she smiled nervously at the crowd, who all looked slightly confused but also impatient for the music to resume.

One of the band members, a short guy wearing thick Buddy Holly glasses and holding a trombone, tapped his foot loudly on the wooden floor, clearly agitated. That pissed me off. Hey buddy, cool it, you play the freaking trombone for crying out loud. A year from now she'll be selling millions of records and you might be playing at bar mitzvahs. Might.

Once she got the microphone down to the level she

wanted, Judy turned and nodded at the drummer. The guitar player shook his head, but tapped his foot in a three count anyway, and then started to play.

Was it a disaster? No, I wouldn't say so. Could anyone in that room that night predict that she would, in just a few short months, go on to become one of the most famous singers in the country? No. Definitely not.

The song wasn't one of hers and it seemed, to me, an odd choice. Not fast enough to be a dance song but also not slow enough to wrap your arms around a partner and sway to it either. No one seemed to know exactly what to do. A lot of couples simply walked off the dance floor, others stayed and tried to make the best of it by shuffling around half-heartedly. I heard one of the girls who were still sitting on the bleachers, dance-partnerless, ask her friend why she was singing such a tired old song. I didn't understand what she meant by that but I was also wondering why she was singing it, it just didn't fit her. It didn't fit her voice.

I'm not a musician, I don't have a trained ear, but I didn't have to be to know that there were a few slight bumps in the instrumentation. And they seemed to have been deliberate. After the second hiccup, both the guitar player and the drummer looked at each other and smirked. If Judy noticed, that she was being deliberately sabotaged, she didn't let on that she did and she didn't let it rattle her either. She'd been obviously nervous before she started to sing but once she started, all of it fell away and she sang as if nothing at all were amiss right up until the very last note.

When it was over she bowed and thanked the crowd who only limply clapped before roaring again when the singer of the band jumped back in front of the mike.

She looked so crestfallen as she slowly made her way back to the bleachers that I could feel my throat tighten up. She sat in the same spot as before, but now instead of watching the band, she seemed to have grown a keen interest in the tips of her high-heeled shoes. I wanted to walk right up to her and tell her that despite what just happened, in two weeks time, she was going to give a performance that would be so incredible, so unforgettable, that in fifty years thousands and thousands of people from all around the world would still be seeking it out and watching it every single day. Teenagers who wouldn't even be born for another thirty years would find that video and go on to cultivate a love for sixties music because of it. That's the effect she would have on people. This day, no one would remember.

But just as I couldn't console the boy who'd been rejected, I couldn't do that either.

But I could do something.

"Hi," I said, standing in front of her, my hands stiff and cold despite the uncomfortably warm air, my legs trembling so bad I didn't know if I'd be able to get through this without collapsing. "I...I just wanted to say I thought you did great up there."

She looked up from the floor at me with those eyes. The clearest, lightest shade of green I'd ever seen. And smiled. A genuine smile, dimples and all, but a smile that also said "Come on, we both know I tanked, but it's kind of you not to say so."

"Thank you."

"You're welcome. May I?" I asked, pointing to a spot beside her.

"Certainly."

As I sat I could smell, only faintly, her perfume. Hairspray too, she was definitely wearing a lot of hairspray, but underneath the slightly acrid scent of chemicals, there was a delicate feminine scent that made me glad I no longer needed to support myself on shaky legs.

"So what was it? Did you dump one of the boys in the band and this was their revenge?"

"What do you mean?"

I nodded my head toward the stage where "The Bobby's" (according to their hand-written sign taped to the bass drum) were now belting out another dance song. Sounded like crap to me but the dance floor was once again packed and jumping, so what did I know? Also, I'm probably a little biased.

"I could tell they weren't too thrilled with you being up there."

"It was that obvious?" she asked, as if there were any question.

"Yes. It was."

"Oh. Well, no, I didn't break up with anyone. My uncle Norman, he's Peter's family dentist," she said, pointing to the drummer. "He set it up. He's always trying to be helpful, he knows how much I want to be a singer."

"So it was a favor."

"Yes."

"But why would they be so upset about you singing one song?"

And why did you never bash them in any of your interviews? You always made it sound as if the flop was completely your fault when clearly it wasn't. You had the world's attention to call these mean-spirited boys out. Rub it in their faces that you made it and they obviously didn't (After all, who's ever heard of "The Bobby's"? They don't even know how to use apostrophes correctly.) but you never did. Why?

She shrugged her shoulders. "Because it's really tough, getting booked in one of these clubs, it's competitive. You don't want someone else taking up your time, sometimes people who work for recording studios come in, to listen to new bands, looking for talent. And once in a while they even get to make a record, and sign with a label."

"Ah, I see. So if someone walked in while you're up there

and not their singer..."

"Yes."

"Still, that was pretty mean."

"It's okay. It was nice of them to give me the chance."

I get it now. You never badmouthed them because you're basically the Tenderheart Care Bear.

"And was that a song you wrote?"

I knew it wasn't, I was just trying to keep the conversation going. And as soon as it was out of my mouth I realized my mistake.

"No," she said, turning to me and giving me a quizzical look. "Was I that bad that you didn't recognize it? It was all over the radio last year."

Luckily her puzzled look turned into a knowing playful smile. "You knew that."

I returned the smile. "Yes, of course I did, I was only joking, trying to cheer you up."

I've got to be more careful.

"I would have loved to have sang one of my songs but that would mean them having to learn it. I couldn't ask them to do that, so I just sang what they chose."

"So not only do they make you sing a year-old song no one wants to hear anymore, they also deliberately mess it up. Unbelievable," I said, shaking my head while staring down Buddy Holly.

When I turned back to her, her brows were drawn together, not in a confused way, but in a look that said she was touched that I'd be upset on her behalf. Then her brow smoothed again.

"It's okay. It's probably time I give up on singing anyway and go to college like my parents want me to. I always knew it was a long shot." I only panicked for half a second before I realized that my being here tonight didn't matter. I hadn't changed anything. This night had been disappointing for her regardless and she'd still shown up at the concert. She wasn't ready to pack it in just yet. But I offered up my encouragement anyway. Couldn't hurt.

"Nah. I wouldn't give up on it if I were you. Maybe don't ever sing that song again though." She took it as the joke it was meant to be. She smiled and shook her head. "But I think you have a great voice."

"Thank you."

"I'm Evelyn, by the way."

"Oh, my gosh, I'm sorry. My name's Judith."

"But...you go by Judy right?"

"Oh, no. I don't like that name. I think it sounds childish, don't you?"

Huh. Interesting.

"Yes," I agreed, "it does. Judith, then."

After that we chatted about all the things girls chat about. Clothes, music, TV, movies. It's a good thing Evelyn wasn't a nun or I'd have been in trouble. She had all sorts of memories in there I could access. I still felt guilty about prying, but, I had to admit, it was getting easier to cast those feelings aside. And besides, I rationalized, clothes and makeup are hardly personal. And since I was never going back, what did it matter?

I hope you're enjoying 2010 Evelyn, there's a 1990 Chateau Latour in the wine cooler, live it up. I'm sorry, I know you've been robbed of eighteen years but look what you get in exchange. A house four times larger than the one you left behind with central air instead of a fan. Need to get in contact with someone but you're at the beach and they're out shopping? No problem. There's a grey shiny thing in your pocket that to you is going to seem like magic. Want to know which pubs you can visit in Dublin that the locals patronize? Impossible unless you actually know the locals in Dublin? Nope. You have internet now. Look it up, it'll take you two minutes. If you happen to see something on TV that fascinates you, a type of candy, say, that children in Japan eat and they make it sound so delicious you wish you could taste it for yourself but how in the world are you going to get your hands on some obscure item only made in a country clear across the Pacific? It's called Amazon. And you can have it at your front door in two days. And don't worry, you have credit cards even though you're single. Yeah, that's right, a bank can't refuse to issue you one just because you don't have a husband. Neat, huh? And, also even though you're single, you can go on the pill if you want, that's up to you, it's perfectly legal. I didn't need it, obviously, you might have figured that one out by now. And uh...I apologize for that. That must have been quite a surprise for you. And what are my friends going to think? Gay all my life and all of a sudden I'm coming out as straight? It's usually the other way around. But hey, your body, your call.

Anyway, yeah, I think it's a fair exchange. You left me a fan that blows warm air and doubles as a hair dryer, a library with a card catalog, and a rotary phone. The clothes are nice, I'll give you that. But if you miss them, again, Amazon.

What was also getting easier, besides putting my guilt aside, was gaining access to the memories. As the night wore on I no longer had to pause for a second to think about them, to ask for the information. They were starting to come to me without any thought, as if they were my own. Which was a good thing because Judy, or Judith, had asked me if I was okay when she'd asked which school I'd graduated from. It took me a full five seconds to retrieve the name. But she forgot about it when she realized we lived in the same town.

"But that's in Leyfant. You don't live here in Dallas?"

"No, I live in Leyfant."

"So do I! What a coincidence. But I graduated from Leyfant High. Not your fancy private school."

"Oh, it wasn't that fancy." But it was, it was pretty fancy.

A few minutes after that exchange we were interrupted by

a pair of boys, or men, I should say, since they both looked to be right on the cusp of the age limit of twenty, who asked us to dance. We each declined, politely, and the guys seemed to take it in stride. They'd been at this longer than the nervous fidgety boy who'd asked Judith to dance earlier. So I didn't feel quite as bad this time. But I did the next.

A boy, I swear he couldn't have been older than fourteen, tapped me on the shoulder because I was too engrossed in my conversation with Judith to notice him standing just off to my left. When I turned to look up at him, there he was, bow tie, freckles and all.

"Would you care to dance?"

I almost laughed. The scratchy-voiced woman who'd taken my dollar at the front door must be right, I really must look younger than twenty.

And I almost didn't have the heart to turn him down. But if I didn't, that could open up a whole other can of worms. And that's the last thing I needed, more worm cans.

"I'm sorry, I would, I really would, but I can't. I'm going steady with someone. I'm really only here for my friend," I said, pointing in Judith's direction.

"Oh, okay. Well, then would you like to dance?"

"I'm going steady with someone too. Sorry," Judith said, with an apologetic smile.

"Okaysorrythanks." At least that's what I think he said. He mumbled it and took off in the direction of the snack table. I was starting to understand that although the sign dangling off of it read "Refreshments", it was really just a euphemism for "Rejections".

"Thanks a lot," Judith said, nudging my shoulder with hers while trying to keep a straight face. I could tell she wanted to laugh but was keeping herself from doing it, in case the boy, who was already stuffing a cookie in his mouth, thought she was laughing at him.

"Hey, at least I made sense. I said I was here for you, why

would I be here for you if you couldn't dance either? You don't make a very good partner in crime."

This time she couldn't keep it in. Her laughter, which I'd heard before, but never this clearly, made me resolve to myself then and there, that I'd try to make her laugh at least once every single day for as long as I knew her.

Fortunately for me, snack table gossip seems to travel at a pretty quick clip because we weren't bothered anymore after that. I wondered, briefly, what was being said about us. Don't bother asking either of those two to dance. Because we're frigid? Stuck up? I doubt the word lesbian was being whispered behind cupped hands into ears. That concept was probably harder to fathom for them than if someone said we might be Martians and didn't want to stand up because we were hiding the fact that we each had three legs.

Let them think what they want. It made no difference to me. Judith picked up the conversation again right where we left it when we'd been interrupted and said, since we lived so close to one another, we should get together to go see a movie sometime or carpool the next time we came to the club. Although she didn't use the word carpool. That also didn't matter to me. I'd just been saved from having to come up with some ridiculous way to see her again. "Oh hey! Listen, I think I might have the mumps so you should go see your doctor just in case, they're highly contagious. What's that? How did I know where you live? Well, it wasn't by following you home that night, I can tell you that. It was by some other very reasonable, respectable...okay-go-see-your-doctor-talk-to-you-later-bye!"

When the club shut down, at midnight, which was a surprise to me, I walked with Judith to her car, a pretty navy blue and white one, don't ask me the make or model, I have no idea, but it was a whale just like all the others in the lot, so we could exchange phone numbers. If this were 2010 I would have asked if she wanted to go someplace else, have a drink, a cup of coffee, it was only midnight after all. But this was 1964, I was twenty, and she was nineteen, so I bid her good-night and walked to my car, fighting the urge to rush to it and follow behind her. She'd be taking the same route back to town as I would, I presumed, and it wouldn't hurt to make sure she got home safe, but I didn't. I had her phone number now, and following her for miles would definitely be creepy, so I walked to my car and then drove home with the radio off replaying our entire conversation in my head and, now that I was alone and really had the time and space for it to sink in properly, hyperventilating a little. I had just spent the evening with Judy Paige. "I just spent the evening with Judy Paige!" I yelled in the privacy of my car and thumped my hand on the steering wheel.

I hadn't been in awe earlier this morning, seeing a long gone earlier decade live and in living color, but I was now. Not only because I actually got to meet and talk to a woman who would be world famous in a very short time but also because earlier today, or what seemed like earlier today from my perspective, I had been standing in front of her grave. A grave that I knew, now that I'd met her, I was going to do everything I could to make sure didn't exist until much later than 1991.

As soon as I got home, I made a pot of coffee.

In a stove top percolator.

Once I figured out how to light the stove without burning the house down. (I really should figure out that zero on the phone.)

The entire time I thought of the brand new programmable Cuisinart coffee maker I'd just bought before my time-traveling trip. It had a built in coffee grinder. I also thought of the fresh coffee beans that would be delivered to my doorstep on Sunday by the local coffee shop that roasts their own beans in house. But I guess burnt coffee with coffee grounds floating around in it is just as good huh?

I'm not complaining. I'm really not. In fact, the reason for the coffee? I wasn't going to sleep. I was afraid that now that I'd done what I came here to do, the moment I drifted off to sleep, I'd be yanked right back to that cemetery. I know I can't stay awake forever. Eventually I'll have to sleep, but if that's the way it works, if I lose consciousness and that's what triggers a return trip, then I can at least try to stay here one more day.

With a tiny cup of coffee in my hand I returned to the living room and turned on the TV. And got static. I forgot I was at least twenty years away from all night television. So I scrounged up some magazines and books from the extra bedroom, sat as upright as I could on the couch, and began to read. I managed to drink six cups of coffee (2010 two cup equivalent) and got quite a ways in to The Grapes of Wrath by 4:30 in the morning.

It wasn't until 4:45 or so that my eyes started to droop, and it was 5:22 a.m. when the book fell out of my hand to my lap and then to the floor as I rested my head on the back of the couch, my eyes closed, and everything went black.

CHAPTER TWELVE

It was the ringing of the phone that jerked me awake.

I didn't have time to think about where I was. All I thought was: Judith.

"Hello?"

"Evelyn, sweetheart, it's me, are you okay?"

A rush of emotions hit me so hard that I nearly dropped the phone and left me unable to speak for a second.

"Evelyn?"

"Yes...yes, sorry, I'm fine Mom."

"Oh good, well, I was just worried about you, you missed church and Frannie told us you canceled your plans with her yesterday because you were ill."

Damnit, what is this Frannie's problem?

"Yes, I did, but I didn't feel that terrible, just not well enough to go out. I feel better today."

"But not well enough to go to church?"

Oops.

"I must have forgotten to set my alarm."

"Alright, I'm sure the Lord will forgive you since you were under the weather. Pastor Hayes, on the other hand, may not be so forgiving. But you don't worry about him. You don't have anyone to answer to but God."

My eyes were threatening to well up again. I could feel the complete and unconditional love this woman had for her daughter. Felt it at the first sound of her voice. Dozens of memories, in images and sounds and smells and textures were pouring over me like warm water. She never missed a night of tucking me in, of kissing me goodnight, even curling up in bed with me until I drifted off if I asked her to because I'd been scared of the dark for a while there. Until I got too old for that and told her to stop. (Why? Who ever gets too old for that?) The smell of pancakes and syrup coming from the kitchen every morning for two months straight when I went through one of those phases kids go through of declaring they'll never eat anything else, ever. The feel of her fuzzy pink housecoat, the smell of her skin lightly coated with talcum powder, that day she wrapped me in her arms when I ran in the house crying after witnessing our neighbor's cat get hit by a car. She'd held me, my head against her chest, her hand on my head, for as long as it took for my hitching sobs to diminish into silent crying, and then wiped away my tears with her hands. Never once did she tell me I was being foolish, that I needed to toughen up, that I was acting ridiculous.

I knew I'd missed out on certain things, certain experiences, not having a decent mother. I just never felt how much until now.

"Yes ma'am."

"Your voice sounds funny. Are you sure you're feeling better?"

I cleared my throat, wiped my eyes, and tried again.

"Yes Mom, I promise, I feel fine. I feel real good."

"Good enough to come down to Carver's? Your father and I just put in our orders."

Actually yes, I would love to drive to Carver's cafe, I knew where it was, we'd been there hundreds of times. Straight after church, along with half the congregation. To sit with my mother and father, eat an omelet or a bowl of oatmeal with fresh fruit in it, and just soak it all in. All the memories of picnics, Christmas mornings, beach vacations and birthdays. It wouldn't even bother me this time, when my mother would place her hand on my back to correct my sitting posture. Because she would. She always does.

But as much as I wanted to, I knew it wasn't a good idea.

"No Mom, you enjoy your meal, I'm not even dressed yet, your food would be cold by the time I got there."

"Okay honey, I better ring off now, someone's waiting in line for the phone. Call me if you need anything, we'll be going home straight after we're done."

"I will. And Mom?"

"Yes?"

"Thank you. For checking up on me."

"Of course. Bye, Evelyn."

It took a few minutes of sitting on the couch with a blank stare on my face to come out of that daze. But eventually I did when it hit me that I'd made it through the night. I was still here.

"Thank you," I said, up towards the ceiling, though I had yet to see any indication that Mr. Smith could hear me or was even listening.

The phone cord was only long enough for me to scoot the table it was on a couple of feet closer to the bathroom, so I took the quickest shower I could, and still turned the water off every minute listening for the sound of the ring. I did the same thing with the fan while I brushed and dried my hair. Off. Listen. On. Brush. Off. Listen. Nothing.

Of course there was nothing. We only just met. Why would she be calling me the next morning? She might not call at all, ever. It was probably just one of those things, hey, we should get together sometime, one of those things you say at parties to someone you meet and then regret the next day.

But you never know.

And I had her phone number anyway. I'll give it some time. By sundown, definitely. I was sure I could come up with a good enough excuse to call her by then. If I got desperate enough, the mumps might actually work. It could just be a false alarm. Easy.

With a good plan in place, I relaxed and made myself a large ham and cheese omelet, some toast, and more coffee and ate it all while watching Jeopardy! on TV. I had no idea the show, a favorite of mine, was that old. I half expected a ten year old Alex Trebek to walk on set with index cards in his hands but it turned out to be hosted by a man named Art Fleming. Or Bart Felling. I can't be sure, the TV kept crackling every time a car drove past the house. I was on my way to bang the side of the set once more when the phone rang again.

"Hello?"

"Hello. May I please speak to Evelyn?"

"Hi Judith, it's me, this is Evelyn."

"Hi. How did you know it was me?"

"I recognized your voice."

"Really? You must have a great memory."

"Yeah, I guess I do." Let's go with that, and not that I've heard your voice hundreds of times over the past week. Both the way it sounds now, girlish and sweet, and the way it'll sound in twenty years, lower, with just a touch of huskiness to it.

"Um. Well, I hope I'm not bothering you, but I just wanted to know if you're hungry?"

My eyes turned to the empty plate sitting on the coffee table and back again.

"I'm famished."

I rushed to get dressed, this time choosing a white sleeveless dress with a pink and blue flower design and matching blue heels, then stood by the window, peeking through the venetian blinds, waiting.

Judith offered to drive since my house sat between hers and the diner she suggested and I wasn't about to say no. Extra time is extra time, even if it was just a few minutes drive. I kept checking my watch as I stared past my lawn to the street. Every time a car came into view my pulse quickened, only to be disappointed when it just rolled on past.

"Shut it, Janice," I whispered to myself. No, time-travel hadn't addled my brain but I knew if my friend were standing here now, she'd have her arms crossed over her chest and a smirk on her face. "Never had it bad huh?"

It seemed to take hours but in reality it was only twenty minutes and she was right on time.

"You must think I'm a little odd, calling you so soon after we met," Judith said, as we pulled out of my driveway.

I was relieved to see she was also wearing a dress. A light pastel green one that matched her eyes. I had begun to worry I was overdressed when I saw a group of young girls from the window walking past the house during my wait. All four of them had been wearing pants, one of them was even in jeans.

"No, not at all, I'm glad you called or I would have been stuck at home watching As the World Turns."

"Do you normally watch that show?" She was trying to be polite, in case it turns out I was a fan, but I could tell, the way she knitted her eyebrows, probably without realizing it, that she definitely wasn't a fan. So I told her the truth.

"No, I don't, I don't like soap operas. Never have."

"Me neither, I think they're silly."

She went on to tell me that, the reason she called, was that most of her girlfriends had gotten married soon after their high school graduation. Two of them within the week of. They still phoned and invited her out, but it wasn't the same. The hot topic of conversation was marriage and babies and white picket fences. And if that wasn't enough, they were beginning to look at Judith with pity in their eyes. Poor thing, practically on the shelf, nineteen and not even engaged. If she didn't hook a man soon it would be all over. So she didn't see them as often as she used to, they'd slowly drifted apart.

"I just think it's ridiculous, being tied down so soon."

Sure, that's the reason why you didn't marry right out of high school the way all your friends had, the way all my friends had. The way everyone expected you to.

It was difficult, keeping the amusement off my face as I nodded, but I tried, and she took it the wrong way.

"Oh no. I put my foot in my mouth didn't I? You're engaged aren't you?"

"What? No. I'm not even dating anyone, much less engaged." I didn't know if this was true or not. The least I could do was not pry into that aspect of her life. That was too personal. I didn't know what I was going to do if a guy showed up at the house expecting certain...things. How was I supposed to handle that?

"Oh."

"Yeah, my mother's not too happy about it, but she tries not to nag me too much."

"Oh boy," she said, throwing her head back but not too far that she didn't keep her eyes on the road, "you're lucky then. My mother doesn't let a day slip by without telling me I need to stop with this singing nonsense and find myself a husband before it's too late."

"And what does she consider too late?"

"Judging by how frantic she's getting about it, I'd say she thinks by the time I'm twenty or twenty-one I may as well start sewing a shroud."

"Imagine that, a twenty-one year old spinster. That gives me less than a year. I guess I better hop to it."

When we walked in to the diner, Lou's, it was called, I could see that most of the after-church crowd seemed to have eaten and made their way home. By now they were more than likely visiting family or mowing lawns or washing the family car. Except for the younger crowd, they'd stayed on, having malts and sodas and fries. Some were still dressed in their church clothes, others had gone home to change so that some of the girls were wearing pants and the boys had slipped out of their suits and now had the nerve to wear something as sloppy as short sleeved shirts, buttoned up and tucked into their jeans. Really, the nerve.

Although there were still a few older people still hanging around. A couple of men sitting at the counter, five stools apart, sipping from coffee mugs and eating slices of pie. And smoking. Every once in a while they'd tip the ashes into the ashtray next to their plates but their cigarettes remained firmly grasped between index and middle fingers the entire time. It was sip, puff, bite, chew, puff, sip, puff. Even the cook, fifties, wavy hair greying at the temples, skinny arms but the beginning of a potbelly, who I was guessing was "Lou", had a cigarette dangling from his lips while he flipped burgers on the grill.

Likewise the two older couples, one in their thirties, it looked like, and the other mid-forties or so, were puffing away as they ate their meals. I was surprised to see that none of the teenagers were smoking. Aside from forks and spoons, they were empty handed. Except for one, a pimply red-headed boy sitting at a table with three girls. So that probably had more to do with impressing the ladies than with being addicted to nicotine.

I should have used a milder word. I wasn't near famished. The smell of cigarette smoke, the four-egg omelet I'd eaten less than an hour before and the excitement and nervousness I still felt just from being in the same room as Judith were all working against me.

When our food arrived, the smallest burger on the menu

for myself (which was setting me back a whopping fifty-five cents), and a cheeseburger with fries for Judith (an extra fifteen cents - like we were made out of money), I wasn't sure I'd even be able to manage keeping a few bites down. And when I looked past the counter into the kitchen with Lou still puffing away at his cigarette, my stomach lurched. Eating a greasy burger on a full stomach is one thing, eating a greasy and ashy burger is another.

Luckily something came along to distract me from that thought. When Judith ordered a "giant Pepsi-cola" along with her burger and fries, the picture that had popped into my head was a tub. Like the tubs that popcorn is served in at movie theaters. But what Betty, our young waitress, brought to our table was a glass that had a red star printed on the side of it with "16 ounces!" written in white across it. Sixteen ounces. Exclamation mark! I wasn't sure what constituted "giant" in 2010, I didn't drink much soda, but I was pretty damned sure it wasn't sixteen ounces. My morning cup of coffee the previous day (and almost fifty years in the future) had been twenty ounces.

"It's too much soda isn't it?"

She mistook my look of "that's it?" for one of "whoa, you're going to drink all of that?" and perhaps she thought I was judging her, so I quickly tried to remedy the situation.

"No, not at all, I was just thinking that for twenty-five cents it should be twice as much."

"Twice?" She looked aghast. "Who on earth could drink that much soda?"

"Doesn't seem possible does it?"

She shook her head then scanned the tabletop.

"She forgot yours."

"Oh, no she didn't, I'm fine with this," I said, reaching for my glass of water.

"Water?"

I glanced around quickly and noticed everyone, even the

mid-forties couple across the way were drinking everything but water. Coke. Pepsi. Grape Crush. One girl, with hair like Judith's, was chugging away at a Diet Pepsi. I'd seen it on the menu. "Try the brand new Diet Pepsi-cola! All the sweetness, none of the calories!" That saddened me. I had some idea that times were going to start changing right about now, and quickly. Some things would definitely change for the better, but not nearly all.

I'd had a Coke the day before. I wasn't in the habit of drinking soda at all and even though I knew it wasn't high fructose corn syrup I'd be consuming if I went ahead and indulged in another, it would be good old fashioned cane sugar, which I had no problem with, but it wouldn't be that way forever, maybe not even for decades, but why get into the habit?

"Yeah, I'm just not much of a soda person." Stick to the truth as much as possible.

"Hm."

Judith ate one of her fries, then took a bite of her cheeseburger and I managed to take a nibble of my own burger before a giant carrot wearing a white bra came bursting through the heavy glass door in front of me. After a second of surveying the room, the carrot locked eyes with me and then called me by name.

"Evelyn?"

Oh Lord. Frannie.

CHAPTER THIRTEEN

Orange pants, orange shirt with a wide white stripe across the chest, and a mountain of reddish orange hair piled on top of her head. A carrot in a white bra. If you were myopic, that's exactly what you'd think walked through the door. I wasn't nearsighted but the illusion was still there.

The dark-haired boy who followed her in was taller than she was but she still had at least two inches of hair on him.

She looked around the room again before she and Ralph made their way over to our booth. Just as she passed one of the men still sipping coffee at the counter, he struck a match to light another cigarette and I half expected there to be a loud "fwoomp!" sound as all the hairspray in her hair ignited at once leaving her with nothing but smoldering peach fuzz.

"No," she said, shoving her brother away just as he was about to slide into the spot next to me. "Sit over there," she said, waving her hand over to the other side of the booth, "she doesn't want to sit next to you."

She wasn't wrong. But I wasn't all that happy about him sitting next to Judith either. He looked put out, at first, then turned to Judith and smiled, thinking maybe sitting on that side wasn't so bad after all. Judith smiled at him but still slid a few inches towards the wall as he sat.

"Hi," Fran said, in Judith's direction, as she slid in to the space next to me.

"Oh, this is…"

"No, don't tell me, you're…" she said, pointing a finger at Judith and then snapping her fingers, as if trying to recall her name.

"What is it, it'll come to me…" Snap. Snap. Snap.

Judith looked at me. I looked at Judith. Fran snapped away.

Okay, this is getting rude.

"Judith," Judith finally said.

"Oh hell, I wasn't even close. I'd never have gotten it. But you were in choir weren't you?"

"Yes, I was," Judith answered her, nodding.

"You two know each other?"

"Not personally, we went to the same high school. You were what? Two grades behind us?"

"One," Judith answered.

The waitress came by and set two more glasses of water down on the table.

"We're not eating, we just ate," Fran said, before Betty had a chance to pull out her pad and pencil from her yellow apron. "We're just in here looking for Dwight. Have you seen him? Was he in here?"

The waitress, who was staring at Ralph to the point of uncomfortableness, said that no, she hadn't seen a Dwight, didn't know who Dwight was.

"How about you? Have you seen him?"

"No," I answered her, "I've been home all morning."

The waitress finally, reluctantly, gave Ralph one last smile before making her way over to a table full of kids calling for her, her blond ponytail swishing left and right as she did.

"Oh that's right," Fran said, before snatching the burger off of my plate and taking a bite out of it. A pretty large bite. Then set it back down in front of me. If I had actually been hungry I'd have been annoyed, but as it was, she was helping me out, so I let it go. "Too sick to go to the movies yesterday.

Thank you for that, by the way. Had a great night listening to my dad snore on the couch all the way through Hootenanny. And too sick for church this morning."

"Yeah, um," I said, as I nudged my plate closer to her. She took the bait. If she had just eaten, like she told the waitress, it didn't seem to have been enough. As soon as she took another bite I gave Judith the look. Just play along, I wasn't at the Saturn and Sun last night, I'll explain later. Hopefully that look works just as well in 1964 as it does in 2010. It must, because she quickly changed expressions and made an attempt at appearing casual by sipping on her tiny-giant soda.

"It might have just been something I ate," I said, turning back to Fran. "Or maybe it was allergies, I have no idea, but I feel fine now."

"And you look even better." That was Ralph.

Ah, Ralph. What can I say about Ralph? The memories were all there. Fran's twin brother who, unfortunately for Fran, got all the looks. Tall, dark hair, full lips, and Elvis-like perpetually squinting blue eyes. The kind of eyes all the girls swoon over. He'd been asking me out nearly every week for almost a year now. Not because he was that crazy about me, but because it drove him batty that I kept saying no. There weren't many girls who said no to him. For all I knew I was the only one.

"So what do you say Evelyn? I'm asking a whole week in advance, next Saturday, you can't say you have pl-"

"No, Ralph. The answer is still no."

"Wha- but I, you don't even know-"

I felt lousy for the boys who'd asked me to dance the day before. I did not feel lousy saying no to him. He'd have no trouble getting a date for the weekend. I'm sure there were five girls in here alone who'd jump at the chance, waitress not included.

"Let it go Ralph, she said no, you tried, leave her alone."

This time Fran reached over to Judith's plate and swiped a couple of fries. Judith, who looked so prim, I doubted she'd have said anything if Fran swiped them all, only looked up at me with a surprised smile.

Ralph threw a frustrated hand in the air and shook his floppy-haired head. Like the bottle of Diet Pepsi before, it too was another sign of the changes to come. One of the first guys I'd seen whose hair was more than an inch long. I didn't like it.

"Why are you wearing a dress?"

"Excuse me?"

"You didn't go to church, why are you wearing a dress?" Fran asked, then took a peek beneath the table. "And heels?" She shook her head and rolled her eyes. "I swear you're stuck in the fifties."

Again, why? Why the hell do I choose to hang out with this crass woman? It wasn't as if I'd waltzed in here wearing a ball gown and a tiara. Meanwhile you stick a few well placed black triangles on her shirt and she's a jack-o-lantern. Hey look lady, my hair is as stylish in 2010 as it is now, so suck on that. And this, this bouffant you have? That will never be repeated. Ever. I know it's called a beehive for a reason but hers really took it to the next level. It barely even resembled hair, it looked like an actual orange colored beehive had been glued to her scalp.

Between her and Ralph, I was starting to get angry. Not only because of their behavior, but also because their intrusion meant I'd hardly had any time at all to talk to Judith. I still wasn't sure how much time I had left. I started to think it was high time to cut some ties.

I would have said my good-byes then and there but Judith still had half a burger to eat even though her fries were disappearing at a pretty fast rate. So I gritted my teeth and instead of insulting her hair or outfit, I pointed out to Fran at least six other girls in the place who were wearing dresses or skirts. I did not, however, point out that Judith was also not wearing pants. If she insulted her, that would definitely have been too much for me to keep quiet about.

But Fran wasn't interested in hearing it, her attention had been drawn elsewhere.

I'd been too distracted by my growing irritation to notice that a woman and her daughter who'd just entered the diner, had all eyes on them.

The woman was still dressed in what I guessed were the clothes she'd worn to church. A knee length slim off-white sleeveless dress with a lace design on the upper half of it and a wide silk band around her small waist that ended in a bow in the back. Her shoes, beautiful matching satin heels. Her hair was swept up in a simple updo, showing off her slim neck and the string of pearls around it, on top of her head was a pillbox style hat, and in one of her hands was a cream colored purse. If she'd been wearing white gloves I think I might have cried. She looked that elegant. And her daughter was just as pretty. She looked to be about seven or eight, so no heels for her, only white shiny Mary Janes and thin folded over socks, but she still looked every bit as graceful as her mother.

Lou put down his spatula, grabbed a greasy towel from a hook next to the grill, wiped his hands, threw the towel over his shoulder and walked around to the front, to the counter, to deal with them himself.

"Go on Betty, I'll take care of this." Betty did as she was told, obviously happy to walk away.

"Now you know better than this, go on," he said, flapping his hand in the air to the side, in the direction of the door. "I don't want any trouble."

"I'm sorry, sir, but I didn't see a sign in the window," the woman told him.

"That don't matter, you see any more of you in here?"

The woman didn't bother to look around before

answering.

"No sir."

That's when it hit me, what the scene playing out before me was all about.

The woman, and her daughter, were black.

"Well then?"

"I'm not trying to cause any trouble. My husband was called in to work so my daughter and I had to walk to church this morning and now we're on our way home. She only wants an ice cream soda, we won't be long."

I turned my head to look behind me. Some people, the two adult couples and a pair of ladies who were sitting at one of the back tables, had the decency enough to look uncomfortable. They had their heads down, pretending to eat, but I could see they were only pushing their food around their plates. The kids and teenagers had gone back to their burgers and conversations, kids are kids, after all. But the two men still at the counter had no trouble at all staring right at the woman and her child, their loyalty obviously with Lou.

"I don't care if all she wants is a glass of water, you can't sit in here."

The woman placed her hand on the side of her daughter's head, pulling her closer to her so that the little girl's head lay against her thigh. I noticed where she placed her hand. It was over her daughter's right ear, her left ear was against the fabric of her dress. She didn't want her to have to hear what was being said.

"Please, sir, it's only an ice cream soda. It's hot out, we wouldn't be but ten minutes."

"Lady, I'm not telling you again."

One of the men at the counter, the one at the far end of it, fifty-ish, decent looking, jacket and tie, pink clean-shaven face, planted his feet on the floor as he slid off the stool. "You want me to take care of this Lou?"

He took a step forward and the woman jerked back two.

"No, sir, I apologize. We'll be leaving now."

I couldn't believe what I was witnessing. It wasn't real. Couldn't be. I had to be watching a movie. Everything in me was telling me to say something, do something. For all my 2010 bluster, all the speaking my mind I did back there, when there really wasn't that much on the line, here in 1964, where it actually mattered, where it actually made a difference, I was just sitting there like a powerless cowardly moron.

"You sit down! And you, you can't do this!" Fran was up on her feet and making her way toward the counter. She pointed her finger first at the asshole who'd stood up and then at Lou. "It's against the law. Ma'am? Ma'am, please don't leave." But the woman was already at the door. She placed her hand on her daughter's head and they walked out. The bell above the door jingled as it closed behind them.

"Against the law?" Lou asked, and snorted. "What country are you living in?"

"In a changing one. Haven't you heard? Don't you read the paper? The filibuster is over. The Senate voted it down."

Lou turned to his customer, who had backed up next to his stool but remained standing. He nodded at Lou, she's right.

"That don't mean nothing. The bill still has to be approved and then signed. And in case you haven't heard, Kennedy's dead."

"Hey now!" Someone shouted from the back.

Lou waved his towel at whoever it was without turning his head. "And there ain't no way in hell Johnson, a Texas man, is gonna sign it. No way in hell. Not if he knows what's good for him he won't."

"Yes he will!" Fran walked closer to the counter directly in front of the cook until her stomach was pressed against it. "And if he doesn't, the next one will."

Lou smirked and stepped forward, leaning over so that his and Fran's heads were no more than a foot apart. "Be that as it may," he said, then raised the side of his upper lip in a sneer. "No nigger's ever gonna sit at my counter, in one of my booths, bill or no bill, law or no law."

"Oh I'll see to it personally, you fucking jackass!" Fran looked ready to climb over the counter to scratch Lou's eyes out and might have if the man who'd sided with Lou hadn't spoken up.

"Alright, hey! That's enough! You have quite a mouth on you missy."

"You shut up baldy!"

His eyes bulged, his already pink complexion went fuchsia. "What did you-" He started advancing towards her, his hand curled into a fist, but jerked to a quick stop when Ralph jumped up out of the booth and stepped in front of his sister.

Ralph was younger, taller, and outweighed him by at least twenty pounds.

"Forget it Ralph. Come on!" she shouted towards us. "We're leaving! And so should everyone else!"

Both Judith and I stood up, as did the two women in the back.

"That's it?" She had a scowl on her face as she looked around the diner, glaring at everyone who remained seated. "You all should be ashamed of yourselves."

This she said to the room at large before zeroing in on one of the boys I'd seen earlier.

"I saw you smoking Jimmy! If you don't get up right now I'm telling your mother!"

Jimmy got up.

"You'll regret this," she shouted at Lou. "Can't even make a damned soda for a thirsty child. What the hell is wrong with you? We'll be taking our business elsewhere and I'll make sure everyone I know never comes in here again!" Satisfied she'd made her point, she turned and started stomping towards the door.

Okay. I see it now. I see why we're friends. Abrasive and loud, yes. A touch rude, definitely. But I liked her. I liked her a lot.

Before she made it to the door she turned back.

"Judith! Come on, what are you waiting for?"

"We...we haven't paid our bill," Judith said, timidly, afraid of bringing down Fran's wrath on herself.

"Oh for crying out loud!" Exasperated that her dramatic exit had been disrupted. "Well, go on then," she said, waving her hand in front of her. "We're trying to fight injustice here not land in jail for food theft."

CHAPTER FOURTEEN

Judith and I walked out of the diner five minutes later just in time to see Fran kick the bumper of a red Ford Fairlane parked near the front of the door.

"Ow! Goddamnit!" She yelled, raised her leg, grabbed her shoe in her hand, and hopped around on one foot around the parking lot.

"I need a ride home, it's your sister that kicked me outta there, so you owe me."

"Yeah, yeah, fine," Ralph said to Jimmy and pointed to his car behind him then turned to me. "How about the Saturday after next Evie? Two whole weeks in advance. A burger, just a burger, it won't even-"

"Sorry Ralph, that's my nana's birthday, I'll be at her house all day long."

"Oh boy Ralph! Your car is ace!" Jimmy shouted, while running his hand over the shiny green hood.

"Just get in before I leave you here!"

Frannie hobbled along behind me and Judith as we walked to Judith's car. Without a word, she opened the door, hopped into the back seat and proclaimed "I'm in the mood for a sundae."

Both Judith and I were too intimidated to argue, she was still peeved at Lou, so we drove over to Maybell's Dairy on the edge of town, the last stop before the interstate, and had some ice cream. Not fat-free yogurt, not soy-based mash with a heap of guar gum and carageenan in it, not artificially flavored chocolate frozen coconut milk that's more ice crystals than anything else, but real honest-to-goodness ice cream. Egg yolks, sugar, whole milk, heavy cream, and actual vanilla beans. Full fat. And why not? I'm twenty years old, who needs to worry about heart disease? The second hand smoke would probably get me before my arteries had a chance to clog up anyway. May as well enjoy it. And I did, every last delicious drop, even with my still half full stomach.

The ice cream even managed to calm Fran down until she remembered why she was at Lou's in the first place. She'd been quiet for a few minutes, watching the few people who walked in or walked out. A couple of kids for ice cream cones, a woman wearing a pink and blue polka-dotted kerchief over her hair for some butter and eggs. Then she'd turned her attention to the parking lot and the sidewalk just outside the large window we were seated next to. Her sundae sat in front of her, half-eaten and melting. I didn't pay her much mind, at least she'd finally quieted down after talking non-stop and gave me and Judith a chance to have an actual conversation for the first time since she'd stormed into the diner.

But it didn't last.

"Where the hell is Dwight?" She raised her hand then let it fall heavily to the table which made her spoon rattle in the glass bowl. A young blond woman, sitting with her husband and two children across the floor from us turned our way with a scowl. "He was supposed to meet me after church."

She caught me unguarded, in the middle of talking to Judith.

"I don't know, Fran, jeez. Why don't you just text him?"

"Do what? Test him? Test him for what?"

"No. No...telephone. I meant...phone him, you know

telephone him. There's a booth right outside."

"And how am I supposed to phone him when I don't know where he is?"

Darn the past is hard.

Luckily I was saved by the jingling of the bell above the door.

"Michael!" she shouted, turning towards the door. "Have you seen Dwight?"

The boy who walked in looked less than delighted to see Fran in all her orange glory but answered truthfully regardless.

"Uh...yes, about thirty minutes ago, outside the rec center. With Fred and...I think Pete."

"What? What's he doing...never mind, come on, I need to talk to him."

She got up, limped over to the entrance and held the door open, waiting for him to follow.

"What?" he asked.

"You're going to take me to the rec center, come on."

"But...my mom sent me here for milk."

"Well buy your milk and then let's go, gah!"

She stood at the door, tapping her good foot and shaking her head. When I met her eyes, which were blue, just like her brother's but a darker shade, so not as noticeable, she gave me a look "Can you believe this guy?" As if it were he that was putting her out and not the other way around.

Michael, milk in hand, slumped his shoulders when he turned from the counter at the back, after receiving his change from Maybell, and saw that Fran was still waiting for him at the door.

"It's hot outside! If I bring home spoiled milk I'm sending my father to your house."

"Yeah, yeah. Bye Judith. Bye Evie, I'll see you at work tomorrow."

And they were gone.

Work?

WORK?!

Bryant's. Clothing store.

Later. I'll have to think about that later.

"Uh oh, whoever Dwight is, he's going to get an earful isn't he?" Judith asked.

"I'm sure he is."

I didn't elaborate because I wasn't sure who Dwight was either. When I thought about it I could see a boy, or a young man, who I seemed to think was Fran's boyfriend, but, and I should probably be ashamed of myself for thinking this, he seemed way out of her league. Not that Fran was an ogre, not at all, but compared to the guy I was picturing, who bore a resemblance to a young pre-car accident Montgomery Clift, she was, well, a bit plain.

That sounds horrible. Really horrible. I decided to change the subject.

"Did you see the poster outside? Big concert, lots of bands?"

"No, I didn't." She turned her head to look at the large window beside the front door but the poster was taped to the glass from the outside. "But I know which one you're referring to."

"Do you wanna go?"

"I'd love to, but we can't. Here, try some of mine, it's delicious." She pushed her bowl to the center of the table.

"What are those red and white specks in it?"

"Just taste it, it's new."

I tasted it. Peppermint. Okay.

"So those red and white bits are peppermint candy crushed into it?"

"Yeah," she said, and her eyes lit up with delight like a child discovering something new. "Neat huh?"

"You're right, delicious." How could you not delight in that yourself? Wonderment at bits of hard candy in ice cream.

Just a few months ago I'd gone with a friend to a local gourmet dessert shop and had had a bowl of fried chicken and waffles flavored ice cream and hadn't batted an eye.

"So why can't we? Go to the concert?" I asked, as Judith slid her bowl back towards herself.

"They're not selling any tickets. It says so right on the poster."

"They're what? Why would they put on a concert and not have anyone go to it? Are the bands just going to sing to a bunch of empty chairs?"

That couldn't be right, I heard the audience roar when her song was over, even if I never saw them. Canned roaring? Do they have that yet? And the story was that the kids in attendance started calling stations to request the song which is what caught the studios' attention.

"No, no there'll be people there, but it's only going to be teenagers. They gave all the tickets away for free, handed them out at a few high schools both here and in Dallas. I have no idea why. But it's going to be filmed, so we can watch it on TV."

I knew why, but I couldn't very well tell her. I couldn't tell her that just a couple of days ago I was chief marketing officer for a growing company so I knew a few marketing tricks. The producer didn't want a bunch of old fogies in the audience. Old fogies don't buy music. Teenagers do. And if teenagers see a packed room full of other teenagers enjoying something, they'll automatically think it's something they should be enjoying as well. But if people who are old enough to be their parents are enjoying something, well, that's a turn off. It doesn't appeal to their rebellious nature.

"Yeah, you're right, but it won't be the same."

Something else I couldn't tell her. That I'd already seen it on video, over and over again, what I wanted was to see it live.

I was getting better at the past. When Judith asked what I felt like doing when we left the dairy, my immediate thought was shopping (one lousy fan just wasn't going to cut it). But I immediately realized I'd have to wait for that. No shopping on Sundays. I could buy gas, grab a bite to eat, maybe get a few groceries, but anything else was off the table. Everything was closed. So instead, Judith parked her car in my driveway and we went for a long walk. We picked up a few people along the way on their own walks who decided to join us. Neighbors. Friends. Some of them I knew, some of them she knew. Not that Leyfant is that small a town that everyone knows everyone else, it's not, but when you have three channels on TV, you can't shop, or you can't sit in front of a computer all day long, alone, updating your Facebook page, this is what happens. You go out and actually talk to people.

By the time we got back to the house we'd made two new friends and had half a ham nestled in an orange Tupperware bowl courtesy of Mrs. Luskin from three blocks over. We ate ham sandwiches, we watched a bit of Walt Disney's Wonderful World of Color...in black and white, and now we were in my bedroom.

Judith was busy combing through my stuffed closet, while I sat on the bed, fiddling with my alarm clock.

"What do you think? This one?" she asked, turning around holding a dress to her chest with one hand.

"Sure, looks great."

One of the more conservative dresses in the whole bunch of course. I'd probably seen every picture of her that existed on the internet but it wasn't until I forced myself to look at the newer ones, when she was almost forty years old, that I found out she has a sprinkling of freckles across her chest. Before then I don't think she showed the world more than half an inch of skin below her neck. Meanwhile, back in 2010, Lady Gaga is licking a telephone in a jail cell wearing nothing but a few scraps of crime scene tape.

Was it the loosening of morals over the years? Hardly. Just take a look at that famous Sophia Loren/Jayne Mansfield picture. It was taken in 1957. People were in an uproar over something Janet Jackson did in 2004 that Jayne had already done forty-seven years earlier. That famous photo wasn't the only one taken that night. There are others. And it happened.

So no, I didn't really think it had anything to do with any societal moral code that kept her from dressing in a more provocative way, it was just her personality. And I think I liked her even more for that.

"And you weren't going to wear it? Are you sure?"

"I'm sure. Take as many as you want, I can only wear one dress at a time."

She turned back to the closet, contemplated it, then shook her head.

"No, no I shouldn't, this should be okay."

She draped the dress she'd chosen over the bedpost, carefully, not letting it touch the floor, then sat on the bed with me.

"How do you have so many clothes?"

"My last name's Bryant. Bryant's clothing store? My father owns it. And I work there."

Aha. Very successful store in an affluent area of Dallas. That explains the fancy shmancy private school I attended.

"Oh wow. I know where it's at, but I've never been, I'd never be able to afford a dress from there," she said, then quickly added, "not that I think your father is in any way-"

"I know you don't," I said, dismissing her remark with a wave of my hand. "Now what time is this birthday party you're singing at tomorrow? The one you'll be wearing the dress to?"

She grimaced. "Maybe I shouldn't borrow it after all, now that I know how expensive it is. What if a kid spills punch on it?"

"Then I have you arrested Judith. I call the police, they

hunt you down, and then they haul you off to prison for staining a dress."

For a second she actually looked alarmed before she smiled at the sarcasm.

"It's at noon. The party."

Drat. I'll be at work. Unless...I call in? I was supposedly ill yesterday, maybe I didn't fully recover? Perfect. I set the alarm clock for six in the morning and sat it atop my nightstand. That should be early enough to call in someone else to replace me before the doors opened up at nine.

"Do you think I can come along? To the party? Not for the entire time, just to hear you sing?" It wasn't the concert, but it was something.

"Sure, I think it'll be okay, but why would you want to?"

Stick to the truth as much as possible. "Because I'd like to hear you sing. Your songs, not an oldie from way back in 1963."

"You think they're going to let me sing my songs?"

"Well, yeah, what else?"

"It's a birthday party, Evelyn, for fourteen year olds. They want to hear The Dixie Cups and Mary Wells not Judith Paige. But you're still welcome to come if you want to hear me sing The Shoop Shoop Song."

I tried not to laugh, I really did.

"What's so funny?" she asked, grinning herself.

"Nothing, nothing. And yes, I still want to go. If I can't go to the concert, still mad about that, by the way, then Shoop Shoop it is."

"You know you wouldn't have been able to go to the concert anyway, even if they were selling tickets," she said, then lay back on the bed and draped her hands across her stomach. The hem of her dress rode up above her knees.

"Why not?" I hoped I didn't look unnatural. I probably looked unnatural. Keeping my head level, trying to keep my eyes on the bedpost and the dress hanging over it.

"Because it's on your grandmother's birthday, you'll be with her all day won't you?"

"I will?"

"That's what you told Ralph at the diner."

"Oh, that's right, I did. Yeah, that was a lie."

"You lied?" As if I just confessed to hiding a dead body in the spare bedroom.

How the heck did she ever survive the music industry? 1960s or not, I'm sure it's just as ruthless and cutthroat now as it must be in the future.

"Yes, I lied. But I'm pretty sure he knows it was a lie, he's heard plenty of them already. I once told him I couldn't go to the movies with him because I'd been mauled by a tiger in the parking lot of a Texaco."

Her laughter echoed around the room.

"You did not!"

"I did."

"How did you explain not having any injuries?"

"I told him the tiger was very old and had lost all its teeth and claws. But that I was traumatized by the experience nonetheless."

Once she stopped giggling she asked, "I know that's not a true story, but why?"

"Why what?"

"Why do you keep turning him down? I mean, I went to school with him. I didn't know him, we weren't friends, but I knew who he was and I can tell you at least half the girls in the school would have killed to go on a date with him. My friend Sue, a week before she got married told me if he asked her out she'd call the wedding off."

"What a lucky man your friend hooked, that's going to be a lovely marriage."

She smiled but was still waiting for my answer. I wasn't getting out of it. So I shrugged.

"I'm just not attracted to him."

"Not attracted to him? Gosh, you must have really high standards. Who are you waiting for? Warren Beatty?" It's a good thing she'd turned her eyes back up towards the ceiling and didn't catch my expression. I thought of the Warren Beatty of 2010.

"No, it's not that at all, I think Ralph is very good looking and I also think he's a great guy. Maybe a touch pompous, from all the attention he gets, but nice. He's not the problem."

Judith rolled over, propped her elbow on the bed and then her head on her hand. "Okay," she said, and then waited for me to tell her what the problem was exactly.

So I took a deep breath and did.

"It's not just Ralph I'm not attracted to. It's boys, or men, in general, that I'm not interested in."

She became so still, so quickly, she probably stopped breathing mid-breath.

"I don't think I under..." The look of bemusement dropped from her face as she sat up. "You don't mean..."

"Yes, I do. I'm..." I trailed off trying to think. Is the term "gay" part of the sixties vernacular? Didn't sound right. But neither did lesbian. Queer? Ew. "I'm attracted to women, Judith."

Even though we were at least a foot apart on the bed, she still leaned away from me. That kinda hurt.

"I'm sorry, I didn't mean to shock you or..."

"No, no, you didn't, but, um..." She stood and pointed towards the alarm clock. "It's already nine and I've been gone all day so I really should get going."

"Because of what I just said."

"No. Not at all, it's just that I still have some things to do, for tomorrow, so..." She was halfway down the hallway before I even made it to my feet.

"Judith, I'm really sorry. I was only trying to be honest."

I followed her to the door but cautiously, like I was trying to approach a skittish deer without spooking it into bolting.

Whether she didn't hear me or just chose to ignore it, I don't know.

"Thank you, Evelyn, for going to the diner with me today and for the walk and everything else. It was fun. I'll see...uh...bye."

"You forgot the dress!" I shouted at her from the porch just as she was opening her car door.

"That's okay! I'll just wear one of mine!" She didn't peel out of the driveway but she'd made her point.

Boy, that did not go the way I thought it would.

I figured she'd be relieved to know she wasn't the only person in the whole world who felt the way she did (it's what I felt as a teenager, and that was in the eighties). I thought she'd be happy to have someone she could talk to about it, to finally have even just one friend she didn't have to lie to constantly. I never expected her to run out of here like I had the plague. Or the mumps.

But hey, I wanted to know her story and now I'd just gotten a small piece of it. She hadn't figured things out this early. She didn't actually come out, officially at least, until the eighties. Could be another sixteen years.

I was happy to learn something new, but not so happy that I probably blew my chances at finding out if it was just a joke or if there really was an actual song called The Shoop Shoop.

CHAPTER FIFTEEN

I woke up the next morning thankful that I was still here and with all the lyrics of The Shoop Shoop Song playing in my head. Betty Everett, of course. I'd heard it plenty of times.

I didn't even have to think about it.

There were a lot of things I didn't have to think about. Like going to work. I had no problem finding the place, I had no problem recalling all of my co-worker's names, I even knew several of the regular customers. I worked both on the floor selling ladies dresses and slips, and also in the back offices, when needed, to answer phones, type up correspondence...and make the coffee. My 21st century brain seethed at that, but I had Fran to seethe along with me, so it wasn't all that bad.

I also met, for all intents and purposes, my father.

I saw him before he saw me, I already knew what he looked like. Taller than average, lanky, his dark hair already thinning, soft brown eyes behind the half black-rimmed glasses that matched his brown suit and shoes. Not the most handsomest of men, a big nerd in school who was still growing out of it, but he looked like a good man. No, I knew he was a good man. A man who loved his daughter and didn't deserve to be deceived.

I managed to keep it together, when the memories and

emotions hit at the sight of him. It's a good thing, that to him, today was no different than any other day. He'd seen me just three days ago, at the end of work on Friday, so there was nothing dramatic about it, our meeting. All I got was a "Good morning, honey" and a quick squeeze of the shoulder before he had to attend to a busy workday.

What could I do? I certainly didn't want to hurt anyone, but I had no control over the situation. I didn't choose to be someone else. And even if I wanted to go back, and let her return, I was starting to think I just flat out no longer had a choice in the matter.

When ten o'clock rolled around, I thought about calling Judith, to ask about the party. I could slip away from work for an hour, hell, my father owned the place, but decided against it. Clearly I'd made her uncomfortable, she wouldn't want me there. But she'd also probably be too polite to say so, so I made the decision for her.

To keep my mind off of it, I made smalltalk with the ladies who came into the store to buy expensive gloves and girdles. I teased Fran about having to wear a dress to work. I studied the paper when I had a few spare minutes throughout the day, and made plans. Fran and I walked to the Woolworth's three blocks down the busy streets at lunchtime for a couple of bacon and tomato sandwiches with apple pie and malted milks. My treat. Not just because the entire bill was less than two dollars but also because I got paid almost twice as much as she did even though we both had essentially the same job. She was not aware of that fact and I thought it best to keep it that way. I rather liked having functioning eardrums.

It was bad enough when I asked her if she'd managed to find Dwight the day before. She hadn't and she let me know just how teed off she was about it. Me and half of the

Woolworth's lunch counter.

All in all, by the end of the day, I think I did pretty well. I only slipped up once early in the day. When I guessed a woman's size at a four and I got a funny confused look. There was no such thing as size four in the women's department. She was a size twelve. No one was trying to appear thinner by slapping a smaller number on a label. What women did in these days to appear thinner, was, well, be thin.

By the time I pulled into my driveway at the end of the workday I was thinking about one of those hypothetical questions we've all asked or been asked before.

If you traveled back in time and had to do without modern conveniences, which one would you miss the most? Which one would you not be able to live without?

I don't think I would have hesitated in giving my answer before I actually did travel back in time. The internet. Of course.

But now that I was here, I thought, as I walked through my front door after driving straight home after work and roasting in my metal tank of a car under the Texas sun, I knew better.

The answer is central air.

Screw the internet.

And above that, even above refreshing cool air, at least for this particular moment, the answer would have been an answering machine. Even a ten pound 1985 clunker of an answering machine would have been wonderful. Just to know if she'd called. What's a little heat stroke after all?

If I did have the internet, I'd be able to look it up and learn that there are in fact answering machines around in 1964. Large impractical monstrosities that cost an arm and a leg, but they do exist. But who cares, that information wouldn't have done me any good anyway.

What was going to do me good was another shower. My second of the day. Thank God I hadn't been accidentally shipped off to 1804 or I'd have had to make do with a bucket.

After my shower I had the last of Mrs. Luskin's ham. I watched a little TV. I read. I washed Mrs. Luskin's Tupperware bowl and dried it. I thought about walking over and returning it but without a cell phone, I wasn't going to risk missing a call.

By eleven o'clock, after pouring over the business section of the newspaper once again while the phone remained stubbornly silent, I gave it up as a lost cause, took one last quick shower, and called it a night.

The next day I met Dwight.

I was surprised to see he was every bit as handsome, if not more so, than I had pictured. And even more surprised to see Fran transform into a fifteen-year-old schoolgirl in front of him when he and Ralph showed up at the store right before lunchtime.

It was embarrassing really, all the giggling and batting of eyelashes. I'm pretty sure she was going for sultry but that fell apart when one of her fake eyelashes fell off mid-blink.

"Hello Mr. Englewood, Mr. Ellison, here to buy every tie I have in stock?" my father asked. He placed a hand on each of the boy's shoulders and winked at me playfully.

"No sir, Mr. Bryant, we're here to take Evelyn and Fran out to lunch."

"Sorry Ralph, but I'm afraid Evelyn has a date with me this afternoon. Evelyn? You wanted to speak to me?"

"Yes, sir."

"See you later Evelyn," Dwight said, and then clapped a deflated Ralph on the back, "come on, cheer up buddy, we can still go have some lunch."

I smiled and waved at all of them before following my father back to his office.

"Hey! Just because Evie isn't going doesn't mean I'm not still hungry!" Frannie shouted across the store behind us. Ralph and Dwight were already halfway outside the door.

"So what's this about honey? Everything okay?"

"Yes, sir, everything's fine," I said, as he opened his office door for me. "I've just been thinking about something, and I need your help."

"Okay, I'm all ears."

I entered his office, pulled the newspaper out of my purse, and hoped he wouldn't laugh too hard at what I had to say.

That evening was a repeat of the day before. I drove straight home after work, even though I was going to have to risk going to the grocery store soon. There were a couple of TV dinners in the freezer but believe it or not, they looked just as bad as anything you'd find in 2010. And there was no microwave. That meant having the oven on for thirty or forty minutes. In this heat? With no air conditioning? Puh!

No calls, except from my mother, who told me not to worry, I'd get what I asked for, she'd see to it. And another from Frannie who'd reverted back to her old self now that Dwight wasn't around.

"What a damned disaster today was!"

"What are you talking about?" It couldn't be about her lunch date, she'd already vented to me about that at work. Seems Dwight didn't pay her enough attention and instead spent too much time talking to Ralph about cars or baseball or some other ridiculous topic.

"My father's car broke down, so after waiting outside the store for half an hour before getting the call, I had to take the bus home, and very nearly took my eye out when I was trying to put my eyelashes back on and we hit a damned pothole."

"Why didn't you call me? I'd have come back to drive you home."

"How could I? You wouldn't have been home."

"True, go on."

"So there I am walking the three blocks to my house from the bus stop sweating my tail off and here comes old Mr. Goldstein's dumb dog yapping his fool head off and almost takes a chunk out of my calf. Well the last thing I need is rabies so I tried to swat at him with my purse and that's when my heel gets caught in a crack in the sidewalk and it snaps clean off! Now I've got a broken shoe and a twisted ankle."

"Hello? Evie? I can hear you laughing!" She was laughing herself, so it didn't come out as angry as she wanted it to.

"I'm sorry Fran, that's horrible, it really is."

"Yeah, you sound real torn up about it."

"How about I buy you a new pair of shoes?"

"No, what I need is for you to tell me who the hell I call to fix potholes and to keep that hellhound off the street."

"He's a poodle."

"He's a nuisance."

Now that I wasn't cracking a rib I was anxious to get her off the line, if someone were trying to call they'd only get a busy signal, so I told her to call city council. I have no idea if that's correct but she seemed satisfied with that answer and finally let me hang up the phone.

Not that it made a difference.

By the end of the workday on Wednesday my resolve to give her space and time, to let her contact me, if she ever wanted to again, that is, was crumbling. I drove home on autopilot, my brain busy working out how I could casually bump into her. Grocery store? That's good, yes, but I don't know where she lives. There are several grocery stores to choose from. And even if I happened to pick the right one, I could spend all day hanging out in the produce department squeezing oranges and thumping watermelons when she's already been and gone while I was at work.

I could try going to the Saturn and Sun again on Saturday, that was a possibility. But she never did say whether or not she goes every weekend.

This is bad. This is cutting it close. I only have a few weeks before she's off and running hobnobbing with Mike Douglas or Ed Sullivan and I'll be back here with Fran, Mrs. Luskin, and a rabid thug of a poodle.

What can I do? What can I do? I was thinking, as I rounded the corner on my block. What other option did I have? None. I'll just have to call her. I could try the "Oh, sorry, I must have dialed the wrong number...but...how are you?" ploy. That could actually work, after all, it's probably new, no one's had time to catch on to it yet. For that matter I might be the first person to ever even use it.

This is what was going through my head when I pulled into my driveway, so I didn't notice her car parked on the curb, nor did I see her sitting on the front steps until I was only a few feet away, twirling my key ring on one finger.

"Hi," she said, looking up at me.

She was sitting on the bottommost step with her knees tucked close to her chest and her arms wrapped around her skirt and legs for modesty's sake.

"Judith, hi. Is everything okay?"

"Yes, I just...I needed to apolog-"

She'd abandoned her modest pose and was now leaning both legs off to one side at a sharp angle, she had one hand planted on the step beside her and the other stretched out straight in front of her. Without the help of a railing she was having a hard time getting any leverage.

I watched her struggle for a few seconds and tried, unsuccessfully, to keep the smile off my face, before I said anything. "You're trying to get up aren't you?"

"This...jeez...this-"

She managed to lift herself about an inch off the step before her shoe slipped and she plopped right back down.

157

She let her head fall back and laughed. "I can't get up, this skirt is so tight!"

"How did you even manage to sit all the way-"

"Are you going to help me up or are you just going to stand there giggling?"

She held her hands out to me and I pulled her to her feet.

Once she was standing we were only a few inches apart. It felt awkward, given what had happened on Sunday, but she didn't step back so neither did I.

"Thank you."

"You're welcome."

"And I'm sorry, Evelyn, about-"

"No, there's no need, you didn't do anything wrong."

She nodded. Underneath the bright sun, and this close up, her eyes were...stunning. I tried not to, but I couldn't help but to stare at them.

Probably a mistake. She shifted her eyes to her right, towards my car, then cleared her throat before looking back at me.

"It's hot out here." She squinted up towards the sky and back. "And I've been waiting on you for over an hour. So can I come in? Have a Coke?"

"No, you can't. I'm sorry."

"Oh." The small smile she'd given me after asking her question vanished. "Uh...okay...I understand, I'll just-"

"My refrigerator is empty. Come on, hop in the car, we're going shopping."

"Not funny," she said, but the smile that reappeared on her face as she followed me to my car said otherwise.

"You know, the nearest grocery store is always too crowded this time of day. Why don't we go to the one you normally shop at?"

This time I wasn't taking any chances.

CHAPTER SIXTEEN

We went shopping that day.

And the next.

Instead of a fan I bought a window air conditioning unit that brought the temperature inside my house (or at least half of the living room) down from a scorching ninety degrees to about a soupy seventy-nine, but still, Judith and I sat on my couch that evening drinking iced tea out of frosted mugs and luxuriated in it. Now that's living. It's the little things.

On Friday, the three of us, Fran, Judith, and I, finally went to see the movie I was supposed to have seen the previous Saturday night. Viva Las Vegas. It was horrible. But watching it was hilarious.

Every time a scantily clad woman popped up on the huge drive-in screen (which was approximately every five minutes) I could see Judith watching me from the corner of her eye. She was sitting right next to me, with Fran on her right, in the front seat of my car. At first I tried to keep my face neutral. Which should have been easy, because believe me, nothing on that screen intrigued me in the slightest, no offense to Ann-Margret. But with Fran there, something was bound to happen.

"Boy, that gal is really shaking it isn't she?"

That's when I cracked. When Fran said that. I had to cover my mouth with a closed fist to keep from laughing.

Then I decided to have fun with it. Every time Judith tried to catch me ogling, I ogled. I started making exaggerated facial expressions. Those cartoonish jaw dropping eye popping ones. At first she thought I was being serious and would snap her eyes back to the screen, embarrassed. After a while her looks grew suspicious. By the time she figured it out, that I was messing with her, the movie was ten minutes away from ending. I was mouthing the word WOW when she finally bumped my shoulder with hers. When I turned to her she was facing the screen but she was smiling and shaking her head.

On Saturday I met my mother.

I'd been invited over to my childhood home, for lunch, and to discuss this harebrained scheme of mine.

But before I get to that, my mother.

The woman with hazel eyes who'd given me the housecoat I'd put on when I arrived.

Every day I spent here, the more entrenched I became in the world around me, in this life, as Evelyn Bryant. That other life, who I once was, was slipping away, hour by hour, minute by minute. This was it for me now, I was no longer stealing someone else's memories, I was creating my own. I'm the one who went to a dance hall on a Saturday night and met Judith, I'm the one who sat and ate a sandwich with Fran at the Woolworth's on Monday, I'm the one who sat and ate a bowl of vanilla ice cream with my friends at Maybell's. These were my own memories, no one else's. My own experiences. And isn't that what makes a person? Their experiences and memories? I no longer had to fake being someone else. I was this someone else. Evelyn Bryant, twenty years old, two inches taller, fancy private school graduate, Leo and Elizabeth Bryant's daughter, all of it.

And, as I said before, what other choice did I have?

I hadn't heard a peep from Mr. Smith.

Maybe he'd heard my request, that I wanted to stay here.

And maybe Evelyn, or Karen, I should say, she was Karen now, wanted to stay there.

Or maybe he's just forgotten about us.

Either way there didn't seem anything I could do about it.

So yes, instead of telling this woman the outlandish truth which she wouldn't believe anyway, and possibly break her heart when she realized her daughter might have to be institutionalized, I returned her hug when she greeted me at the door and felt only the slightest twinge of guilt as the memories flooded through me ten times stronger than they had at only hearing her voice over the phone. Then I walked in. I had memories to create.

I ate the pork roast, it was delicious, but I passed on the salad. It was encased in green Jell-O. Really. Green gelatin with cauliflower, cucumbers and red peppers stuck right in the middle as if floating in mid-air. I had memories of eating it before, even enjoying it, but even though 2010 was slipping away, I still knew that there was a reason why Jell-O had ceased to be included in savory dishes.

"I just don't understand Evelyn, you've never shown the slightest interest in this sort of thing before."

My father set his spoon down on the table and wiped at the corner of his mouth with a napkin, after finishing his Whip'n Chill dessert. I passed on that too.

"Yes I have, I just haven't spoken to you about it."

My mother, who was sitting directly across from me, was busy gathering dishes from the table and stacking them neatly off to the side, presumably lost in her own thoughts, not hearing a word of what was being said around her. But I knew better.

"It's not the money, I just think it could be put to better use. Something practical and safe. A college education, for instance. The stock market is volatile. No matter what you may have read or heard."

Yes, I could agree with that. But when you have the knowledge I do, it's a pretty safe bet.

If I was a sports fan I could have made quick money, and a lot of it, but I knew exactly diddly about sports. I couldn't have told you who won the Superbowl in 2010, I couldn't even have named either team who played. So there was zero chance I'd recall who won a horse race, the World Series, or a single boxing match in 1964.

What I did know about was the market. I'd invested quite a bit in that old long ago life, and even if I hadn't, you don't have to be a financial genius to know Google's doing pretty well for itself and investing in them early on would have been a damned good idea.

Of course Google is decades away, but others such as IBM, Xerox, Polaroid? They're here now and they'll be taking off. Some of them will tank later on, of course, but the risk, when you know when that tank will happen, is virtually nonexistent. Pretty soon everyone was going to want to watch TV in color, they were going to ditch homemade meals for fast food, we were all going to sit and watch the moon landing in 1969, which would end up costing over twenty-five billion dollars for the entire Apollo program and thanks to my nerdy interest in science, I knew which companies would end up with those very lucrative contracts.

I knew McDonald's would be going public in a year. I knew Walmart was a single store at the moment somewhere in Kansas or Arkansas, I wasn't sure which, but that didn't matter, all I needed to know was that they wouldn't be a one store mom and pop operation forever. I knew people would scoff at the idea of cell phones in the beginning. Pretentious, they'd say, who needs to carry a phone with them everywhere they go? Ridiculous. Why would you invest in that?

Because I knew.

"Yes, Dad, I know but I've done my research, I'm not just being flighty."

And, I thought, I don't want to sell pantyhose for the rest of my life. Or become an airline stewardess, which, if you read the ladies section of the paper, was about the only option open to me. That, or nurse, and I don't have the stomach for a career in medicine. Plus I already had a college education, I couldn't see putting myself through that torture again.

"Still, sweetheart, what do you really know about these companies? It's not as if they have readily available information for you to study-"

"Leo, dear, did your father ask you what you knew about dresses and girdles before he loaned you the money to open a store, or did he just trust and believe in you?"

There wasn't a trace of confrontation in her voice when she said it. But there was a finality to it. And, as if to punctuate that finality, Elizabeth Bryant grabbed the pile of dishes from the table and disappeared with them into the kitchen.

My father said nothing, he only took off his glasses and wiped at them with his napkin, but the crooked smile on his face as he did it told me everything.

I spent the rest of that Saturday with Judith. Mostly in my virtual icebox of a living room, listening to music, watching TV, talking. We made an upside down pineapple cake for Mrs. Luskin (now that I had AC, I was no longer afraid of turning on the oven, but the TV dinners still went in the trash) and walked it over to her, returning her bowl, and then quickly walked back before we melted. I attended church with my parents on Sunday, had a great meal at Carver's afterward, and then met Judith's parents and brothers when she invited me over to her house for dinner.

That was her mother's idea. She wanted to meet this girl her daughter was spending so much time with. She was not impressed. Not married? Not engaged? What's wrong with you? She didn't ask that, not in words anyway, but that slow shifting of her eyes when I answered her questions told me all I needed to know. How was she going to get her daughter married with such a bad influence hovering around?

On Monday, after work, it was back to Maybell's. Judith really had a thing for that Peppermint Stick ice cream. I stuck with plain vanilla because I still couldn't get over how good it tasted.

It was then that she brought up the subject we'd both been avoiding since the previous Sunday.

"Do you, um, date?" She kept her head bowed and swirled her ice cream with her spoon, mashing it up, breaking apart the small red and white pieces in it. The skin at her hairline turning a bright pink.

"If you're asking if I'm dating anybody right now, no," I answered truthfully.

Here's the thing, I broke my promise. About not digging. I dug. And what I found out was that Evelyn did not have a boyfriend. And didn't want one either. That was too much of a coincidence to think it wasn't planned. Mr. Smith had done a great job of picking the right person. My friends back in the future wouldn't be getting a shock, nor would Evelyn (or Karen) herself. And I wouldn't be having a guy come knocking at the door with puckered lips and roses in hand. Thank God.

"How does that work? Do you ask a girl out or does she ask you? How do you know who's supposed to ask who out?"

I smiled at her even though she still had her eyes squarely on her now soupy bowl of pink mush.

"There's not an official rulebook on the subject. It doesn't have to be the short-haired girl with the leather jacket and boots on that asks the girl in the skirt out or anything like that."

"Girls wear boots?" She finally raised her widened eyes. Oh, she was going to have so much trouble with the future.

"It's just a stereotype. I guess girls wear boots, I don't know. I'm just saying it doesn't matter who asks who out. You just tell someone you're interested in them, the rest takes care of itself. If," I said, punctuating it, "you know they're of the same persuasion. I'd never make a pass at someone who was not interested in women."

"Never?"

"No."

On Tuesday, just as I was beginning to worry that my being here had ruined everything, that maybe instead of being by the phone when the call came in, she'd been in my living room swapping 45s on the turntable and had missed out on her big break, I got the call. Judith telling me one of the performers scheduled to play at the upcoming concert had pulled out, and she was in. Thanks to her uncle.

I didn't see or speak to her for the next three days.

Not until Friday night.

"Seven hundred and fifty dollars! No fucking way! For a TV? You're out of your datgum mind Bill."

There was a knock at the door.

"Did I hear you cursing?" Judith was standing in the glow of the porch light with a disapproving look on her face when I opened the door.

"Did you know a TV set costs seven hundred and fifty dollars?"

"Are you watching The Price Is Right again?"

"Twenty-one inches, seven hundred and fifty dollars." And no remote control, I thought, but kept that to myself.

"But they're in color and come with a radio. And a record player."

"Oh, okay, well then that makes sense." No it didn't. What was that the equivalent of in 2010 money? Forty-five hundred? Five thousand dollars? "Come in, what are you doing here? It's almost ten o'clock."

"I'm too nervous to sleep," she said, stepping into the living room while I switched off the TV. The knob making a big clunking sound. It always made me wince, I was sure the whole thing was going to snap clean off every time I did it.

"You could have left it on, even though you're terrible at guessing the prices."

"Of course I am, how can I not be? A TV costs almost eight hundred dollars but a washing machine costs a nickel."

"Can I have one of those?" Judith asked, pointing to the beer bottle on the coffee table as she sat.

"You've been smoking haven't you?" She looked up at me from the couch when I returned from the kitchen and set a cold bottle and a glass in front of her.

"Yes, a little. Today," she admitted.

I was going to tsk-tsk her but you don't tsk-tsk someone for smoking in the sixties. They're more likely to tsk-tsk you for not smoking. Instead I went back to one of the kitchen drawers for an ashtray and placed it by her beer before sitting next to her.

"No, that's okay, this should be enough." She raised the beer to her lips, the glass remained on the table. She swallowed, then asked "Why haven't you called?"

I was surprised she'd even noticed.

"I don't know, I thought you'd be too busy with rehearsals, I didn't want to bother you. How did they go by the way? Are you all set for tomorrow? Excited?"

She shrugged her shoulders.

"That's it? I thought you'd be a little more enthused than that."

"I am, I am. But right now I'm more nervous than excited."

"I can tell." Her beer bottle trembled each time she brought it to her lips and she was doing that nervous shaking of her hands thing whenever she set the bottle down on the table.

"You can? How?"

I pointed to her hands. "That. I saw you doing the same thing right before you sang that Saturday night at the Saturn and Sun. Before then, when you were sitting on the bleachers, you seemed to be fine."

She looked at her hands, then back to me.

"You were watching me before I sang?"

"Um." I took a drink from my own bottle. "Yes. I was sitting next to that boy, the one who asked you to dance shortly before you sang? Anyway, he was acting strangely, when he was sitting there, next to me, which is why I was watching him when he approached you. So I was really, you know, watching him more than..." I trailed off and took another drink.

She nodded with the tiniest of smiles. I could tell she didn't buy my flimsy excuse. But she was too polite to call me out on my lie.

Awkward.

"So come on, tell me all about it, the rehearsals, which songs you're going to sing, all of it," I said, perhaps a little too cheerily, but I wanted to get off the subject.

She nodded her head again, took another drink, then told me all about it.

By the time midnight rolled around, over two hours later, there were four beer bottles sitting in front of her, three empty, one halfway there. The alcohol had helped steady her hands, and she'd only had three full beers, but I'd never seen her drink before. I was beginning to worry I was going to have to drive her home and then drag her up her parent's front steps in a drunken lifeless heap. That would make a wonderful impression on her already distrustful mother.

"I know the concert isn't until tomorrow and you still

have plenty of time before you have to be on stage but not that much time," I told her and then pointed to the bottle in her hand.

"You're right," she said. She leaned over, ready to set the bottle down, hesitated, then brought it back to her lips. I could hear the glug-glug-glug as she nearly emptied it in one go.

"Judith, no, jeez, you're killing me," I laughed and reached out to take the bottle from her hand. "I will not be responsible for you not singing tomorrow, no way."

"I'm not drunk," she said, as I placed the beer on the table. I straightened up, thought about it, then leaned over again and slid it all the way over to my side.

"But," she continued, wiping away a drop of beer from the corner of her mouth with a finger. "I probably shouldn't be driving."

"I can drive you, I've only had one. Fran and I can get your car to you tomorrow morning."

"Can I just stay here tonight?" she asked.

"Sure, if you don't mind sleeping on oversized sheets, I haven't gotten around to buying linen for the spare-"

"That's not what I meant."

I froze. It was the way she said it.

"Then what do you..." I knew exactly what she meant.

"I meant with you. In your bed."

Is it possible for someone to hear the thudding of your heartbeat from a foot away? Sounds impossible, but at that moment I thought it would be impossible for her not to hear it.

She's not thinking clearly. She's been drinking. I can't take advantage of that. Can I?

No. No you can't. Stop it.

"Judith, you've had a few drinks, I don't think you know what-"

"No," she said, shaking her head. "I'm not drunk, and

I've had plenty of time to think about it. Ever since that Sunday I've been thinking about it. And all this time we've spent together...it's made me realize...that it's what I...and you said you would never make a...so I...look, you don't know how nerve-racking this is for me, how difficult it was for me just to come here tonight, so please say something."

"That's why you came here tonight?"

She couldn't meet my eyes, instead she looked down to her lap, plucked a non-existent piece of lint off of her skirt, then smoothed the material down.

"Yes," she admitted, finally looking up at me. "It is."

"Why didn't you say anything before now?"

"I don't know, I suppose I wanted to be sure."

"And you're sure now?"

She inhaled deeply. "Yes. I think."

"You think?"

"Well I've never done anything like this before, how can I be sure about it?"

"Okay, you're right. But are you sure this is the right time for something like this? With the concert coming up tomorrow..."

"Why would that matter? It's just a show."

"It's not just...it seems pretty important, I just don't want to interfere, get in the way of anything."

"You won't be." Her hands were starting to shake again.

"You don't know that. You don't know how it will affect..."

"What? I'm just singing, I'm not performing surgery."

"If I'd known, I-"

"Oh my God!" she shouted and threw both hands in the air. "Why is there so much talking? Is this in the rulebook? That girls have to talk for an hour about it before anything can happen?"

If I hadn't been in love with her before then, I was now.

"No," I said with a smile before kissing her.

The tip of her tongue, from the chilled beer, was still cold, as it met mine. Her hand too, as she reached out to curl her fingers around the curve of my neck. I don't know how long it was, seconds, minutes, hours, before I felt her slide her hand up through my hair then gently pull on it. I ran my own hand up her waist, up to the side of her breast and then over it. She inhaled sharply, put her other hand on top of mine, and pulled away.

"I want to do this," she said, her forehead resting against mine, "I do. But I don't know what I'm doing."

"No one does, their first time, but it still gets done doesn't it?"

She smiled, shakily, maybe out of relief. As if I'd call everything off due to her lack of experience.

"Come on," I said, standing, taking her by the hand and leading her to my bedroom.

I could feel her hand trying to shake in mine.

"You don't have to be nervous."

Useless, I know. Telling someone not to be nervous is like telling someone to take a breath under water. Your body just won't cooperate. But the thing about Judith, I would come to learn, is that she would always be nervous before an event, before singing, before climbing the steps onto a stage no matter how large or small. But once she began to sing, that anxiety would fall away in an instant. Apparently the same goes for whatever's making her nervous.

When I kissed her again, by my bed, I felt her hands slip under my shirt, her palms gliding over the skin of my back. She unclasped my bra, and then ran her hands around to my breasts as her breath grew quicker. Gone was the shy timid girl the world would always assume she was.

She was worried she wouldn't know what to do, but when she pulled my hand to her, later, in bed, to her rising hips and then lower, it was without hesitation and free of any inhibition, which made it that much harder for me, to go slow. Not that she wanted me to. "Don't stop, please, don't stop," she kept whispering in my ear until I felt her body spasm beneath mine.

After a few seconds, of her staring into my eyes, her breath still heavy, tiny beads of perspiration still clinging to her temples, she said: "You know, I wasn't really sure."

I opened my mouth in surprise but then she cupped the side of my face with her hand.

"I'm sure now."

CHAPTER SEVENTEEN

Saturday morning. It's all going to change after today. Not for a few more days, maybe even a week or two, but it was coming, I knew it. So I took a couple of minutes to watch her lying there beside me, the thin sheet pulled up underneath her collarbones, her bare shoulders moving slightly with each breath.

If only I could tell her.

It's not going to last. You're going to get everything you want. But it's not going to last, so slow down, don't take any of it for granted, enjoy every second of it.

Part of me wished I had disturbed something and she wouldn't become Judy Paige, because isn't having everything and then losing it worse than never having had it at all? I know the saying, better to have loved and lost, blah blah. That's a crock. You can't miss what you never had. And what if the loss of it all is what sends her into a downward spiral? Was a few years of stardom worth it?

But that was all moot now. What's done is done. And it wasn't my place to take it from her, to change the future. Not all of it anyway. I planned on changing at least part of it. And if the future had a problem with it, well that was just too damned bad.

I propped myself up on one elbow and leaned over her. "Judith."

"Hm?"

"Good morning."

She opened her eyes, the pale green somehow even more striking without the usual eyeliner to highlight them.

"Good morning." She pulled her head up from the pillow and kissed me, I kissed her back and felt all the blood instantly rushing from my head. I moaned and pulled away from her. If we got started there was no way I would be able to stop.

"Shouldn't you get up? Last minute rehearsals and all that?"

"First you get me out of my clothes and now you're trying to get rid of me?"

"I got you out of your clothes? I remember it a little different-"

Her nose crinkled as she laughed and wrapped her arms around my neck.

"I don't want to go," she mumbled, with her lips against the skin of my neck. "I'm not going."

"Okay, sure," I said, patting her hip with my hand beneath the covers.

She pulled back, but kept her hands behind my neck, her fingers slowly running up through my hair, distractedly.

"Really. I'd rather stay here."

I turned my head, and looked at her sideways.

"All of a sudden you don't care about singing?"

"No, I do. Just...not at this particular moment. This seems more important."

"This?"

"Yes, this." She let go of my hair and rested her head back against the pillow. "Us. It's probably not a big deal to you," she said, and shrugged her shoulders.

She was wrong about that and I was going to correct her but she quickly went on.

"You've already, you know, but me, I..."

"I understand."

She turned her head away for a second and then back again.

"What if I...singing has been all I've ever cared about...until now. And what if I put so much emphasis on it because it was all I had?"

"What do you mean?"

"You know, in school, weren't all your friends obsessed with boys? I know mine were. And when I didn't get it, didn't understand what all the fuss was about, I guess I just felt like I needed to obsess about something. It never crossed my mind that I could...obsess about girls."

"Really? You really actually didn't know?"

"No, I didn't. Where would I even get the idea? Father Knows Best?"

"Ah. So that's why you tore out of my house that day, slammed the door on me, peeled out of the driveway, nearly took down my neighbor's fence, their mailbox."

"I did not!"

"So what are you telling me? You'd rather stay here and give up the biggest opportunity you've ever had?"

"I don't think it's going to be all that important. After all what really can come out of it? No one is going to see me, I'm going on second, way before the headliner, half the people won't even be in their seats yet. I think it'd be a lot more fun, staying here, don't you?" She raised her eyebrows and gave me a hopeful smile.

If only I knew for sure. If only people had cared enough to find out what had caused that dark period in her life. I could stop it right now. But I didn't know.

"Oh believe me, if I didn't think it was important you would not be leaving this bed for hours."

Her smile grew larger.

"But." Then it dimmed. "This isn't one song at a dance hall in front of a few dozen kids. People are going to notice if you don't show up. I don't think it's the type of thing you can pull out of at the very last minute. And your uncle, I'm sure he had to call in a lot of favors for it to happen. He's probably going to have to work it off for a month."

"Ugh! I know, I know. Fine. I'll go. But can we leave right after I finish my songs? You don't want to stay for the entire thing do you?"

"What do you mean? I don't have a ticket."

"If anyone backstage asks, you're my voice coach."

"I'm going to be backstage? I finally get to hear you sing your songs?"

"I wish you weren't so excited, that just means you're going to be that much more disappointed when you do hear them."

"Oh, I won't be. Come on," I said, turning away, getting ready to hop out of bed, but she pulled me back by my waist.

"Where are you going?" she asked, looking over my shoulder to my nightstand. "It's only seven, we have plenty of time."

When her hand slid from my waist to my abdomen and then between my thighs, I didn't have the will to argue.

"I can't believe I'm actually here, I can't believe I'm going to be singing in front of this many people!"

For all her earlier talk, now that she was here, backstage, in the middle of all the hustle and bustle of a large live show, she could barely contain her excitement.

"I feel like I'm going to be sick. I really do. What if I'm sick out on stage?"

Or her nerves.

"Relax. Breathe."

"What?"

"I said breathe," I shouted.

Besides the noise of the house band warming up, the

175

clanging of cymbals and thumps on bass drums, various horns blowing intermittently, there was also the noise of the audience (who were all present and accounted for, seats full) echoing around the large auditorium. The sound put me in mind of a large wasp's nest, that constant droning buzzing sound.

Judith had already seen it, during rehearsals, so she wasn't surprised by the size of the venue, but she hadn't seen it like this, with thousands of kids already shouting and hopping around in their seats, anxious for the show to start. I, on the other hand, was surprised by it. The clip I'd seen on YouTube never showed the audience. I knew there were more than just a handful of people, judging by the screams I heard when she was done, still, I wasn't prepared for just how many there actually were. I began to get nervous for her, but tried not to show it. She didn't need me adding to her anxiety. She really did look like she could start spewing any minute and that can't be a good look, going on stage with puke on your skirt. Why didn't they have several buckets strategically placed around the joint?

She was shaking her hands again, the way she had at the Saturn and Sun, the way she had last night, only this was an exaggerated version.

"I've never sung in front of this many people. And it's going to be filmed! If I mess up it's going to be on film."

"You're not going to mess up, I promise."

"Oh, I'm sorry!" A girl, rushing by the pair of us, too nervous or excited to watch where she was going, bumped into Judith, and I had to do a double take when I realized I recognized her. She was one of the three girls in pink dresses I'd seen in that picture, around a microphone, singing and snapping their fingers. The other two, I saw when I turned, were off to the side, looking every bit as frantic as Judith was.

"That's okay," Judith said to her with a shaky smile.

"You'll be here right? You won't leave?" Judith turned

back to me, her face full of anxiety.

"Where am I going to go? Of course I'll be here, right there," I said, pointing off to a spot behind what looked like a giant black suitcase with silver trim.

There were dozens of people wandering around. Men, women, young, old, some clearly performers by the way they were dressed, some carrying around musical instruments, others in more practical clothing messing with wires and microphones, or curtains and light switches. No one was paying me any mind, no one had said anything to me, no one was looking at me suspiciously, so I thought I was safe, that I was actually going to get to see this.

I wasn't going to be getting the best view in the world, the only spot I thought I could get away with standing at during all the chaos of a live show was at an oblique angle to the stage. I'd be able to hear Judith fine, but unless she turned and sang directly to me, I would be staring at her back the entire time. Better than nothing.

"Okay, okay, okay." Judith placed one hand over her mouth and her cheeks puffed out.

Uh oh.

"You were wrong!" I shouted, thinking quickly, trying to distract her, keep her breakfast, the little she'd managed to consume, from staying in place. "It is a big-" Just then the drums, the cymbals, the horns all fell quiet.

"It is a big-" I continued in a lower voice until I was interrupted.

"Excuse me, you, young lady? Do you need to be back here? Are you part of the show?"

From behind a young guy walking away with his arms full of a bundle of cords came another older man with a clipboard in his hand and a large sweaty forehead pointing at me. He was so harried his tie was loose, the top button of his shirt was undone and his sleeves were rolled up. For the sixties, that was practically falling apart at the seams.

No! I have to see this! You can't make me leave. I'm just about to witness something amazing. Not only Judith's incredible performance but actually seeing something live, that I'd seen almost fifty years in the future. The magnitude of that would make anyone's head spin. But what could I do? I couldn't lie.

"No, sir, I'm not."

"Good. Someone took a ticket and didn't bother showing up, there's an empty seat out there, I need you to go out and fill it." He started flapping his free hand in the air, toward a small set of steps behind me. "This is being filmed, how would it look with an empty seat out there? Like the show wasn't a success. Go on."

"You mean go out and sit in the audience?"

"Yes," he said. He also gave me a look that said I might be the slowest person he'd ever dealt with. "Third row, you can't miss it, it's like a missing tooth out there."

He stood by, waiting.

"You're going to be great. Trust me." It's all I had time to say to her before Mr. Clipboard wrapped his large damp hand around my arm and led me a few feet away to the stairway and practically shoved me down the first few steps before pointing, indicating for me to turn, once I got down to ground level.

The first act, four guys from Oklahoma who, judging by their hair and outfits, were trying hard to be Beatlesque, wasn't too bad. And the young girls beside me hadn't worked themselves up into a frenzy just yet so my hearing was fine when it was time for Judith to come out on stage. The announcer, a guy wearing black slacks and a green sparkly suit jacket walked up to the mike, and introduced Judith. As Judy Paige. Probably thought Judith sounded too schoolmarmish for the tone of the concert and decided to change it. So that's where it came from. The tiny twists that change the course of history. Incredible.

The audience clapped but only perfunctorily. No one had ever heard of her. Judy Paige? Who's that? I smiled to myself thinking you're about to find out. You and millions more are about to find out. I looked around me at the rows and rows of seats going up and up and all the kids seated in them. All of them, at the moment, clueless, so that they were all mostly still, there was no excitement or anticipation on anyone's faces. They had no idea what they were about to witness. But I did. And I have to admit I was feeling pretty darn smug, having that knowledge. Sitting there knowing what was about to happen.

Judith emerged, from off to the left, just as I'd seen in the video, still nervous, looking down to the ground, then up, swallowing, trying not to be sick. The band started up, louder than I expected. The act before her played their own instruments, a grand total of four of them, while she was being backed up by what looked like an entire orchestra. At least twenty of them off to the side, off camera. So I could hear, loud and clear, those same four familiar beats to the beginning of her song "One Day You'll Leave Me", the same four beats of music that had brought me here. It was surreal, to see her acting out right in front of me, the video I knew so well. I'd seen it too many times to count and I knew every gesture. As she slowly walked up to the microphone I thought, she's going to look off to her left, she looked to her left, now she'll look to her right, she turned, scanned the audience to her right, and then she's going to...

The smile froze on my face. My stomach tightened up and the music began to fade out and echo at the same time.

She's going to find someone, in the audience.

Her eyes glided across the aisle I was in, then locked on to mine and her lips turned up into a slight smile.

The thin film of sweat at the very top of my forehead turned cold in an instant.

She's going to wave.

She raised her hand up close to her chest and wiggled her fingers. At me.

Exactly as I'd seen on the video.

A video I was apparently a part of.

In the unseen audience.

Impossible.

CHAPTER EIGHTEEN

I missed the whole damned thing. Which was a shame. Only the one song had actually been recorded, the producer didn't seem to want to waste film on someone no one knew so the rest of her performance was a one shot deal. Either you were there to see it or you were out of luck. I was there, but I was still out of luck.

I just couldn't concentrate on anything else. Is this some sort of weird loop thing? I'd seen the video in 2010 before I'd come here, before I knew her, how is it possible for me to be a part of it? But as this was 1964, and 2010 comes after...but seeing it is what made me come here in the first place. It's not kill your grandfather paradox, but a paradox nonetheless isn't it? Whose seat had I taken? Whoever had sat there is who Judith had waved at. No she waved at me. But that doesn't make sense.

It had been empty. Someone hadn't shown up. Someone who couldn't show up because they were now in the future? Evelyn? No. She's not in high school. And neither am I, but I was sitting there. Maybe she and Judith already knew each other, she'd come along for moral support and had been asked to sit there just as I had? That couldn't be it either. Judith hadn't recognized me at the dance hall. They could have met between then and now, or even that night. Again, no. She'd had plans to go to the movies with Fran, not out dancing. I'm the one who lied about being sick and changed my plans. I sought her out. They still could have met anytime after that. But that was stretching it wasn't it?

By the end of her third and last song everyone that I could see was on their feet screaming at the top of their strong teenage lungs. And there were thousands of them. That's a lot of damned screaming, it was deafening. And I was no closer to figuring out what was going on but I had to put it all aside for the time being, deciding to take my own advice. Slow down, don't take anything for granted, enjoy every moment. So I stood along with everyone else and clapped and watched Judith glowing up there.

The first time I'd watched her up on that stage on a tiny screen, in black and white, with tinny speakers, I remember thinking that it was probably the happiest she'd ever been in her life. But here now, seeing her bow and wave at the huge crowd, nearly every single boy and girl screaming and waving back at her, as the applause went on and on, I knew it was.

"You seem a little distracted, you didn't like my songs did you? I told you not to get too excited about them."

"Are you kidding me? I loved them. Especially the first one. But..."

"But?" Judith asked as she scraped at her ice cream bowl with a spoon. Her pale yellow jacket hanging on the seat behind her.

Straight after she'd left the stage I'd abandoned my post (Mr. Clipboard wasn't going to be too happy about that), and found Judith backstage hopping around in a tight little circle.

"That was amazing!" She covered her mouth with both hands but not out of fear of vomiting this time. "I wish I could have sang ten more songs! My hands are shaking! Look, look!"

"You're gonna break a heel."

"Who cares? That was incredible! And people were clapping for me! For me! Can you believe it? All those people!"

How could I ever have thought of taking this away from her?

I thought she'd want to hang around, greet the fans, soak in all the adoration, but either the thought that anyone would want to meet her hadn't even occurred to her or she just didn't care. Once the singing part was over, and once she'd calmed down enough to walk, she'd seemed eager to leave.

I wanted to take her out somewhere special, to celebrate, I felt like we needed to mark the occasion somehow. She felt like ice cream.

So here we are.

Maybell's, home of the famous Peppermint Stick ice cream.

"Maybe I'm a bit jealous," I said, in a lower voice so the two women over by the counter, perusing the ice cream case, couldn't overhear. "Who's this someone who's going to leave you one day? Are you sure you weren't just a teeny tiny bit obsessed with boys in high school?"

"Yes, I'm sure. I dated a little, yes, but I did not write that song for a boy, believe me. I don't even remember why I wrote it. Probably picked up the idea from all my friends moaning about their boyfriends at the time."

"And when you say dated..."

"Movies. Holding hands. That's it."

I tried to play it off by eating some of my own butterscotch ice cream. I'd moved on from vanilla.

"Why are you laughing?"

"It's just, that's...holding hands. It's cute."

She gave me a strange look but went on.

"And what about you? Did you date any boys in high school?" A cheesy grin on her face.

"I went to an all girl's school remember?"

183

She set her spoon down. "Oh." The grin was gone. She puckered her lips, tucked her chin in and raised her eyebrows. All she needed was to cross her arms in front of her chest to complete the look.

Even though she was going for mock jealousy, I could tell there was at least a trace of the real thing in there somewhere.

"I take it you don't want to know any more?"

"No, I do not." She did it. She completed the look. She crossed her arms across her chest, raised her chin, and turned away from me to stare out of the window beside us.

"Are you sure, because there was this one girl who..."

She cracked. The smile was back.

"It doesn't matter," I said, again lowering my voice. "Whatever happened, before I met you, doesn't matter." And not just because I can never tell you about it, I thought, but because it's the truth.

Her smile softened as she turned to face me.

"So it was okay to use that word earlier today?"

"Which word?"

"Us."

I smiled at her and nodded.

"That's what I was trying to tell you at the concert, before you went on stage and wowed everyone."

"You'll have to remind me, that half hour before I actually began to sing is one big fuzzy nervous blur."

"I was trying to tell you that you were wrong. Before. About this not being a big deal to me. It is. I wanted you to know that."

Judith leaned over the table, temporarily forgetting where we were, but caught herself when Maybell, in her white apron and white paper hat, walked past our table, across the black and white tiled floor, and stopped at the door. She opened it, nodded at the two women as they stepped outside, then flipped the sign dangling on it over to "CLOSED".

"Looks like we're being kicked out."

"Yes, well, it is pretty late," Judith said.

I took a look at my watch. "It's only six."

"No, it's really, really, late."

"What are you talking about? We left the concert way before all the other acts and we've only been here-"

"Evelyn."

"What?"

"Let me see your watch."

I raised my wrist and she pulled it towards her then started fiddling with the dial.

"See there?" she asked, turning the watch face towards me and tapping at it with her finger. "Nearly midnight. I'm usually in bed by this time."

"Huh? Just because you changed...ohhhhh."

Judith was clueless about what was going on behind the scenes the days after the show. First there were calls to radio stations, most of the kids remembered the name of the song, some remembered her name, and others just had "the song the girl with the green eyes sang" or "the one in yellow". After enough phone-in requests, the calls to studios began. Station managers wanting to know who this Judy Paige was and why hadn't they been sent this record everyone wanted to hear? Agitated and worried that kids were going to start switching over to other stations searching for it if they didn't play it. Of course I knew what was coming, only this time, unlike at the concert, I wasn't feeling smug about that knowledge. On the one hand, I could hardly wait to see her excitement, to have a front row seat to it all, to be able to watch her achieve this dream she'd had for years, but on the other hand was the apprehension. I had a feeling that after just a short while, I'd have to pack up and move on down to a third row seat, and then a sixth...and eventually I might just be lost somewhere in the shadows up in the balcony.

But there was no use fretting about it, the ball was rolling, and there was no way to stop it now.

I also tried not to fret about what had happened, at the concert. Could that possibly be how I'd known her eyes were green before I'd ever even seen a colored picture of her? Is that the way time travel works? Is time just one large loop and everything that's going to happen has already happened? It still seemed too paradoxical to me. Hearing that song is what led me to look the video up in the first place. Had I not looked it up, I never would have come here. I didn't spend too much time on it, trying to figure it out. It made absolutely no sense to me. And I was scared to, to think about it for too long. Because when I thought about it, I thought of Mr. Smith and how he was probably the only person who could give me any answers. And, as much as I wanted answers, I didn't want them half as much as I wanted to stay here. Now more than ever. What if by thinking about him, he took notice of me? For all I knew, he really had forgotten all about his fun little pet project. He might have gone on to larger, more important business. Drowning Hitler as a child maybe or making sure the lead car in Franz Ferdinand's procession didn't take a wrong turn. If I summoned him somehow, made him take notice of me again, well, I wasn't willing to risk it. So I put it out of my mind. It wasn't important. And it was probably too complex for me to comprehend anyway.

It only took a week, for Judith to be contacted. She was ecstatic about it, in the beginning. When she was rushed into the studio, recorded four records in two days, signed to the BlueRock record label (right there in Dallas), it's all she could talk about. And when we were walking back to my house one evening, only six days after she recorded it, and heard her song blasting out of a convertible rolling down the street, she nearly lost it.

"That's my song! It's on the radio! That's me!"

She took off her heels and, maybe for the first time in her life, hiked her skirt halfway up her thighs and sprinted the rest of the way to the house.

"Stop running! You're going to..."

But she was already half a block away, flip hairdo flowing behind her, as much as a flip hairdo can flow. I thought about the zero on my phone. And decided a busted knee wasn't that much of an emergency. She made it somehow, with knees intact, but not in time to hear the rest of the song. She had to wait a whole hour for it to come on again.

After that, there was no looking back.

I tried to prepare myself for it. I pictured a tornado with Judith at the center and everything else, her friends, our friends, everything that represented her life up until then, including me, as detritus swirling around her at high speed until eventually it all, we all, would be flung away like so many roofs and car doors. I thought of the blushing Mr. Peters. He's out there somewhere right now, a scrawny twelve year old kid with a crew cut. Soon he and millions of other schoolboys, all across the country, would be dreaming of asking her out, fantasizing about taking her to the school dance. Which, of course, were of no concern to me. What did concern me is that there would also be thousands, I'm sure, of girls and women out there secretly wishing for the same thing. And I was also sure that at least some of them would be bold enough to tell her so. That's a hell of a lot of temptation.

She was going to be a part of a different world now. Tours, TV shows, movies, concerts. Glamorous parties with movie stars, raucous ones with other famous singers and bands. How could I compete with that? Where would I fit in? I wouldn't be a part of that world. It's not as if I could show up to events with her, hand in hand. No, it was inevitable, that she would be swooped up, carried away, and lost. At least for a time. I told myself that I'd wait. I could wait until it was all over. It would be three years, three and a half at most, and then it would be over. Not completely, but it wouldn't be mobs of fans, teen magazine covers, and sold out concert arenas forever. I could wait. And, of course, that was assuming she'd even want to. Come back. To me. But if she did, I'd be there.

In the meantime, while the storm clouds slowly rolled in, as her record climbed steadily up the charts, she was able to lead a semi-normal life for a few weeks. Yes, there were radio interviews and a half dozen or so appearances at fairs and amusement parks here and there. Houston, Austin, even Oklahoma and Arkansas, but she'd be back the same day or the next.

And while fans showed up on her parent's lawn, as many as thirty or forty at a time, it was nothing like I expected. I was thinking in 2010 terms. These were 1964 fans. Fans that showed up with their markers and record sleeves unannounced and camped on her front lawn, but who also waited patiently without pushing and shoving as she signed every single thing she was asked to. Fans who thanked her afterward, then picked up any soda bottles, napkins, or candy wrappers they may have dropped on the grass while they waited and then walked on back to wherever it was they came from. Yes really, polite fans who picked up after themselves.

No, people in 1964 aren't angels, but they're generally more well-behaved than they will be in the decades to come, so in the beginning, for the first month at least, she was pretty much left undisturbed as she did what she had been doing all along.

We drove Fran around town on her many bids to try and track Dwight down. We fixed up my spare bedroom with linen on the bed, a brand new pillow, a couple of art prints on the wall. (This became the bedroom Judith slept in on the many nights she stayed over - wink wink.) We loaded up three cars with friends and drove up to Lake Lewisville for a couple of days of camping on the beach. Cars, beer, tents, bonfires, all on the sand just a few feet away from the water without a single beach patrol storming in asking us just what the hell we thought we were doing and citing rules and regulations.

I was glad Ralph couldn't get away that weekend, he was back home counting hammers and wrenches at Kirkman's Hardware, but not so happy Dwight had to pull out at the last minute as well. He had to attend a family wedding so I had to listen to Frannie complain for three days straight.

"What a waste! A brand new bikini and no one here to see me in it."

I temporarily got her mind off of it by pointing out a sign near the entrance to the beach. It read WHITES ONLY BEYOND THIS POINT with a cartoon drawing of a pointing finger.

"There's a crowbar in my trunk."

She began to smile.

I tried to make as many memories as I could, while I could.

The second weekend in August, while she was away for a couple of days in New Mexico, I made Judith a cake on the day she was planning on returning. As soon as she walked in the door that evening I covered her eyes and walked her to my tiny kitchen table.

"Ta-da!" I said, as I dropped my hand. Maybe too much fanfare for a cake, but this one was special. I felt it deserved the dramatics.

"A cake?" She undid the top button of her wrinkled blouse and blew a few strands of hair away from her eyes. The bounce was gone, the upturned edges of her hair were now laying flat, cascading over her shoulders, causing her hair to look surprisingly modern. Or should I say futuristic? Traveling long distances in these days is not as easy as it will be.

"Yes," I said, "a welcome back cake and not just any old cake, look." I picked up a knife and sliced into it. "It's an ice cream cake!" I stepped back with a smile and waited for the amazement.

"Oh. Like an Ice Cream'n Cake Roll, but in a round shape."

"What? Ice cream and what?"

"Ice cream rolls, you know, the ones they sell at the supermarket?"

Proof that the sixties could still throw me some curveballs. How dare they invent ice cream cakes before me.

"Isn't that where you bought it?" she asked, then picked up a spoon from the table and scraped at the ice cream. "Are these new? I've never seen one with pink in it."

"No," I said, completely deflated, "I didn't buy it, I made it." Now she'll notice how lopsided it is.

"You made it? Wait, is this..." She raised the spoon to her mouth, placing the ice cream on her tongue. "This is Peppermint Stick."

"Yeah, I talked Maybell into selling me her entire batch. She grumbled about it a little, asked what she was going to do when other people came in for a cone but I might have mentioned your name, greased the wheels a little." I pulled out a chair and sat, now that there wasn't going to be any clapping or pronouncements of what a culinary genius I was.

"But Maybell's is way over by the highway, how'd you get it home without it becoming a puddle?"

"Oh that," I said, tapping my fingers on the Formica tabletop, thinking about the fiasco. "I was at Maybell's before I thought about it so I had to drive all the way back here, beg all the neighbors for their ice trays, you owe Mr. Jacobson's niece an autograph for his, by the way. I emptied out all the trays into that metal wash tub after scrubbing it clean, wrapped the whole shebang up in a couple of blankets so the ice wouldn't melt on my way back to Maybell's. I drove back to the dairy, hoping Maybell hadn't gone and sold thirty scoops before I returned. It worked, somewhat, the ice cream still melted partway so I had to refreeze it but I couldn't fit the bin in the freezer so I had to go back out into the neighborhood and ask Mrs. Weber and Mrs. Landau for all of their Tupperware bowls, portioned it out, emptied the freezer, and managed to stuff it all in there before it poured out onto the floor. But then I had to go back out and ask poor Mrs. Weber and Mrs. Landau to now store all the stuff that was in this freezer in theirs. You might have to give the neighborhood a free concert."

After she didn't say anything for several seconds I looked up and found her smiling at me. She set the spoon down on the table, then pivoted and sat on my lap.

"You went through all that trouble just to make me a cake?"

I shrugged. "Wasn't that much-"

"The room service guy at the hotel went all red and huffy because I asked if he could bring me a straw," she said. By the time she finished the sentence, she already had two buttons of my shirt undone.

I looked down at her hands then back to her eyes. "Come to think of it, it was a lot of driving around. I guess it was some trouble..." I thought I was going to get brownie points. This was much better.

"Sounds like it," she said, while undoing the fifth and last button.

"And it was hot too, really hot."

She smiled as she slid her hand between the lace material of my bra and the skin beneath it.

She never did get to eat any of that cake. It was a pile of

goo by the time we remembered it.

But only a few days after that weekend, her song hit number one and she began to slip away.

CHAPTER NINETEEN

"Where is Judith now? England?" Nell didn't have to shout over the music, but only because I was practically sitting on her lap.

"No, that was last week, she's in Australia now."

"Ooh, that's exciting, I bet she's having a blast."

"Yeah, I hope so." But not too much of a blast, I thought. Which was probably unfair, seeing as how I was in the middle of a party myself.

"What was Fran talking to you about yesterday at work?" She shook her head, turned her mouth down.

"In the back, by the dressing rooms, she was flailing her arms all over the place, getting all worked up about something." I asked not because I was nosy, I just wanted to get off the subject of Judith and the fact that she'd been gone for eleven days now. Which in turn reminded me that in the past nearly three and a half months since Mack Stevens, Leyfant's most popular DJ, had announced Judith's song had made it "Number one, folks! Our very own Judy Paige is on top of the charts!" she'd been more gone than not. And it was just going to get worse. She already had another song out that had hit number nineteen in only two weeks.

"Oh, yeah, she's been trying to get me to go eat with her at a diner. After Henry turned her down for the fourth time, she started asking me."

"Ah. Lou's huh?" I had to smile. Fran had been right, President Johnson signed the bill just as he'd promised. Lou must be steaming.

Nell took a sip of her drink then nodded her head. "Yes, that's the name. I'd tell her no, but she can be a real..."

"Bitch?"

Nell chuckled and slapped at my arm with her free hand. "No! I wouldn't say something like that."

"I know you wouldn't that's why I did." I turned towards my kitchen, where Fran's mountain of orange hair was bopping away to the music as she and Peg made up another batch of cocktails. "Her heart's in the right place, of course, she just needs to work on her diplomacy. But still, however well-meaning she is, don't you let her bully you into going. That's your decision to make, not hers. And if I were you-" There's no way Fran could hear me, but just to be on the safe side, I leaned in closer to Nell and lowered my voice before going on. "I wouldn't do it. Not because I don't think you have the right to sit anywhere you damn well please but would you really want to eat at a place that's only serving you because they're being forced to? I don't think I'd trust the food not to come with a little extra something mixed in the gravy."

Nell looked confused.

"You know," I said, then mimed spitting onto an imaginary plate.

Her jaw clunked open. "No! You don't think someone would do anything as horrible as that do you?"

Sheesh. I'm glad I went with saliva.

"Don't worry, I'll have my dad talk to her, tell her to stop harassing all of his employees. Poor Henry, isn't he only sixteen? That's a gutsy boy, turning Fran down."

"Shh! Here she comes."

"Here you are Evelyn, I made yours special with an extra olive." Peg handed me a cold martini glass just as the phone began to ring. Eleven o'clock at night, it could only be one person.

"Thanks Peg, excuse me. Ugh, Nell, give me a push, will you, I'm stuck." With a drink in my hand and five people wedged onto the small couch I wasn't going to make it. All I could do was stretch out my arm to try to get some leverage and wiggle. Before Peg had a chance to grab my outstretched hand, Nell pushed me from behind and I popped right up.

"Hello?"

"Hi."

"Hi! I was just thinking about you."

Either there was crackling on the line or she'd taken a deep breath. "Are you just saying that or were you really?"

"No, I was, I was thinking about the day you were waiting for me on the front steps."

Whatever she said to that I couldn't hear over Fran's yapping.

"Judith? You'll have to speak a little louder, I can't hear you too well."

"What is all that noise?"

"It's the record player, hold on a second. Fran! Fran turn it...turn it down! Mary! Can you turn it down a bit?"

Mary, one of the girls Judith and I had met on our first walk together, managed to stumble her way past Fran, spilled half her drink on the floor, and momentarily turned up the volume as high as it would go, realized her mistake, and then lowered it. To the same level it was at before.

"Mary! You didn't...you need to...oh forget it." She'd already flopped back down on the couch, which was roomier now that Nell had gotten up. She was now standing by Fran next to the record player and had her hands on Fran's hips. I didn't know what the heck that was about. Either I'd had too much to drink and I was seeing things, or this party had just taken a very interesting turn.

"I'm sorry Judith, that's as good as it's going to get."

"What's going on?"

"Hm, oh, I see, Nell is trying to teach Frannie a dance. It's either the Watusi or the Mashed Potato, I can't tell which, Fran just looks like she's having a seizure. Dwight and Ralph are...I don't know, I think they're outside smoking. I don't know why, there's a thick enough fog in here already, they'd just be adding to it. Peg, Michael, Nancy, and well, you know, just everybody, are here too. I don't know how it happened, but apparently we're having a party."

There was a long empty pause. I thought we might have been disconnected but before I could ask, she came back on the line. "Peg is there?"

"Yeah, she's been here all day, helping me swap out all the curtains, why?"

"All day just to switch curtains?"

Was that jealousy in her voice? I'd ask, but I wasn't sure I wouldn't be overheard, even with the music at high volume just a few feet away.

"No, not just curtains, we also tried making soufflés. Which did not go well. There's chocolate on the ceiling."

I thought that might get a laugh, but no, just silence.

"Judith?"

"Yes."

"What time is it there?"

"Two."

"As in tomorrow two?"

"Yes, it's Sunday here."

"Why is it...hold on just a second." I covered my other ear with my hand and managed to stretch the curly phone cord until I was two feet into the hallway. If that thing snaps, which it very well could, I was going to get one hell of a lump on my head from the springback, but at least I could hear her better.

"Aren't you supposed to be on a show right now? Aussie Bandstand or something? Or is it Kangabaloo?"

Finally a small giggle, which came with a bit of static over the international line.

"I am, I'm here."

"I don't hear anything, why is it so quiet?" It sounded so still on the other end, so empty, I swore I could hear an echo. Unlike the ruckus coming from my living room. Dwight and Ralph had just walked in the front door, laughing at something or other and letting a gust of unseasonably cold November air in while Mary was shouting at Nell to change the record.

There was another long pause before she answered.

"I'm in a dressing room. Waiting."

"Oh."

I knew what that meant. I'd gone along with her to a few of her gigs, one right there in Dallas, one in Ohio, and one all the way in New York City. You'd think they'd be exciting and glamorous, especially the TV show filmed in New York, that was my expectation anyway, but they really weren't. Long nights, early mornings. Lots of self-important brusque men in skinny ties running around barking orders. Hot bright lights. Sound checks, air checks. Make-up, hair. We need you on stage for rehearsals, no scratch that, sound techs aren't ready, go on back and wait, we'll call you when we need you. That was a large part of it. What she was doing now. Waiting. It could be minutes or it could be hours. And without someone to sit with you in those small dingy impersonal dressing rooms, I imagined it could get pretty dismal and lonely. I don't know how Judith felt, but me, at the end of those days, I felt like an old penny. Gritty and grimy, like I'd been handled by too many people. All strangers. With smarmy smiles. And that was me, I was a nobody, I was mostly ignored the entire time.

"We haven't even started rehearsals yet, and I've been

here since-"

"Come on Evie!" Peg shouted. "Come dance, you're missing all the fun!"

Nell had just switched the record from Do Wah Diddy Diddy to Shirley Ellis singing The Nitty Gritty and everyone was up on their feet in an instant.

By this time I'd been here for five months and I felt well and truly ensconced by now, not much fazed me anymore, and yet, every once in a while, a moment like this one still stood out. Still struck me as amazing and made me remember just what an incredible opportunity I'd been given. If you've never heard the song, you're missing out. If you've never seen the dance, that's a shame. But to hear it on full blast and watch, right in front of you, a roomful of your friends dancing to it, in 1964? I just don't know if that can be beat.

"Oh my God, everyone looks so happy, especially Fran. Dwight's drunk so he's really giving Bobby Banas a run for his money. I hope he doesn't try to flip her like the last time." I covered the mouthpiece with one hand. "Hey, move away from the table, if you're gonna fling her in the air scootch over, I just replaced that coffee table!"

"Evelyn?"

"Sorry, I'm back. I really wish you were here to see this!"

She sniffed before answering after several seconds.

"Yeah, me too."

Even with the music, the thumping of shoes on the carpet, the laughter from the impromptu dance floor, and the wind howling outside, I could hear something in her voice.

"Are you getting a cold? Or is that from too much singing?"

It was neither. She was starting to cry.

"Oh no, I'm sorry, I didn't mean to...hey, it's okay. You'll be back in a few days. And where's your mother? Shouldn't she be with you, keeping you company?"

She sniffed again. "She's out souvenir hunting."

Typical.

"I promise, when you get back, we'll have another party, a proper one. I don't know that seeing Fran dance would cheer you-"

"I love you Evelyn."

This time it was my turn to pause.

This moment had nothing whatsoever to do with which decade I was in, but it still struck me as amazing.

"I love you too Judith."

If anyone heard that, well, I just didn't care.

CHAPTER TWENTY

She returned from that trip five days later. I stepped out onto the porch just in time to see her pull into the driveway in her brand new car and hear her bumper thump into mine. She left the door open as she rushed out, raced up the steps, and pulled me into a hug that felt more like someone clutching at a life preserver. Her nails digging into the small of my back. Next door, Mr. Jacobson was pretending not to notice anything, he kept his head down and continued to sand the railing on his own porch.

"That bad?" I asked.

She only nodded her head silently but I could feel her chin bob against my collarbone.

"Okay, Judith, I'll do it, I should have done it earlier, I'm sorry."

The "it" was to quit my father's store, let her pay the rent on the house, and travel with her as much as we could get away with. She'd been asking ever since her first royalty check came in five weeks before.

It was only dumb pride that kept me from agreeing until now. I figured it would only be a few more months until I started seeing real profits from my stock picks anyway, I could quit then. But hearing her cry on the phone had decided it for me.

"Really?" Her voice was muffled, her head still buried in

the hollow between my neck and shoulder. "You're not joking with me are you?"

"No, no jokes."

She laughed anyway, softly, and I could feel her warm tears as they fell onto my skin.

Seven months later...
June 1965

"How long has this been going on?" I tossed the newspaper on to the bed. The large black and white picture facing up. A picture of Judith in a cream colored sleeveless dress, her hair elegantly swept up, the pair of diamond earrings I'd given to her for Christmas the past year shining with the flash of the camera. And him. Warren Cabot, young, blond, white gleaming teeth, wearing a tuxedo, standing at least a foot taller than her...with his arm wrapped around her small waist, holding her so close that she had to lean her head slightly away from him to keep her hair from being flattened by his lapels. Both of them smiling at the camera.

Judith shook her head and sighed heavily before sitting on the bed beside it.

"Two months," she admitted. "Since filming that movie in California. When you stayed home to watch over Fran, when she was sick."

I nodded. "How convenient."

She said nothing to that. She kept her head down, staring at the picture.

"At least your mother will be happy."

"I'm so sorry." She took the paper in her hand, folded it in half so that it looked, for a moment, as if the picture Judith and the picture Warren were about to kiss, then she tossed it away across the room and onto the floor.

"We've only just moved into this house." I turned away

from her and towards the large window. We hadn't even gotten around to putting curtains up yet so I could see directly into our very spacious but empty back yard. "We haven't even had a chance to have a housewarming party."

"What does that have to do with anything?"

"Well," I said, turning around and throwing my hands in the air, "if you're going to marry this guy, I'm assuming we won't be living together anymore."

The corners of her mouth began to twitch.

"We don't live together now."

Technically true, I'd kept the rental house as my official residence. For appearance's sake. I'd even planned on sleeping there whenever Judith's mother decided she'd like to see Denver or Phoenix with her daughter, alone, and I stayed behind. Keep the weak illusion going, why not.

"And I used to worry it would be a woman that would steal you away. But a man? A man, Judith?" I walked over to the bed and grabbed one of the small decorative pillows off of it. Keeping my eyes on her the entire time.

She ignored the question, and me. She bowed her head and began tracing her finger along the blanket beneath her. Tracing over the flower design, over and over. We hadn't even slept underneath it yet. "Even if I do, marry him, it doesn't mean this has to be over does it? Me and you?"

"You've got to be kidding me."

"Why not?" she asked, shrugging her shoulders. "People do it all the time, don't they? Have affairs."

"Is that the kind of person you think I am? A person who goes around sleeping with married women?"

She raised her head to look at me. "I never said anything about sleeping."

"Oh, that's cute, real cute."

She ducked when I threw the pillow at her but not fast enough. It caught her on the shoulder. She laughed, picked it up off the floor, and threw it back at me.

The pictures and fake stories bothered her way more than they bothered me.

Although, of course, they did bother me somewhat. Especially if I were there when she'd be pulled aside and posed with whichever young dashing eligible bachelor happened to be in the vicinity while the cameras snapped away.

But they didn't happen that often. After all, her record label wanted her fans to think she was dating a couple of guys, not bopping every man she came across.

It didn't take very long for the bigwigs at her record label to figure out a few things. Shortly after I started traveling with her on a regular basis she was told, none too politely, that who she was sleeping with was her own business but if she breathed one word of it to the public then it became BlueRock's business and contract or not, she'd be gone. And furthermore, if she didn't want to spend the rest of her days singing in the parking lots of Publix grocery stores she'd keep a lid on things.

So she kept a lid on things.

The public was left in the dark about that.

But not everyone could be.

My parents, while it wasn't all sunshine, lollipops, and rainbows when I told them, eventually came to terms with it and never once did they express any anger or disappointment with me. Judith's parents weren't so understanding. It took nearly five months for her father just to speak to her again and even then it was mostly in grunts or clipped two or three word sentences. Her mother, on the other hand, didn't skip a beat. She kept on treating Judith the same as always, nothing changed. Because in her mind, nothing had. She flat out refused to believe any of it.

"You're lying. Stop lying. That's a sin, to lie, so stop it," is all she ever said about it. That, and "I don't ever want to see that woman again." Meaning me.

What a peach.

Telling our friends was a much simpler task, especially when it came to Fran.

"Thanks for telling me Evie, but you're a few months too late."

"You didn't know! How did you know?"

"I'm not blind, Evelyn. Judith can have her pick of any man she wants and she chooses to spend all her time with you? You're not that funny. Or charming. The best I can figure is you must be great in the sack."

She always was a woman ahead of her time.

Ralph, instead of angry, was relieved. "I knew it! I knew it couldn't be me!"

I'm not going to say it was easy, those years, having to keep our relationship hidden, because it wasn't. That part was harder on me than it was on Judith, of course it was. Unlike me, it's all she'd ever known. Like the proverbial fish that doesn't know it's in water. I felt the water every single day. But would I give it up to go back to a time when I could freely walk down the street holding my partner's hand? To maybe get married in a few years? To not be labeled as mentally ill, unnatural, and deviant? Not for a second. Some things are worth sacrificing for.

And anyway Judith had other things to contend with that I didn't. There was pressure on her to lose weight (to match the made up 108 pounds they ascribed to her), to fix her nose, change her hair, lower her necklines, shorten her dresses.

"I don't get it, they insist on calling me Judy, like I'm a ten-year-old, they want me to lose weight so I'll appear even more childlike, yet they want me to prance around on stage half naked!"

And she was being serious about that.

"I don't think I'd consider a hemline half an inch above the knee half naked. Not even a third naked," I told her.

"Do you want me getting more of those disgusting fan letters?"

"I don't know, they're kind of entertaining."

And they were. Real eye-openers too. I was right when I thought there'd be plenty of women out there who'd be crushing on her right along with the boys, and some of them were not shy about expressing it either, and graphically.

She never changed the way she dressed, didn't prance around on stage naked, which to her meant having the first two buttons of her blouse shamelessly opened. It reminded me of a comment I'd read on one of her videos in the land of YouTube. "She's really hot, but why is she wearing a housecoat?" Except this was YouTube, so the comment was more along the lines of "shez rly hot but whyz she wering a houscoat?" For the record, it wasn't a housecoat. I was there. I can attest to it. It wasn't the most form-fitting of dresses but not a housecoat. She didn't "fix" her nose (I never got that one, thousands of boys out there didn't think there was anything wrong with it, and neither did I). She didn't stop eating her ice cream, but she did comply with one of those requests.

I liked her old hairstyle but the new Jean Shrimpton-esque do wasn't too shabby either. Didn't require half as much hairspray. That was a plus.

She never changed, period. Everything I needed to know about the way Judith's singing career would go I could have picked up on the very first day of it. The day of the concert. She didn't wait around to bask in all the attention then, and that never changed. Her dream had been to be a singer, it was never to be famous. Or maybe it had been at one time until she found out what all it entailed. I would say she endured her career, not reveled in it. She endured it because she loves to sing, that passion remained, but she didn't revel in it because she was uncomfortable with the attention. Which is one of the reasons why, back in the world of laptops and ISPs, I had been so frustrated with the lack of information on her, the lack of pictures and videos. It's because she never gave them anything to snap or capture.

Her life, the kind of life she wanted to live, was in Leyfant. The people here grew used to seeing her around and, like everything else in life, she became commonplace to them after a while. Yeah, she's on TV and sings on the radio but I've got things to do, I can't stop and ask her for an autograph every time I need to go get gas or run to the library. So she tried to stay home as much as she could, which was surprisingly a lot.

I was wrong when I pictured her being swooped up and carried away by all the trappings of success. Of all the glamour of being a famous singer wanted by thousands, all the hobnobbing with the Hollywood and Broadway types. She wanted none of it.

It surprised me. When I pictured it, years ago, I thought her singing career, being on TV and touring, the fans, the records, the screaming mobs, was going to be the most important part of her life. That it would consume her, take precedence over everything, change her, and turn out to be that one bright shining moment in her life that she would mourn forever. That she wouldn't be satisfied once it was over. That she would spend the rest of her days trying to recapture it.

In the end, it turned out to be quite the opposite. It turned out to be a very small part of her life. It was almost like a part time job. She filmed four movies in the first two years and then turned down the rest, she was offered her very own television show and turned that down too. That would have meant moving away. Broadway show? No, thanks. New York is nice, but my life is here, in Leyfant. She refused to go on any more long tours, anything that would keep her away for more than three or four days at a time. Which angered and frustrated her manager, her publicist, the record label. They only tolerated it because her music was that popular that heavily promoting it didn't seem to matter, people still lined up at the record stores to gobble it all up. Whether or not that would have continued, I don't know, I'll never know, because by the end of 1968 she'd endured all she was going to endure.

She quit.

It hadn't been the changing of the times, her refusal to wear mini skirts, the war, or the hippies, she was still popular, even had a song in the top twenty on the charts when she decided she wasn't going to sign another recording contract. Which left both her agent and the record label dumbfounded. Who gives up a singing career? Don't you know there are thousands and thousands of people out there who would kill for this opportunity? She knew, she just didn't care.

She didn't quit singing, she'd never give up singing, but of course, with no new records, all the hysteria surrounding her dwindled, which she happily welcomed. The royalty checks dwindled right along with it, but by then I was making almost three times as much as she was so that didn't matter either. (In truth, she never made very much money at all. BlueRock did, the songwriters did, and they'll keep on making it for years, even decades.) She was free. Free to spend all her time with our friends instead of strangers. Free to wear whatever the hell she wanted to wear, eat what she wanted, keep her nose from going under the knife. And, most importantly to her, besides being home, free from having to be the fake Judy Paige everyone thought she was. The girl who was always just on the verge of marrying this guy or that one. It's why she rarely granted interviews for print or in front of a camera. Everyone was obsessed with who she would settle down with.

"It's bad enough I have to pretend to be someone I'm

not, every single time I get up on stage, every time I have to sing one of those songs they make me sing, about boys," she'd always said. "That's not really me up there, it's who they want me to be. And those words I'm singing aren't my own, they're someone else's. So they can't be considered actual lies. But during an interview, those are my words. That's when I actually become a liar. They force me to be dishonest."

I wasn't complaining. In the beginning I was obsessed with Judy Paige. I fell in love with Judith. I was happy to have her back.

CHAPTER TWENTY-ONE

1968 was a tumultuous year. I cursed myself for not paying enough attention to history when it was history. All I could recall of Martin Luther King Jr's assassination is that it happened in Memphis on the balcony of a motel and that he was shot by a man named James Earl Ray. I'm ashamed to say I couldn't have told you the name of the motel or the exact date. Truthfully, I would not have even been able to tell you the year. I can now. April 4, 1968. And it was the same for Robert Kennedy. I knew it was at a hotel. Which one? No idea. He was shot by a man named Sirhan Sirhan, that I knew, but for some reason I had always believed he'd been shot while delivering a speech. In a kitchen. Why would he be giving a speech in a kitchen? He wasn't. He gave a speech, then left through a kitchen hallway. The date was June 5, 1968. Although even if I had known all the details beforehand, what could I have done about it? Who could I call? Who would listen to Evelyn Bryant, a twenty-four year old woman from a town in Texas no one had even heard of? How do you stop something like that?

It was also in the last month of 1968, after being here for four years, that I saw something that shook me and left me scared for several months afterward.

It was Mr. Smith.

I think.

A man, grey suit, white shirt, grey tie, black shoes, sitting at a bench across the street from Maybell's seeming to be looking directly at me through the window as I sat with Judith and Fran and Dwight and Ralph.

"All that campaigning we did," Fran was saying as she shook her head. She was still taking both assassinations pretty hard. "I really thought we were making a difference."

Dwight reached over and rubbed her back consolingly. Even that didn't bring her out of her funk. Usually she would have melted.

"He made a difference," I said to her, "you just can't see it now but-"

The spoon in my hand clanked to the table and then to the floor.

"Evelyn?"

It's him. He's here. He's taking me back.

No, it's not. He's too far away, I can't be sure. And It's 1968, there are plenty of men who wear the same exact suit. But why is he turned this way? He's looking at me.

"Evie? What are you-"

The front door opened as a boy and his little sister walked in, gloved hands linked together. A cold gust of wind followed them in.

"It's the year 2019," the little boy said.

My stomach dropped. No. It's...2014, back there, it's 2014, why...and how did he...what's happening?

When I turned back to the window Mr. Smith, or the man who looked like Mr. Smith was gone. The bench was empty. I'd only turned for a few seconds but there was no sign of him. That doesn't mean anything, I said to myself. There were plenty of cars passing by. He could have been picked up by any one of them. Or maybe a bus passed by and he waved it down. It wasn't him. I scanned the street anyway, scared to see him crossing between cars, heading this way.

"Evelyn?" I felt Judith's hand cover mine. "What are you looking at? What's wrong?"

"The little boy, did you hear him? What did he say?"

"What boy?"

"You didn't see a little boy and a girl just walk in?"

She shook her head.

Both Dwight and Ralph had amused looks on their faces as they stared at me but they were quickly turning to looks of concern.

Now I knew it was him.

He can't. He can't take me back. Not now.

"He was talking about that Dick book," Fran said, her frown disappearing as she snickered at the word.

"A what book?" Dwight asked her, his eyebrows almost disappearing into his now shaggy hair.

"That crazy sci-fi sheep book by that author, Philip Dick." She nodded her head in the direction of the counter towards the back.

I turned and there they were, just two ordinary little kids bundled up in hats and gloves but still staring longingly at all the new ice cream flavors. Trying to decide which one to choose. "Yeah," the little boy was saying to his sister, "he wants to own a real animal, because in 2019, there won't be any more real animals left. Or not a lot of them. Only real rich people will be able to afford them."

"I'm going to have a real animal then," his sister answered him.

For weeks I was scared to go anywhere. Scared to turn a corner and bump into him. Scared to go to the library. What if, when I leave, he's waiting for me in the parking lot leaning against my car? I was afraid I'd see him strolling down the grocery store aisle, heading straight for me.

"You've had your fun, you got your answers, why don't you come with me, we can have a cup of coffee. We need to discuss what happens next."

I was scared to sit outside on our front porch swing.

For weeks Judith had no idea why I insisted we sit on our back patio instead.

"It's nicer out here."

"Not really," she said, "I can't see the neighbors walking by."

"Yes, which means they can't see us either. That's what makes it nicer."

"How is that ni-"

I leaned over to kiss her.

I knew my logic was faulty. If he has the power to transport people between decades, surely he can knock on our front door or open a gate to the backyard. He'll find me no matter where I go.

But he never did.

I never saw him after that day. Maybe I never did.

Or if I had, if it was him, maybe it was just a check-in. Still want to stay? Yes? I see you've made a life for yourself here, you look happy. You're not hurting anyone, you're not out trying to change important world events, you didn't set yourself up to become filthy rich. If you want to stay, I don't see any harm in it.

After a while, a month or two later, I began to relax.

By June of 1969, when we read about the Stonewall riots, I'd put it completely out of my mind.

"You think any of this is going to make a difference?" Judith asked me, holding my hand tightly as if she desperately needed me to say yes.

"Yes, I do. It can't stay this way forever. People can only be held down for so long before they get fed up with it and rebel. This is just the start, believe me. And who knows, one day we might even be able to get married."

"Okay," she said, shaking my hand with hers, "change, yes, more acceptance, certainly, but marriage? That will never happen. That's a little too far-fetched even for you. I know, once we're engaged, we can call all our friends to tell them the news on these magical telephones in our pockets you think are going to be all the rage." She shook her head and gave me the same smile she always gave me whenever I made any of these wild claims. "Pocket phones," she said, as in, sure, of course, one day we'll live to be five hundred years old too.

In July of that same year we threw a party and had a houseful of our friends with us as we stayed up late into the night to watch, in awe, as Neil Armstrong stepped onto the surface of the moon. I'd seen it before, of course, on YouTube. But there's nothing like being there, with your friends, all holding their breath, their eyes glued to the screen, holding each other's hands out of nerves or excitement, or fear. It's so easy to be blasé about such things when they're far in the past but when it's happening in real time and the people around you are shaking and even crying as they witness this incredible accomplishment, there's no way you can be indifferent to it.

There were just so many things I got to experience or witness with her in such a short amount of time. Some good, some not so good. The Manson murders, Richard Speck, the draft.

We had to say goodbye to several of our friends. Judith's oldest brother Carl, our friend Michael, even George, the first person I'd met upon coming here. I cried when he left. And I cried even harder when I learned later that he wouldn't be coming back. Ralph and Dwight were lucky. Even the lottery in late '69 didn't get them. Both of them had very high lottery numbers.

By 1970 Ralph was married and expecting a baby. Fran had grown drunk with power when she'd managed to get several potholes fixed and decided she was going to run for city council. And I started to watch Judith very closely.

I didn't know what I was looking for so I looked for everything. Is she sleeping more than usual? How many drinks did she have at last night's get together? Who was she talking to on the phone? Anyone shady? Selling drugs? Maybe all that talk about her losing weight before had caused her to become anorexic. I watched what she ate, to see if she was skipping meals or eating only salads. I insisted she have a check-up every three months. I'd have been happier with every month but she grumbled about the three. "I'm twenty-four years old! My heart's not going to burst in the middle of the night."

It had been so long, my memories from that other life were now so faded I started to think I might have remembered it all wrong. Maybe I'd blown it up in my mind to be worse than it actually was. Perhaps she lost a pound or two, changed her hairstyle, wore different makeup? The lighting might have made her appear sickly when in fact she was just a little worn down? Those videos I'd seen weren't great quality. At least one of them, I'd read in the description, had been a VHS transfer. The colors were flat and muted. The sound even warbled in places.

And what if it was me?

That thought gave me hope.

Maybe I changed things in a way I wasn't even aware of. And I had to have didn't I? Of course. She'd led a completely different life this time, with me, instead of whatever she'd done before. I had no idea what would have transpired if I hadn't been here. Maybe she'd had a girlfriend, maybe not. There was of course, never anything in the media about that. What was her life like before? I'll never be able to know. She most likely had a completely different set of friends. Maybe people she'd met during her career. People who'd influenced her in the wrong way. So was it drugs?

I didn't shorten her career, that happened regardless. But behind the scenes there could have been dozens or even hundreds of differences I wasn't aware of. I just couldn't be sure. It was so frustrating. There were no clues at all.

And as 1970 started winding down, it seemed more and more likely that she was going to escape whatever befell her before, because there was absolutely nothing there. She was as happy and as content as I'd ever seen her. She was in no way depressed about her career, in fact, she often turned down offers to sing at large events, preferring to keep to her light schedule of singing at nightclubs every once in a while, a small musical in an obscure playhouse here and there. She didn't drink any more than usual. She hadn't lost any weight, she didn't seem concerned at all about what she ate. She'd quit smoking two years before. I couldn't figure it out. I was hopeful, and growing more and more confident with each passing day, that whatever she'd gone through before, was not going to hit her this time.

But I still watched.

By November 14th, 1970, we'd been together for over six years. And we'd managed to get through all six of them without any major fights. Neither one of us ever packed a bag and our pillow and spent a week at a hotel or on a friend's couch. Arguments, yes, the usual: cap left off the toothpaste, you left the milk out, why are there muddy footprints on the carpet? (We could thank Fran and her platform shoes for that one.) When Peg moved to Canada but continued to write to me, Judith was sure she and I had "fooled around" as she put it. She wasn't too far off the mark. Not that I ever even contemplated it, but yes, Peg had tried to kiss me once when Judith was off traveling up and down the east coast for four days with her mother. It didn't happen, but it took at least a week for me to convince Judith it hadn't. They were silly, our little squabbles, nothing every couple hasn't gone through, but the one exception were our arguments about her mother. Those sometimes got testier than I'd like.

This was one of them.

It had started the day before. There was a little yelling, a slammed door or two, cold silences, then back to shouting, then, by the end of the night, resignation. Nothing was going to get resolved, so we each called a truce. A strained one.

For Judith, this morning, it was over, for me, it wasn't.

"This is still the best ice cream in the world. Mmmm, Peppermint Stick."

I was upset with her but I still smiled. I couldn't help but see that sweet timid nineteen-year-old girl with the flip hairdo who'd sat across from me that Sunday so long ago.

It was easy to do here, at Maybell's. The place hadn't changed one bit. Except for Maybell. She'd been replaced by her son. Fran swore up and down he wasn't as generous with his scoops as his mother was, but then again she also swore she and Dwight were going to be getting married any day now, so you really can't trust her judgment.

After a second, I let the smile slip and turned to watch the cars through the window, as they waited at the intersection, for the light to change, so they could head on up the ramp and on to the interstate. The bench had disappeared a year ago. I no longer even thought about it. Him. That day.

Judith set her spoon down on the table and wiped her mouth with a napkin.

"It's only one day, I'll be back tomorrow."

"Judith, you know that's not why I'm upset."

"Yes, I know."

"It's been almost five years now that you told her. Is this really the way it's going to be forever?"

She sighed. "We can't keep going over this. There's no use. I can't change her mind. I've tried, you know I have."

Judith pushed her still half-full bowl away. "She wants to go on this one trip, she's never been to Illinois, and it's the last before the end of the year. It's one day. Please, I don't want to fight anymore."

"I'm not fighting, I just…I don't think you've ever been as upset about it as you should be. It just makes me…I'm disappointed."

She nodded, she checked her watch, and then rose from her chair.

"That's hurtful. I wish you hadn't said that, but I can't keep talking about it right now. I have to go. I'll see you tomorrow, straight from the airport, I'll drop my mother off, I won't stay, even though she'll ask. I might even be home before you wake up."

She lingered for a few seconds, waiting for me to turn to her. I didn't.

"I know you're upset right now, but…I love you," she said, quietly, so that the elderly couple heading for the door couldn't hear.

I kept my eyes on the cars as she walked away.

"Hey Frannie."

"What's wrong with you gloomy?"

"Nothing. Judith's mom."

"Pfft, that? Still? She's as bad as you used to be, lost in some other decade."

"Hey, I wear jeans now. I am with it."

"Sure you are," she said, and I could hear her transferring the phone from one ear to the other. "But really, are you two okay?"

"Of course we are and you're right, I don't know why I let that woman bother me. I really shouldn't."

"No, you shouldn't."

"Anyway, I don't want to talk about her, what's going on?

Why are you calling? You're not calling to ask to come over are you? Try to seduce me while Judith's away?"

"Ha! You wish! Oh my God, I know you've been lusting after me all these years, but no, it's not going to happen, sorry."

How could I ever have thought she was obnoxious?

"No, I was calling to tell you about that man, Nelson? You know the one who kept coming by the store, asking me out?"

"Yeah?"

"Well, he's back. I forgot to tell you yesterday. He showed up again last Friday."

"And did he ask you out again?"

"Yes, he did."

"Go out with him."

"What? No. I can't."

"Why not? Because you're in love with me?"

"Because I'm with Dwight?"

"Uh huh. Put that aside for a second and tell me, are you in any way attracted to him? This Nelson guy?"

She was quiet as she thought about it.

"He's not bad looking, I suppose. Nice hair. He's tall, I like that. But he's no Dwight."

I'd have to take her word for that, I'd never seen him, but that didn't change things.

"Frannie, sweetheart, go out with him."

"Evelyn, honey, what kind of a girl do you think I am? Cheating on-"

"No, Fran, honey, you don't understand. I've never said anything all this time because I didn't think it was my place to, but I can't let you waste any more of your time. Sweetie, Dwight is gay."

Silence.

"What the hell are you talking about?"

"It's been over six years. What man is going to wait six

years to have sex?"

"He wants to wait until-"

"Until you get married, yeah, yeah. Why does he always pull out of engagements with all of us when Ralph won't be there? What happened at Ralph's wedding? He got so drunk and belligerent they had to lock him in his car so he could sleep it off. What did he do when you told him Ralph was going to have a baby?"

She paused again.

"He...that was the day he was arrested for punching a hole in the wall at Arnie's."

"You were so quick on the uptake with me and Judith, I thought you'd have figured it out by now. He's been in love with Ralph for years."

The longest pause yet.

"That son of a bitch!"

It took twenty minutes to calm her down but I finally got her breathing normally and to agree to take it easy on him when she confronted him about it. Somehow I had the feeling she was going to break that promise.

I'd just have to wait and see.

In the meantime I hung up the phone and went to bed.

The next morning, before I could even open my eyes, I knew it was going to be a bad day. I could hear, in the distance, the sound of thunder and felt a cold drop of water land on my wrist.

Oh come on! I thought. What an inconvenience, first Judith's mom and now this, having to deal with a leaky roof. Can it get any worse?

When I opened my eyes, I realized that yes, it can.

I was sitting in front of Judith's grave.

CHAPTER TWENTY-TWO

"No. No, no, no."

I made it ten feet away before I had to stop, bend over, and be sick on the grass.

She's not dead. She's not dead. She's just in Illinois. She'll be home soon. She's not dead. The thought just kept repeating over and over in my head as I remained there, clutching my knees, retching.

Mr. Smith waited a few minutes before he stood and walked up behind me.

"I told you you'd have to come back."

"Six years!" I yelled at him, wincing at the pain in my raw throat.

He nodded.

"No. This isn't happening."

But it was. There behind him, plain as day, her headstone. Judith Lynne Paige. May 10, 1945 - October 18, 1991.

"Six years," I repeated as I straightened up. "You never said I'd be there for six years. You can't do this. You can't."

He pursed his lips and then sighed.

"I was clear in that-"

"No! No you weren't at all, you weren't clear about anything. Oh my God, oh my God."

I turned away from him, walked a few feet away, turned back, saw the headstone behind him, and turned back around.

I couldn't look at it.

"I was there for six years. Six months is long enough to form attachments, but six years...I...had a life. I had..." My instinct was to turn back to the headstone but I stopped myself.

He walked around to face me. "Karen, there's something..."

Karen. Who the hell was that? I'd stopped being Karen long ago. My name is...

"Evelyn," I said, then quickly looked around as if expecting to see someone else, a woman, a woman in her forties. Forty-four to be exact. But she wouldn't be here. She's...

"No. Is she going to wake up back there in an unfamiliar house, six years older, in my...our bed?" The thought made my stomach flutter again. The thought of someone else...and then another even worse thought came to mind. When Judith gets home, what is she going to come home to? A stranger. Someone who looks exactly like me but who won't know her. What's going to happen?

"No. She won't. No time has passed. Look around, Karen."

I did as he said just as more droplets of water fell from the sky. It was beginning to drizzle. The sky above was grey, just as it had been that day six years ago. And we were in the same cemetery. I was wearing the same clothes. The older couple and their granddaughter I'd seen that day were just now making their way up the paved path lined with cars. The girl still a teenager in a crude t-shirt, not a young woman six years older.

"What are you saying?"

"I'm saying it's 2010. The only time that's passed has been the few minutes since you...came back."

"You can't be serious. Are you saying what I just experienced, what I felt to be six years was all in my head?

That that entire world and everything in it was just some sort of a fabrication?"

"No, not at all. 1964 through 1970 definitely happened. And you were there."

"Then what? What does that mean? If no time at all has passed here, does that mean that...Evelyn," I said, extremely uncomfortable in talking about her, even thinking of her, as a separate person, "did not experience any time passing? That she's going to wake up completely clueless? In the blink of an eye, for her, it'll just be six years in the future?" That would be horrible. At least if she'd lived six years here, she'd understand what was going on, she'd have some sort of an idea of what was happening. And she might have been able to work out the situation with Judith. Maybe let her down easy. Or would she? Would she let her down? She might not. After all, she was also...no, I couldn't think about that.

"No, that's not going to happen either."

"Then what is? She'll wake up...in 1964 exactly as she would have? On that day, with George mowing the lawn and she'll be none the wiser? It'll all play out as if I was never there?"

If that's what he meant, then from her point of view, Judith never met me at all?

"No, that can't be, because she waved at me. It's on the video. I...or Evelyn, was at the concert. I did that. Evelyn, the other Evelyn, had plans to go to the movies that night, she never would have met Judith."

"You're right. You, or she, was at that concert and Judith waved at you, but no, she will not wake up in 1964, nor will she wake up in 1970. Because there is no Evelyn Bryant apart from you. And there is no Evelyn Bryant that exists past that date, November 14th, 1970."

"What?"

"You are Evelyn Bryant."

"Yes, I know, I was Evelyn Bryant."

"No. You are...well technically, yes, you were Evelyn Bryant."

"You're not making any sense."

"You were born on April 11th, 1944. You. What you experienced was your own past, not someone else's."

What could I do? I laughed.

"It's why that song impacted you the way it did. You'd never heard it before, or not in this lifetime anyway. It was a memory. Your memory. A memory you weren't supposed to retain, but somehow did."

It took a long time for me to say anything.

At some point Mr. Smith produced a black umbrella from who knows where as the drops of water started to fall faster and offered it to me. I batted it away.

"My past?"

"Your past, yes."

"As in what? Reincarnation?"

"That's such a...the term doesn't really..." He flicked his hand through the air. "Yes. For simplicity's sake you can call it that."

"That's insane."

"Really? After what you just experienced? This is insane?"

I had to give him that one.

And my mind went back to that day, my second one there, when I'd heard my mother's voice over the phone. How hard it hit me. And even further back, when I'd learned that Judith was dead. That was before I knew her. Or thought I didn't know her.

"So then I wasn't really there? You just showed me something that happened?"

"No. No, you were there, as alive as you are now, and you relived those six years."

I took another long silent pause to think about everything.

"Are you saying that, before this, before I went back, I had another life and in that life I met Judith? That we were together before? That's why I remembered the song?"

"Yes."

"That still doesn't make sense, when I went back I didn't know her. I had to seek her out. Evelyn...I, had plans to go somewhere else that night. I wouldn't have met her."

"You met her anyway. The first time around. If you'll recall you had plans to go to the movies, but first you were going to go out to eat. Which you did, and ran into friends in the parking lot who persuaded you and your friend Fran to go to the dance hall instead. No paradox. The concert."

"So we were together before?"

"Yes."

"So what? I was there, alive, but essentially a puppet? Living my old life thinking I was making choices when I really wasn't? Was it like a movie, with a script that I couldn't go off of?"

"No. You were making choices, and you changed things from the first time, some of them small, others not. But for the most part you kept everything the same. You were still you after all. You just made the same decisions, the same choices, as you did before."

"What sorts of changes?"

"Investing in the stock market for one. You didn't have the knowledge you had this time around. The you before this kept working at your father's store. For a time."

Obvious.

"So I wasn't just living the exact same life I'd lived before?"

"No."

"I can change things, then," I said, half to myself. My brain already churning, already accepting the utter ridiculousness of the entire scenario and focusing on practical matters.

"You could have, yes."

"No, I can."

"No, Karen. It's over. You're back where you belong."

"No, Mr. Smith. It's not. You're going to send me back. I don't know why you brought me back here, to explain the situation maybe, I don't know, nor do I care, but I'm going back."

He looked down at the umbrella still in his hand, twirled it once, then let it fall to the ground where it went from being a solid object, to a shadow on the ground, despite the overcast day, then dissolved altogether like black ink sinking into the grass.

"I'm sorry, but you can't."

"Of course I can, I went back before, you have the ability. So I can't? Or you won't do it? Is this some kind of morbid game you're playing?"

He shook his head.

"It's not a game, but there are rules. Rules that I cannot break, however much I'd like to."

"You're going to have to explain better than that."

"You want to go back, you want to wake up on November 15th, 1970, and continue on just as before but I cannot make that happen."

"Why? You sent me back to 1964, how much harder can it be?"

"Don't you understand? You never left."

CHAPTER TWENTY-THREE

"I never left?"

"That's right."

"Are you saying there's a," I did the math, quickly, in my head, "sixty-six year old version of me, Evelyn, running around out here now?" I turned my head to the side as if expecting to see her...me, older, walking down the path with a bundle of flowers in a wrinkled, age-spotted hand. It wasn't as far-fetched as it sounded. Perhaps I never left the area and I visited the grave of the woman I loved once upon a time often. Or would I? Remembering back, she and I weren't together when she died. She'd been with another woman. We'd broken up? I couldn't believe that.

"No, there's only you. No separate Evelyn. You," he said, pointing towards his head, "what makes you, you, your consciousness, cannot exist in two places at once. Which is why I can't do what you've asked. I can send you back to 1964, or 1969, even 1945 if you wanted, but you will never make it past November 14th, 1970. Not as Evelyn Bryant."

"Why? What is so important about that date! I don't get it!"

"What's the date approximately nine months after it?"

Just the mention of "nine months" made me realize, I didn't need to calculate numbers to know.

"My birthday."

He nodded.

"It was the night you were conceived."

I should have stopped asking questions.

"Are you saying I died that night? Is that what you're saying? I was a healthy twenty-six year old! Young people don't just suddenly die in their sleep."

"No, you didn't die." For the first time since I'd seen him in the cafeteria a week ago, or six years ago, or however you look at it, he looked uncomfortable. He fidgeted with his hands, rubbing at the knuckles of his left hand with the fingers of his right. "This is the part that's hard to explain and it'll be hard for you to hear."

"This part? What the hell can be worse?"

"It does usually work that way. A death, a rebirth. A clean slate. A new life. In your case, there was a new life. But no death. It was, to put it simply, an error."

"An error?"

"Yes."

"An error?" I repeated, dumbfounded.

"Yes."

"Erro-"

"These things happen. They are exceedingly rare, but they happen."

"What things happen? I still don't understand."

"You didn't die, you just...ceased to exist as Evelyn Bryant the moment you were conceived and were eventually born as Karen Stephens."

"Ceased to exist? This is...that's..." I threw up my arms. I had no words.

"Yes. You remember the ball don't you? A glitch. It was in one spot one second, in another the next. I know, I understand, you're a human being, not a ball," he said, seeing the look on my face. "It's not supposed to happen, it rarely does, and it's not taken lightly. We learn from these...mistakes, and maybe one day it will never happen again. As it is now,

227

every ten years give or take, it does. One out of half a billion births or so. I know that makes no difference to you. It's no comfort."

"Is that why I remembered? Because I didn't die, because I wasn't meant to leave? I lost all the time we would have…"

Mr. Smith turned away as I cried for the first…no, actually, the second time that day.

After a minute he held a handkerchief out to me, which I took, and noticed one still tucked into the pocket of his jacket. I wiped the tears away, which was useless, the raindrops replaced them three seconds later.

"What's going to happen when Judith gets back?"

"Do you mean what happened? That was forty years ago."

Forty years ago. The thought clunked in my brain and made my entire body go cold. It was only yesterday.

"For you it was only yesterday. For her, for all of them, forty years has passed."

"In the blink of an eye? Forty years?"

"It seems that way to you, but I assure you, they didn't experience it that way. They experienced time moving on exactly as you're experiencing it right now. Forty years of it."

Jesus.

"So…when Judith got home, that day, what happened? Was I just…gone?"

"I'm afraid so."

With no explanation. My God, what did she think? That I was kidnapped? Murdered? Or maybe even worse, that I just upped and abandoned her? I didn't even say goodbye. The last thing she said to me, I love you, and I didn't say a word. I didn't even look at her. Fuck. Forty years ago. She must have, for a while, believed that I'd left her. My only comfort, if I could call it that, is that she'd eventually figure out that that's not what happened at all. I might have left her but I wouldn't have left everything. There were others. My parents. They never saw me again either. They lost their only child and they never knew why. They might still be alive. I could maybe...no. How could I explain to them what actually happened? I couldn't.

"I have to go back."

"I told you it's not possib-"

"To 1964. Back to the beginning. Just like before."

"I don't understand."

"I'm not staying here. I can't. You expect me to just pick up where I left off here? With her dead? I can't do that, I won't. You can't break these asinine rules, but you can send me back to an earlier date, you said so yourself."

"Yes, I can, but to what end? You go back and live the same six years over only to end up right back here again?"

"Yes. If I have to, I will. I'll live the same six years over and over and over again. For as long as it takes. Maybe one day, after a dozen times, when I've lived the equivalent of a lifetime with her, I'll be willing to let her go. But I'm not now. I'm not willing to do that."

"Think about what you're saying. You're not the only one who lost something. She lost you too. Are you willing to put her through that again? She's already been through it. Twice."

I hadn't thought about that.

"Your parents, your friends. It affected more than just you."

"Then fix it! This is your fucking mistake! Don't fucking stand there and tell me I'm being selfish when I had nothing to do with it. Why the hell did you come here in the first place? Why would you show me all of this if you can't do anything about it? Don't you think it would have been easier if I had just never found out?"

"That feeling was never going to leave you. That sense of loss. It would have stayed with you for the rest of your life. Do you think you would have been able to live a happy life with it there, always?"

"And you think I can lead a happy life now? I thought you were supposed to be some kind of genius."

"I thought, if you had an answer, as to why, you'd be able to cope with it, understand it, and eventually let it go."

"Really? That's what you thought? How the hell are you peo...whatever you are, running things? Just...I'm going back. End of discussion."

"I don't think that's a good idea."

"Did I ask if you thought it was a good idea?"

"You're upset. You're angry right now. I know, you have every right to be but should you make a decision like this right now? This rashly? You should at least think about it. Really think about things. Take a few days, think about what you'll be putting her through. For you, it's been a few hours. For her, years. She was devastated, yes, but she overcame it, she went on, she was happy aga-"

"Don't. I don't want to hear it. That other life, after me. It should never have happened. It wasn't supposed to happen. It never would have happened if not for you and your damned...no."

I threw his handkerchief on the ground in frustration. It wasn't as satisfying as I thought it would be. It fluttered in the air like a bird, even seeming to form one for a second, before breaking up into a thousand small glowing pieces that drifted to the ground and vanished. I walked off away from him, my head in my hands, thinking. It wasn't fair. He was pinning me up against a corner. Of course I didn't want her to go through it again. But she wouldn't even remember it. Would she? Wouldn't it be like experiencing it for the first time? Maybe. Who knows. I remembered. I wasn't supposed to, he'd told me so, but I had. Even he doesn't know all the possibilities. All the consequences. What if she does? Why did she really write that song? One day you'll leave me. She must have felt something. If there was any chance that I'd be putting her through all that pain again, I didn't think I could do it.

But I had to didn't I?

Because I thought I had all the time in the world before. I thought I'd be there to tell her there was no way in hell she was getting on that airplane. That's all it would have taken. Because I can still change it. Even if I can't stay, I can still warn her somehow. Even if it meant, even if it would kill me, being there, knowing I wouldn't have much time, that my life with her would be too short, knowing I wouldn't be there for her, to help her through her illness or addiction, or whatever it was that…

Of course.

There it is.

The something bad I had been on the lookout for.

For months I'd been watching her. Scrutinizing her every move. Hoping to catch something out of the ordinary. Hoping I'd be able to prevent something I now see was unpreventable.

That something bad was me.

CHAPTER TWENTY-FOUR

I disappeared.

That's what I'd seen on those videos. The weight loss, the vacant eyes, the deterioration. It's one thing to go through a break-up. As heartbreaking as some of them may be, rarely does anyone ever completely shut down because of them. To lose someone to a death, I can only imagine, must be a hundred times worse, and yet people do carry on. Because they know. They can grieve. And every day the pain eases up a little, even if it's just an inch at a time. But to just not know? What must that be like? Is there a constant cycle of hope and despair? Every day you wake up does it enter your mind, today, today he/she may just walk through the door, today we'll find them, today things will get better. But by the end of the evening, once the sun begins to set, is it back to hopelessness? It's been three weeks, two months, a year, they're never coming back. Do you cry yourself to sleep, let it all out, and feel better by the time you drift off only to wake up the next morning and think, today. Today they'll walk through the door. Today it'll get better. And the cycle repeats itself. Like a rubber band being stretched to its limit then allowed to go slack, then stretched again, to its breaking point, then slack again, over and over and over again until it eventually weakens enough to snap.

I disappeared and she never saw or heard from me again. For days and weeks and then, eventually, forever.

She suffered because of that. For a long, long, time.

How could I possibly put her through that again?

"You're right. I should think this through more carefully."

Mr. Smith nodded. "I think that's a good idea."

"How long do I have? Is there some sort of rule about that as well?" I didn't even try to mask the bitter tone of my voice.

"As long as you need."

"And I need to go...home. I don't want to stay here. Is that a problem?"

"No."

"Good. It shouldn't be more than a day or two. How do I contact you when I've made my decision?"

"I'll know. I'll find you."

"Of course you will."

You might think I would have had the urge to drive to our house, to see what had become of it. Were there other people now living in it? A family maybe, with kids. Would there be a swing dangling from a limb on the tree in our front yard? Was it even still standing?

But none of that even entered my mind. To me, I'd only just been there a day ago. Hours, not decades. I had no reason to think there had been any changes at all. It wasn't until I was almost out of town, nearing the interstate, that it hit me, like a punch in the stomach, the actual real time that had passed since I'd last seen her.

I pulled into the empty parking lot, and sat there, listening to the rain thumping on the roof of the car and staring out of the windshield. The image in front of me cutting in and out. Clear and then blurry, clear and then fuzzy, as the windshield wipers swiped the water away from the glass intermittently.

The sign was gone. No more cheery cartoon cow with a red bell around its neck. All that remained was a rusty dented pole. The large windows were completely boarded up and the local graffiti artists had gone to town on them. A pile of soaked debris, beer bottles, plastic bags, an old soiled blanket, an upturned shopping cart with one wheel missing, was lying against the right wall, like a snowdrift. The roof on the left hand side was caving in on itself, the rain surely seeping in and running down the inside walls like tears. I imagined the interior. Musty and dark, mildew growing on the very spot we'd sat at not twenty-four hours ago, in my mind at least. The plonk-plonk-plonk sound of raindrops falling to the floor, echoing in the darkness. The cracked and peeling trim at the edge of the roof was a faded orange and black, not the bright pink and green it was when the sign out front read Maybell's. How many changes had it gone through? Dairies went out of style in what? The seventies? Is that when people grew tired of making a separate trip to a different store just for butter and milk, eggs and ice cream?

It really has been forty years. Forty years since the day she walked out of that door. Only it wasn't a door now, just rotting plywood covered in black, blue, and bright orange spray paint.

If I closed my eyes, I could still hear the click-click-click sound of her heels on the black and white tiled floor as she walked away. I had no image to go with it because I hadn't even turned to watch her leave.

I didn't even say goodbye.

The last words she heard me say to her was that I was disappointed.

She lived for twenty-one years after that day with that being her last memory of me.

Twenty-one years without ever knowing what happened to me.

Going back in time was a jolt. Coming back wasn't quite as jarring but it still took some getting used to. Seeing myself in the rear view mirror was almost as shocking as it was when I'd first seen myself as Evelyn. The small scar on my hand was back, while my ring, the teal blue sapphire, the one Judith had given to me for my twenty-third birthday, was gone. I'd forgotten about changing billboards. It took an hour of driving before I stopped trying to step on the clutch and reach for a gearshift. I stopped to get gas and a cup of coffee. The couple ahead of me in line, holding hands, were two men. There were one or two sideways glances aimed in their direction, but no one was having a fit.

Where are all the phone booths? Oh, yeah, right. I jumped when I heard tinny whimsical music coming from somewhere in the car, beneath me, until I remembered it was a ringtone. I didn't answer. Did you think of me Judith? When cell phones started up? Or had you forgotten by then, our conversation? Did you ever tell her about me? Did you love her as much? Don't answer that. I'd rather not know. Is it selfish of me to hope you didn't? Did it hurt when I suddenly realized that that relationship lasted almost twice as long as ours did? Yes. Fuck yes. Like being pelted by sharp jagged rocks. And then being forced to swallow them.

I drove the four and a half hours back to San Antonio in silence. There was too much temptation with the radio on to switch it over to an oldie's station. And I didn't think I could handle one of Judith's songs, more than likely digitalized, cleaned-up, and remastered, suddenly coming through the speakers. Or even worse, the voice of an overly cheery twenty-something DJ "Let's go aaaaaall the way back to 1964! Here's "One Day You'll Leave Me" by uh...Judy Payne. Big hit back in the day, big hit. What a voice! And Judy, if you're listening, we still love you!"

She's not listening, she's dead, you stupid twit. And it was

Paige. Not Payne. And she didn't like Judy.

Pissed at an imaginary DJ and his imaginary words.

Instead I went over everything Mr. Smith had told me, of how I could go back but couldn't stay. That doesn't mean I can't warn her. Even if I can't be with her, she can live a longer life. But the problem still remained, what possible explanation could I give her for my disappearance? Do it gradually? Tell her I'd fallen out of love with her? That I was leaving? Not to come look for me? It would be painful, I'm sure, but not as devastating. But would I actually be able to do it? Have that kind of willpower? No. Most likely not. And anyway, that wouldn't solve the problem. My parents, Frannie, our friends. I'm sure they'd reach out to her, ask her if she'd heard from me. She's gone. We can't find her. We haven't heard from her, where could she be? That wasn't going to work.

I busted my brain for almost three hours trying to come up with a solution. Of a way to A. Make sure she never boards that plane. B. Not break her heart. And C. Keep her from having to endure years of anguish due to my disappearance.

The answer, of course, was simple. I should have come up with it in less than two minutes. If I'd been presented with the problem as a riddle with say, Bob and Kate as the two main characters in the puzzle, I'd have scratched my head, squinted my eyes, snapped my fingers and spit the answer out. What is that, sixth grade logic level? Come on!

But I wasn't thinking in terms of this hypothetical couple. This was me and Judith. So that simple solution eluded me. Until, after three hours of going over every single scenario I could think of to make it work and not succeeding, my brain, exhausted, began to wander. Going over snippets of our time together.

All those many conversations we'd had on the roof of our

house. I can't even remember now, when or how the ritual had started. But it's a pretty safe bet it had something to do with Frannie. She had a habit of throwing stuff whenever she got into a tizzy about something. More than once I'd had to climb up there to retrieve one of her shoes or a hat. I probably noticed what a great view we had from up there and called Judith up. It wasn't a steep roof, there was never any danger of us rolling off of it so we'd lay up there often, on cool nights, talking, staring up at the stars, pretending we were smart, that we knew which constellations were which.

"That's Ursa Minor, right there," I'd said to her one night, pointing it out with one hand, the other one holding hers.

"No," she said, shaking her head as it lay against the shingles, "that's Centaurus, Ursa Minor's over there." She'd waved her finger off in another direction.

I didn't have the heart to tell her you couldn't see Centaurus from the Northern Hemisphere.

"You're right, it's beautiful isn't it?"

She'd tilted her head so that it rested on my shoulder.

"Yes, it is."

A day in early 1968 when she'd been especially annoyed with one of the record execs when he informed her that she wouldn't be ducking out straight after the private show she was singing at that evening. She would be staying for drinks afterward. And she would be sitting with Burt Coburn (rising film star, also gay, also trying to protect his image). And she would be posing for pictures with him so the world could see just how normal she was.

"I'm so sick of this! I'm not a pair of cuff links they can just pass around! To make men look good in pictures," she'd said, as she marched down the hallway towards me in a huff.

"That's not why they want you to-"

"It doesn't matter, come here!"

She'd wrapped her hand around my wrist, pulled me into

her dressing room, slammed the door shut and started to undress.

"What's going on? What is this?"

"I don't belong to them," is the only explanation she gave me. And before I knew it we were on the couch, her on top of me, as her anger turned into something else.

Did I complain?

No. No, I did not.

To the day just before everything started, on the morning of the concert when I could have stopped it all but didn't. When I'd watched her dozing in the morning sun and thought that I could save her from any future hardship if only I knew what it was that caused it. Now I knew. And now my own words, the ones I'd thought of then, were coming back to haunt me. You can't miss what you never had.

That's the solution.

I need to make it so that she never meets me at all.

CHAPTER TWENTY-FIVE

For three days I checked out completely. Cleaned out the liquor cabinet and stayed drunk. My phone went unanswered, I sent a few text messages to friends: Busy with work. I'll talk to you soon. To my boss: I'll be out for the rest of the month. Family emergency. Replace me if you need to.

Every morning I woke up it was to a split second of happiness. It was just a dream. I'm back. And then that wave of pain hits when I feel the memory foam mattress beneath me and hear the low soft hum of the central air kicking in. No springs or window units here. No sir, this is the awesome future, with five hundred channels, a programmable coffee maker, seventy-two inch high definition television you can control from across the room, cell phones, internet, you name it, you got it. But no Judith. Can't have it all. Sorry.

I'd lie in bed for an hour, torturing myself by going over it again and again. Agonizing over how selfish and petty I'd been the last time I saw her. That was my biggest problem back then, that I didn't have to make smalltalk and eat dried turkey for Thanksgiving dinner with the in-laws. Why did that matter so much to me? So Judith's mother didn't want to be in the same room with me...and? It's not as if she was a bag of cuddly fluffy kittens. Amazing the things we think are problems until an actual real problem slaps you in the face.

After that, I get up, wash up, and take my misery to the

couch. Where I go over it all again. Then a bottle, skip the glass, skip the ice. Even though all it takes is a push of a button and voila! cubed or crushed ice right from the door of my over-sized fridge. All the ice I want. Would have come in handy back then, when I made her an ice cream cake.

That won't be a problem this time around. Because I won't be making her an ice cream cake will I? I won't be having conversations with her on the roof under the stars. No Christmas mornings, her hair sleep-tossled, clapping her hands every time she hands me a sloppily wrapped box. (She was an amazing singer, not so good with scissors and tape.) Even the one I teased her about for months, the one wrapped in paper covered in fat clowns because she thought they were snowmen.

It's not going to be easy. And it's not going to be quick. That would have been hard enough, going there and staying put on that night. Knowing she'd be at the Saturn and Sun, alone, and bummed about the one song she got to sing. I wouldn't be there to cheer her up, get her mind off of it. I'd been there both times, according to Mr. Smith, and that was the thing. I'd met her anyway, he'd said. I'd had different plans, hadn't actively sought her out, but we'd ended up together nonetheless. Which meant what exactly? That we were destined to meet? That we'd meet no matter what? I don't know. I'm not sure. Which means I'll have to stay doesn't it? I'll have to stay to make sure we don't meet. Who's to say I come up with a way to warn her about the future, about getting on that plane, that's easy enough, I'm sure I can come up with a way to do that, and I leave within a week or two. What if we meet a month later? Or two? She never leaves Leyfant, she stays there as much as she can. With or without me, she'll stay because it's in her nature. No, I'll have to stay to make sure it never happens.

That's going to be delightful. I won't be able to escape it. It's not going to be as simple as staying off your ex's social media accounts to avoid having to see them. She'll be all over the place. In magazines. On the radio, in the paper, on television. If I go to a party, someone will put her records on, the cashier at the grocery store while she's jabbing away at the cash register blabbing away: "Did you see in the paper who Judy was out with last weekend?". Am I going to have to put blinders on while driving around because I might pass Maybell's while she's sitting by the window with a bowl of Peppermint Stick in front of her? And eventually I'll see her sitting with someone else. Someone who at first, the entire town will think is "just her friend". But I'll know better. I'll see it before everyone starts to figure it out. Boy, she sure does hang around that girl quite a bit doesn't she? Is she staying at Judy's house? Maybe her own house is being painted and she needs to stay out for a while, you know paint fumes. Wait, I thought she was supposed to be engaged to that actor, it said so in that magazine, but I don't ever see her...ohhhhh. No, they're just friends. Has to be. She's Judy Paige, there's no way she's...yeah, they're just close friends. Let's keep it at that and not dig. Look the other way.

Could I really handle that? Because I'd have to. I'd have to make sure she was happy in a relationship with someone else. Only then would I be able to leave. Knowing that once that was in place I wouldn't have to worry if she met me or not. It wasn't in her to be unfaithful.

Every day I was here I kept thinking that she must be worried. It's been three days, she must be frantic, calling Fran, calling my parents. Wondering what's happened to me. Then I remember that it doesn't work that way. At this point in time, it's over for her. That was forty years ago. She probably didn't think anything of it when she got home that next day and I wasn't there but by the end of the night when I hadn't returned or even phoned? I'd think she'd be more angry than worried. Especially when I didn't come home at all. I wonder if the thought I was with someone else ever crossed her mind.

Maybe I'd gone to Canada to see Peg. That must have sucked. But eventually that anger would turn into worry, and then panic and on and on. But it's over for her now. That was over forty years ago. She has no more worries. Leave it alone. That kept going through my head too. Maybe I need to leave it alone. But then like a pesky gnat that just keeps coming back no matter how many times you swat at it, the thought that she died prematurely kept buzzing in my head. She doesn't have to. But can I really do it? Go back, see her, and not be with her? Stand by and see her with someone else? I can prevent it. Is it selfish to do it? Or selfish not to?

CHAPTER TWENTY-SIX

On my fourth day back, I skipped the alcohol, but only because I didn't have any left. Except for the nine hundred dollar bottle of wine that I once thought the non-existent not-me Evelyn would drink. And I was thinking I should save that for a special occasion. If I ever had any of those ever again. Right now that prospect was looking iffy.

Oh well, I could sit there and postpone all I wanted, procrastinate all I wanted, go over everything, all the pros and cons, the good, the bad, a hundred more times if I wanted, but I still had to eat while I did it. I was going to have to make a trip to the grocery store. So I showered and blew dry my hair and wondered why the heck it took so much time to come up with such a simple device. Maybe, when I go back, I'll team up with an engineer and invent it. Keep my mind off of things at the very least. Will inventing a blow dryer before its time break the universe?

Ever hear of the Baader-Meinhof Phenomenon? If you haven't, now that you have, you will again. And soon. Because of the Baader-Meinhof Phenomenon. The idea is, you go your entire life without knowing something, say the gestation period of a koala bear, which is thirty to thirty-six days by the way, until at age forty when you watch a PBS show about Australia and learn this bit of info. Then suddenly, within a couple of weeks, you hear it two or three more times from random and completely unconnected sources. Everyone, it seems, is talking about koala bears and how long it takes for a female koala to give birth after conception. Some people say it's just coincidence coupled with the fact that our brains are wired to recognize patterns that makes the phenomenon seem significant. Others think the odds are just too high, the coincidences too meaningful for it to be dismissed. Perhaps it's a look behind the scenes, so to speak, at the interconnectedness of everything to everything else. Other people just shrug their shoulders and keep on walking. Eh.

Me, I don't know what I think about it, all I know is that I seemed to have jumped right into a Baader-Meinhof world when I left my house.

At the end of my block, right before turning the corner, parked in the driveway of the house across the intersection was a fully restored shiny green 1961 Chevy Impala. The kind of car Ralph used to drive in 1964. Same color even. As I passed another busy intersection just before the shopping complex I saw a billboard advertising the drug Novmentis. As I walked across the vast parking lot of the grocery store a little girl in a turquoise dress ran out from in between two parked cars and her mother yelled out to her. "Judy! Get back here right now!"

Coincidences. It still made me feel like the universe was taunting me.

At the store, even though I'd been in it dozens of times, maybe even hundreds, I now felt like I needed a map just to find my way to the cereal aisle. It was overwhelming. How many different types of bread do people need? Whole wheat potato bread? Honey wheat, butterbread, split top, roundtop, what the hell is oatnut? Crustless? Really? Sodium sprouted, yoga, oatmeal. And that was just the ordinary packaged sandwich bread aisle. The gluten free sponges were twenty aisles over. Then there was the real fancy stuff at the bakery.

Playing lightly through unseen speakers somewhere above me, Dusty Springfield began to sing Son of a Preacher Man. I'd seen her sing that very song live. It was both hers and Judith's last time performing on the Ed Sullivan show. Judith never went in for hanging with celebrities and neither did I, but we made an exception for Dusty. Because she was Dusty. If you have a chance to party with Dusty you party with Dusty. And also, obviously, she threw our kind of parties. And the one that Sunday night was particularly unforgettable, especially with Fran there. She'd tagged along with us that weekend because she'd never been to New York.

"Evie! Evelyn!" Fran had come rushing over to me and Judith across the crowded room, nudging people out of her way and fanning smoke away from her face. "Some woman just invited me back to her hotel room," she'd hissed, eyes wide.

"Uh oh Fran, I'm sorry, but I did warn you there was going to be-"

"Sorry? For what? Hell, the woman is gorgeous, I'm thinking of taking her up on the offer."

The memory made me smile momentarily, but then I remembered Dusty was gone too. Just like Judith. I needed to get out of there.

I gave up on all the packaged food and decided I'd take my chances with some produce. Hurry things up. Fruit and vegetables are fruit and vegetables, same as 1964 or 1970. Right?

Wrong. No less than fourteen different types of apples to choose from. Nineteen if you counted the organic ones. How exhausting. What if I pick the wrong one? What if that one over there is better than this one? How can I be sure? I can check on my phone. Where I would have a choice of a million web pages to refer to. I could watch a few hundred videos on the subject. I could browse a million pictures to compare them to and make sure they're at their perfect ripeness. I could be there for six hours just trying to determine which apple I should put in my cart. And how in the world does one apple cost two dollars?

Were there really this many heavy people when I left? Wouldn't it be better to walk some of that off instead of riding around on a scooter? And why is it so darn cold in here?

I ended up grabbing some bananas. There was still only one choice of bananas. Yellow. Take it or leave it. Simplicity at its best.

At the check-out, someone had paid for but left behind their carton of ice cream.

When the cashier noticed, just as she was about to weigh my one bag of bananas, she called another employee over to see if they could flag the customer down, but he or she was long gone. Then they started to debate whether or not to put it back in the cold case, how long had it been out? Was it safe to sell? After nearly five minutes of it, and hearing The Supremes start singing Stop! In the Name of Love above me, I'd had enough.

"Could you stop messing with that damned ice cream and let me pay for these so I can get out of here!"

The cashier, a girl, a little blond thing with a ponytail, visibly flinched.

"I'm sorry. I don't...I didn't. You know, I don't um...think I'm going to need these after all."

I left empty handed with the cashier, the other employee, and the customer behind me in line all staring at my back. I couldn't help it. The ice cream was Peppermint Stick.

Outside, sitting on a bench facing the parking lot, I thought, this is it. No matter what choice I make, this is the way it's going to be from now on, when I get back. Everything I'd seen was only coincidences, I knew that. I only noticed the car, the music, the ice cream, because they had meaning to me now. They'd have been there regardless, if I'd never gone back, they'd have just gone unnoticed. There wouldn't have been a pattern for me to pick out. But that doesn't matter, the pattern is there now and will be, for a long, long, time. Probably forever. Everything I see will be a reminder to me of just how badly I'd been screwed over. How badly Mr. Smith had screwed me over.

I was just going to grow angrier and testier every single day until I ended up being the old lady version of the get off my lawn old man. My house will be the one kids dare other kids to approach on Halloween night. "She's a witch, I'm telling you. She never leaves the house. She never wears anything but black, she has twelve cats, her blinds are never open. And my brother Brandon said he saw her on the roof one night. Seriously, he said she was just up on the roof, lying there, looking up at the sky, probably casting spells or something. She's either a witch or a fruitcake." In other words, I was going to end up being just like my mother.

For the first time in my life I had to rub at my eyes and blink away tears at the thought of her. I'd been wrong. When my aunt told me that story so long ago, I'd been twenty. What the hell did I know? I'd never been in love before so I'd dismissed it outright. So she was in love with someone else, her father didn't approve of him, ran him off, blah blah, she married my father out of convenience. And? I had thought then. Get over it. That doesn't make her treating me and everyone else around her the way she did okay. I didn't understand then how overwhelming it can be, that the thought of never seeing someone again can cause actual physical pain. A hard knot in your chest, or that constriction of your lungs, the feeling that you can't breathe even though you know that you are, you are breathing. You aren't actually going to die. Liquor helps, I'd learned that, just as she had. Crying too. Even more than liquor, crying helps, but it's not a cure, it's only a release valve. You open it up, let some of the pressure go, feel momentary relief, but once you close it, that pressure just starts building right back up again. Hard knot in your chest, your lungs start to close up on you. How long did it last for her?

No wonder she was a bitch. No disrespect. She really was. But now I knew she damn well deserved to be.

After a while, I gathered myself, stood up, and told myself I could do this. No more blowing up, I'm in control. Just because I was miserable didn't mean I had to make everyone around me miserable as well.

Then I walked over six stores down to a fast food place and blew up at a teenage boy wearing braces and a yellow paper hat.

Well. He was taking too long getting me my drink and mounted to the wall, above my head to the right, was a TV, a commercial came on advertising the upcoming season of Mad Men. One of the female characters was wearing an almost exact replica of one of Judith's outfits.

Can you blame me?

That's it, from here on out, it's pizza delivery.

Just one more stop. The liquor store. Because crying only helps so much. And then I'm a shut-in. Three blocks over. I should be safe.

Because if I see one more thing. Just one more thing, I might just lose it.

I made it, but the parking lot was full so I had to take a spot at the very end, clear across from the liquor store. Five stores in between it and me. But it was fine. A small Indian grocery store, a beauty salon with posters of very modern looking haircuts in the front window, a Mexican restaurant, a tattoo parlor with blacked out windows, and a shop devoted solely to e-cigarettes and all the paraphernalia that went with it.

I took a deep breath and walked on.

That's when I came face to face with the 2010 version of Frannie.

CHAPTER TWENTY-SEVEN

I stopped dead in my tracks.

"Fran. Wow. Look at you." So in awe of what I was looking at you'd think I was standing in front of Victoria Falls or the Grand Canyon. "You're so beautiful."

There were several other shoppers walking along the pathway behind me but most of them were too preoccupied with the phones in their hands to take notice of me talking to a political poster plastered on the side of a liquor store.

The last time I saw her she was twenty-seven years old, and even though she'd gotten rid of that ridiculous cone head by then, her hair had still been the color of an overly ripe cantaloupe, and now here she was, sixty-seven, white-haired, and one of those women who aren't much to look at when younger but grow prettier and prettier the older they get.

Striking, Janice had called her.

All that time and I never put two and two together.

But how could I? I knew Frannie Ellison, a stampeding loud carrothead. There's no way I could have recognized her the day she walked into that diner as Frances Yates, future Texas State Senator. A woman I had voted for. I had never followed politics very closely, I'd seen her pop up on TV every now and then, sure, but she'd just been background noise, like all the others. But still, I'd waited in line at the library to cast my vote for her because she'd been an early supporter of gay rights. Long before everyone had jumped on the bandwagon, before it was politically expedient to do so. In fact, at the time, way back in 1998, the first time she ran for the Senate, after two stints in Congress, everyone had said she didn't stand a chance. In Texas? You're going with that as part of your platform? Good luck with that.

What I wouldn't give to have heard her reaction to all of the naysayers.

You won your bid for city council then huh? And I wasn't there to celebrate with you. I'm so sorry. Can you be a senator with a criminal record? I'm assuming she walloped Dwight pretty good at some point.

I missed so much.

Six years wasn't long enough.

Twelve years, twenty, wouldn't have been enough.

It took me ten minutes to finally walk away. And by then I'd forgotten all about drowning my sorrows. I needed to know more.

The first thing I'd done, four days ago, when I walked through the door, was grab my laptop and then slid it as far underneath my bed as I could. Now I had to crawl underneath there, moving aside the boxes I'd placed in front of it for good measure and pull it out.

When I'd left for Leyfant that Thursday I thought I'd be gone a day, maybe two (which turned out to be correct, so to speak) so I hadn't even shut down the web browser or any of the tabs I'd had opened before putting the laptop to sleep. So when I powered it up this time, there she was. Pale yellow outfit, flip hairdo, microphone in hand, nineteen years old.

I jabbed and clicked and slid my finger over the touchpad clumsily. Trying to get rid of the picture as quickly as I could. Instead of the tab, I shut down the entire browser. Then it took me a couple of minutes figuring out how to get it back.

It took me nearly three hours to piece together the scant details that were available. I disappeared in the middle of November, right before the holidays. I was an adult, maybe I just skipped town. I wasn't hurting for money, I could easily pull up stakes, move on, settle down in Oregon, maybe the heat finally got to me and I decided Canada was where I needed to be, or Maine. I could be anywhere, France? Mexico? In a world without cell phones to track, where ATMs were only barely starting, where cash was king, what did anyone really have to go on? She'll turn up, eventually. There was no sign that anything bad happened to me. No splintered door frames, no broken windows, no blood. I must have left on my own. That's the impression I got from the very few mentions my case got in the paper. There was a small article that mentioned Judith in connection with my disappearance, of her appealing to the public for help but by that time, her name didn't garner much attention so it faded quickly. It's the holidays, no one wants to hear about missing people, go away and wait, she'll show up.

Mostly the investigation was unofficial. My parents, Judith, my friends. Private detectives, reward money, paper signs taped to telephone poles and placed under windshield wipers. My father eventually lost the store after pouring all of his time, money, and energy into finding me until he passed away only four years later, at forty-nine, of a heart attack. My mother lived to be eighty-four, she passed away only three years ago, in 2007. Her obituary stated she worked, and then later volunteered, for several Texas-based missing persons organizations up until the day of her death. Thirty-seven years of fruitless searching. She never remarried.

Through her website I learned that even now, Fran was trying to pass a bill that would increase funding for the National Missing and Unidentified Persons System, known as NamUs.

Evelyn Bryant was never seen or heard from again after that date, November 14th, 1970, and finally declared dead nine years later, in 1979. Poof.

My father was one of the very few men in the sixties who didn't smoke. He ate a lot of red meat, everyone did in those days, but they weren't all dropping like flies in their forties. How many more years would my mother have had with him if not for all the stress my disappearance caused? My guess was a lot more than what she got.

I can't do it.

I don't have the right to do it.

Make everyone go through it all again.

It's done.

It's over.

She's gone.

They all are.

I decided Mr. Smith was an asshole.

And that I may as well visit the animal shelter in the morning, get started on my collection of twelve cats.

CHAPTER TWENTY-EIGHT

It took me a week to get used to the idea. Not to be okay with it, but to accept it. I still woke up each morning elated to be back and then a second later, angry that instead of a loud annoying rattling noise of a window air-conditioning unit I was met with the soft barely perceptible pleasant hum of the central air unit outside. I went back and forth on my decision at least a hundred times before I even threw the covers off of me and headed to the bathroom. She can live. They'll all die again. She died too young. Thirty-seven years of searching. When I come back, she'll still be alive. Yes, but with another woman. If she lives, when I come back she'll have been with this woman for almost thirty years.

She'd be sixty-five. I would be a long forgotten faded memory. I imagined approaching her in this lifetime. Would she see something? Would she have any sense of recognition? Would I even want to see her? Knowing that the years between twenty-five and sixty-five had been spent without me? No. I don't think I would. I wouldn't want to see her. I'd be content just to know that she was there. That she'd made it.

But this was all just useless rambling going on in a continuous loop in my head. It made no difference. I'd made my decision. As painful as it was.

Our time together was over.

I would never see her again.

I could have changed things. I did change things. I didn't want to see the video of the concert, I didn't want to look at her pictures. But I did want to see one thing. I remembered that interview she gave, it was in Illinois, it was filmed on the very last day I'd seen her. When I'd watched it before, before going back, she had seemed cheerful and happy, perfectly at ease and joking with the interviewer. When I pulled it up this time it's different. This time she doesn't make him laugh at the end of the interview. She's still smiling, she's still answering his questions politely and pleasantly but there's a difference. Probably not noticeable to anyone else, but I can tell, the way she's smiling, with only one corner of her mouth so that only one dimple appears, that she's distracted, and upset. Because of me. I must not have been an ass the time before. At least the last time she hadn't had an unpleasant memory of me.

So I had changed things.
I made them worse.

"Hello?"

"Karen, listen, I know you're busy with work and all but I have some great news!"

Janice. One of the few things in my life here, in comparison, that might get me over the heartbreak.

"Well, I can certainly do with some good news." I tried to keep my voice level. I hadn't heard hers in so long. For the first time since I'd opened my eyes in that cemetery the knot in my chest loosened the tiniest bit. But I felt guilty too. I couldn't remember the last time I'd thought of her. A year? Two?

"Oh, I'm so excited! Okay, so, you remember a certain woman at a certain charity dinner we attended last month?" I could tell I was supposed to by the way she sounded. Like the cat that ate the parrot or mouse or whatever the heck the saying is.

"No, I don't."

"Yes, of course you do, five weeks ago, we paid four hundred dollars for a chicken dinner for Pete's sake."

"We did? Jeez, that's a lot of money, but okay, sure, I remember." Just get on with it.

"Anyway, the woman that was there, the one you kept going on about? The one with the green eyes, the light reddish-brown hair? You have to remember her."

"I can't say that I do."

"Yes you do."

"No, Janice, I don't."

"How can you not remember her?"

Because it's been six years.

"I just don't!" I said, exasperated. "What is the big deal with some woman at a dinner?"

"Karen, come on, you kept bugging me all night long about her. Do I know who she is, do I think she's gay, aren't her eyes pretty, yada yada."

"That doesn't sound like me."

"Well it was. And now you're ruining my big happy surprise."

"I'm sorry. Go on, let me have it, I promise I'll clap and hop around, shout a little."

"Dustin, one of my co-workers was there, he knows who she is, turns out she is gay, and she's single. Long story short, since you put a damper on things, I fixed it all up. You have a date. With her." She didn't say it but I could hear the "ta-da!" in her voice.

"You what?"

"I don't hear clapping. Are you hopping around? It doesn't sound like you're hop-"

"You want me to go out on a fucking date? With another woman? Are you fucking crazy?"

Stunned silence.

"Damnit. I'm sorry Janice. I'm really sorry."

"What's going on?"

"I...nothing. I've just had some really rough days. I had to make some pretty important decisions and I'm not really sure if I made the right ones, that's all."

"Decisions about what? Work?"

"Yeah." Lies on top of lies on top of lies.

"I've never seen you get stressed out about anything, much less work related. Are you sure there's nothing else going on? With this woman?"

"What woman?"

"You said another woman. Which means...you've been seeing someone? Have you been seeing someone? And you haven't told me?"

Sure I have, a woman I'm desperate to get back to. I've been seeing her for twelve years. Six years in one life, then we were on a break for forty years, then back on for another six years in a replay of that life, and now we've been on another break...for another forty years. You know, one of those on again, off again type relationships. Pull up a chair, let me tell you all about it.

"No I'm not. I don't know why I said that, it's...I've been thinking about my mother, it's got my brain all twisted up." At least that was the truth.

"Ah, I see, okay, yeah, that I can understand. I don't know why you waste time thinking about that-"

"No, no. I've been thinking I may have misjudged her, or no, that's not the right word. Did I ever tell you the story my aunt told me?"

I hadn't. I hadn't thought it was worth telling. But I did now, so I told her.

"Well..." she said, after I'd finished, clearly thinking what I had thought in the past. "That's interesting, but it doesn't change anything does it? We've all had teenage crushes that tore our hearts out. And we really thought it was the end of the world at the time, but it wasn't. We got over it and moved on. We didn't all become heartless bleepity-bleeps when we got older."

"Bleepity-bleeps?"

"Well, she's still your mother."

"I know, I know what you're saying and I thought about that too, but I think there's something more to the story. I don't think my aunt told me everything. At the time, when she told me, I didn't give a crap so I didn't question any of it. But now I'm thinking it doesn't sound right. After all, these were two teenagers in love, supposedly, and they were broken up so easily? With hormones flying all over the place? No. Sixties teenagers are no different from today's teens, they just dress nicer, but they're just as rebellious."

"Maybe it wasn't as serious as all that."

"No, it had to have been. No one grows into a heartless bleepity-bleep because of a simple crush, like you said."

We went back and forth on it, which led to the both of us recounting our own stories. High school crushes. Instead of the head cheerleader, Janice's was a quiet studious girl named Brenda.

"She had a perm," she said through laughter. "And not one of those sexy long haired spiral type perms either. You remember those old shower caps? The ones with ruffles? That was it, she looked like she was wearing a brown shower cap. It was basically Richard Simmons hair. And she wore leg warmers! Oh Lord, I'm just realizing I once had the hots for Richard Simmons!"

"Mine," I shared, "was a girl named Jennifer. She was in my biology class. Blond hair, blue eyes."

"Nice."

"No, not really, that blond hair was in a mullet. You know, the feathers up top, the long curls down the back. How in the hell did we ever think that was in any way attractive?"

The same way Fran thought that orange fire hydrant sitting on her head was, I suppose.

"Can you imagine? If we had gotten our wishes back then? If we'd actually gotten to date these girls? Do you think we'd have ended up with the same lives? Would I be with shower cap Brenda right now? I never would have met Melissa."

"No, yes you would, no one stays with their high school crushes anymore. Not like the fifties and sixties when everyone married their teenage sweethearts straight after graduation."

"You know, I just thought about something, going back to your mother and this boy she was in love with..."

"Yeah?"

"I don't know if I should say it, sounds kind of harsh."

"Go ahead, I've been thinking terrible things about my mother for ages."

"It's just that, like you said, if her father hadn't run this boy off and they'd been allowed to continue dating, they probably would have stayed together forever. Gotten married right away, after high school."

"Probably."

"So then she would have married this boy and not your father. And you would never have been born. So...you know, as horrible as it sounds, her heartache kind of worked out in your favor."

"What did you say?"

"Sorry. Was that too far?"

"No."

"Isn't that funny, how just one event can-"

"I have to go."

"Huh?"

"I have to go, I have to go right now."

"What? Why?"

"I have to call my aunt."

"Okay. Um. But wait, what am I supposed to tell this woman I fixed you up with?"

"Tell her I can't make it, I'm going to be away."

The second I hung up with Janice I called my aunt.

"You're not dying are you?"

"I'm fifty-seven years old, not a hundred, I had knee surgery. You'd know that if you called every once in a while."

I thought of telling her phones work both ways but I needed her help, best not to antagonize her.

"Aunt Jane, I need you to tell me the story again, only I need more details this time."

"What story is that?"

"The story of how your father almost single-handedly destroyed my life" seemed a bit too dramatic so I went with "The story you told me, what was it? Eighteen years ago? My second year of college. About your sister Anne, my mom?"

She took a few seconds to answer and I could hear beeps, boops, and what might have been a curtain being pulled open or closed. Heart monitor, privacy curtain. All part of the background noises of a hospital room.

"Why would you want to bring that up again for?"

"Because I was twenty when you told me about it Aunt Jane, I couldn't really appreciate the significance of it at the time. I think I'd be able to better understand it now." While that wasn't the complete truth, it wasn't a lie either.

"What do you want to know?"

"All of it. Everything. And addresses. I know I lived there for a little while but I don't remember the place very well."

"Addresses?"

"Yes, I need the address of where you guys lived at the time. And the address of the place you told me about, where your father went that day."

"What possible reason could you have for needing

addresses? That house probably isn't even there-"

"Because I need to know exactly where to go when I travel back in time to make everything right."

There were more background boops and beeps for a few seconds and then came the sound of her phlegmy two-packs-a-day cackle. That's pleasant. Hell, she might be dying and just doesn't know it yet.

"Alright, you don't have to make up stories, I'll get you the address but you'll have to wait until I get outta here. I don't know how long it's gonna be, damn nurses and their filthy hands gave me an infection."

"No, why can't you just give it to me over the phone?"

"You think I have that memorized? The address of the place I lived at as a kid? That was damn near forty years ago."

"Didn't you ever visit?"

"Of course, but not there. Pop transfered to another department two counties over just as soon as I finished high school and got married. That's where you lived, not the house your mother lived in."

"So where are you going to get the address from?"

"I still have some letters from back then, in my hope chest. In the attic at home."

"I don't suppose you could have someone go to your house and get them today could you?"

Judging by another burst of that delightful cackle, I was guessing not.

"Have someone traipsing all over my house while I'm not there? Dirtying it up, messing with things?"

"Okay fine. I'll fly out there as soon as you're out of the hospital. Call me as soon as you know you'll be leaving."

It's not over until the fat lady with a bum knee sings.

CHAPTER TWENTY-NINE

Eight frustrating days later I was sitting on my aunt's lumpy dusty sofa in her musty cluttered living room. How does it smell like cabbage in here? She's been away for over ten days. She hasn't cooked. She lives alone. No one else has been here, God forbid anyone come in and what did she say? Mess with things? Dirty it up? This pristine castle?

She was sitting with her large dimply bandaged leg propped up on the coffee table and sucking on a cigarette.

"He was black wasn't he? That's the big secret you've been trying to keep from me isn't it?"

"I haven't been trying to keep any secrets."

So she says, but she breaks eye contact with me and pokes at a hole in her armchair with a yellowed fingernail while she says it.

"Well this is the first time I'm hearing this part of the story. And I didn't even hear it, I figured it out on my own."

"You never wanted to hear the story at all, did you?"

This time she makes a point of staring directly at me, with her mouth curved into a sneer.

"Yeah. You're right."

I'd had eight days to sit at home to think about the story I'd originally been told. Just as I'd told Janice, it was hard to believe a nineteen year old guy would just say "Yes, sir," and walk away when he was told to stop seeing a girl he loves. Unless he didn't love her? That was certainly a possibility, but even then, since when do teenagers do exactly what they're told no matter the circumstances? Don't drink. Don't smoke. Don't drive fast. It just doesn't happen, no matter the era. Did teenagers in the sixties disobey their parents by sneaking out of their windows at night to go to wild keggers where they'd smoke pot or pop a few OxyContins and have sex all night long? No. Definitely not. But sneak out to a drive-in movie? Secretly meet up with someone at the bowling alley for a quick soda at the snack bar? Yes.

Why didn't my mother and this boy she was crazy about ever do that? What could have kept them apart entirely?

My grandfather. Of course. Even in the mid-eighties the man acted like a 1920's KKK member. I could only imagine what he was like in 1968 when very few people would have looked down on his behavior. He'd been a racist. And he'd been a cop. And when, as a black man living in Alabama in 1968, you're told to disappear by a white cop, you disappear. Sneaking off at night to a dance hall or a theater with that man's daughter is not cutesy teenage rebellious behavior. It's not even an option.

"Now all of a sudden you're playing detective. Why?"

"I told you. Perspective."

"It's a little too late for that now isn't it?" she asked, then tapped out another crooked cigarette from a crumpled pack and lit it with the one already between her lips.

"It was too late when you first told me, she was already dead."

"Yeah, she was, she is, so why bring all this up again now?"

"What difference does it make if she's dead or not?"

"Because it's over okay? She's dead. Telling you a story isn't going to bring her back you know. What? You think you can tell her you're sorry for misunderstanding her? You can't! You can't apologize to a dead person!" She threw the crumpled up cigarette pack across the room. It thumped against the wall and landed on a pile of old water-logged magazines stacked on the floor.

Okay. She'd never been a bundle of joy, just ask my uncle, if you can find him, but this was a little over the top, even for her.

"What are you talking about? I don't have anything to apologize to her for. I didn't do anything wrong. All I want is-"

She flicked her hand through the air and then pointed to the ground, where her pack of cigarettes had landed.

"Seriously?" I sighed and went to retrieve it. Why ever did my uncle leave this delightful woman?

"All I want," I continued, after she snatched the pack from my outstretched arm, "is to understand her better."

"Yes. Okay? Yes, he was black. That's why my father sent him packing. But times were different back then, it's not like it is today. You can't understand what it was like."

"No, of course I can't."

"It would have caused a lot of problems. And yes, my father wasn't fond of black people back then." Back then? Up until the day he died two years before he was a raging bigot.

"So she was seeing this guy, what was his name?"

"William."

"William what?"

"I don't know, just William."

"Okay fine, William. She was seeing this guy for how long?"

"I already told you that."

"You told me eighteen years ago, how am I supposed to remember? Just, for once, can you, I don't know, try to be pleasant?"

She leaned over and tapped ashes into the ashtray on the

coffee table. Half fell in, half fell on the table, but she didn't notice, she kept her eyes on me the entire time.

Then she told me. The complete story.

The two of them never snuck around after her father became aware of the situation because they couldn't. My aunt didn't elaborate on just what my grandfather did or said to this William fellow but it was enough to scare him away. According to her, he wasn't seen in town any more after he was confronted. He either left town or the state altogether. But he'd promised my mother he'd be back. She was just on the verge of turning seventeen when he made his escape, and when she turned eighteen, he'd told her, he'd come back for her.

They'd get married. Her father would no longer have any control over her.

But he didn't. He never came back.

At least as far as she knew.

She didn't know that he had done exactly as he promised. He came back for her on her eighteenth birthday. William was not fooling around.

On that day, December 6, 1969, he checked into a motel (The King's Court) not having any idea how long he'd be there before he could get word to my mother. Her father had barely let her out of the house since the day he'd run her secret boyfriend off over a year before and there had been no way of contacting her the entire time he'd been gone. Send her a letter? How could he know it wouldn't fall into the wrong hands? Call her? Sure, whoever answered would be delighted to hand the phone over, no questions asked. Get her a message through one of her friends? Yeah, they'd be happy to oblige and go against a violent bully with a badge.

This is why my mother had started dating my father approximately two weeks before her birthday. She wanted her father to think she had moved on. It was the only way he'd let his guard down, not be so watchful of her and to actually let her out of the house. So she went to a movie or two with him, my father, a trip to the bowling alley, maybe a bit of skating at the roller rink. She knew William couldn't just knock on their front door as so many young men did in those days, full of nerves, wearing their best suit, asking to speak to the man of the house to ask for his daughter's hand in marriage. If she was stuck in the house, he wouldn't be able to contact her. This way, when he came back, he'd have a better chance of finding her.

And he did come back, for one day. Someone, my aunt didn't know who, had tipped off my grandfather. He was a cop. He had cop friends. He was a beat cop, he knew every beat cop in town. Beat cops are always on the move, they see a lot. It could have been any of them. It could have been the front desk clerk at the motel. Or a gas station service attendant. A nosy neighbor. Take your pick.

Whoever it was, the result was the same. William was never able to get word to my mother before being threatened, once again, by my grandfather and once again left town. He might have tried again, if he'd gotten the opportunity, but he never did. He was drafted and then he was killed. Two and a half months after he arrived in Vietnam.

All of it happened without my mother even being aware of it. For all she knew, William had forgotten her, met someone else, never really cared for her as much as she thought. But she still waited another nine months after that day, after the thirteen she already had, still hoping he'd show up. But when it was clear he wasn't going to, she finally gave up and married my father. And that was probably just to get out of her father's house. My father, trying to avoid the draft and not being given a choice of which branch of the military he'd be forced to sign on with, joined the Air Force, which is how we ended up in San Antonio, he'd been stationed there at Lackland AFB. He never did serve overseas.

And that was the start of her miserable life.

"No not miserable," my aunt said. "She was actually happy there, for a time. Not as happy as she might have been, maybe, I don't know. But she'd accepted it, that William might not have been able to wait, or that he met someone else, or even that he'd been too frightened to come back. And maybe happy isn't the word. Content perhaps. But she was happy with you, when you came along."

"She was?"

"Yes. Believe it or not, and it would have been a different story if, well..."

She went on to tell me how in March of 1973, when my mother brought me with her on a visit to Alabama, my grandfather went off on one of his drunken rants and spilled the beans. They'd been watching the news on TV, it was the day after the last combat troops left Vietnam. That's what brought it all up again. He told her everything, about how William had come back for her and how he'd roughed him up a bit, and sent him off again. He was proud of it. He was boasting. And then he finished off his story by telling her that she could forget about trying to find him now, the war had taken care of the problem for good.

It was all downhill for her from then on out.

I could definitely understand that.

She'd just been told that the life she'd wanted, the one she should have had, had been unfairly snatched away from her.

It wasn't that he hadn't loved her, it was that he'd been kept from her.

What could have been.

And now, what could never be.

Being left in the dark can oftentimes be a kindness.

It's being told the truth that can sometimes be an act of cruelty.

I ended up staying in Alabama for three days, doing

research. Information is hard to come by in the past, it's not as simple as punching a few keywords into a search engine. I mapped out the different locations I'd need, made sure my aunt was telling me the truth, or that her memory wasn't faulty. That there really was a motel where she said it was at that time. (There was, but these days it was a ratty strip mall that housed a Subway, a couple of nail salons, and a place called "The All-Seeing Eye". A shop that specialized in psychic readings. Although psychic was misspelled. Psycic.) I checked the drive time from one place to another. I only had a small window of opportunity, which was both good and bad. Good that I knew the exact date on which everything came together but bad in that if I messed it up, that was it, my chance was gone. Or, not my chance, really, but my mother's chance.

I didn't have to do anything but keep my mother and father apart on that specific date. November 14, 1970. That was easy. If I had to burn their house down, I'd burn their house down. No one's going to be in a romantic mood when your house has just been reduced to a smoldering pile of kindling are they? Obviously I'm not serious about that, there are easier ways of keeping them apart, but if I got desperate enough? Who knows.

But this was a chance to kill two birds with one stone. I wouldn't have to keep them apart if they never got married. No matter the feelings I had for my mother, the resentment, the hurt, I could put all that aside. In 1969 she isn't who she turns out to be. At that time she'll just be a girl in love. A girl with a chance at a happy future instead of the one she ended up with. If I could make that happen and get to stay with Judith, then that's what I was going to do.

If my aunt had as great a memory when it came to William's last name as she did when it came to the names of motels, what I had planned would have been simple. With his last name I could have tracked him down, found someone living who knew him back then and asked them where it was he ran off to during that year before she turned eighteen or where it was he went to after leaving Lynbrook for the last time. That's all I would have needed. A location. That's it. That's what it all boiled down to. I would have just needed a location. To go to him. Tell him to stay put. I'll bring her to you. Bing-bang-boom, happy ending. But it's never that easy is it? I did try looking up Williams in a list of casualties from the Vietnam War. There are ninety-three by the name of William from the state of Alabama alone. I can't even be sure he was born in Alabama. It was useless. This is all I had. One day, just one day when I knew exactly where he'd be. I had one shot at it. My mother had one shot.

My dumb aunt.

CHAPTER THIRTY

I was anxious to leave but I had to take a few more days after I flew back from Alabama to make sure I had planned for everything and everything was all set. I had to make sure the bank I had in mind hadn't been flooded, it hadn't gone up in flames at some point, hadn't been razed to the ground and rebuilt, no major robberies, no tornadoes eviscerated it, no asteroid strikes, no giant prehistoric irradiated reptiles had gone on a rampage and flattened it at any time between 1970 and 1991. Hey, if I'd learned anything in the past few years it's that anything goes, anything is possible. I had to check histories of law firms and lawyers. There in the sixties? Check. Still there in the future? Check. No sudden coronaries or car accidents? Check-check.

I let the phone ring, I probably didn't have a job any more. I didn't check my e-mail. I didn't bother walking down to the communal mail box down the street.

I skipped the heartfelt dramatic goodbyes to everyone I might never see again. Because it wouldn't matter either way. If what I planned on doing worked, then they wouldn't remember it because it will never have happened, they will never have even met me. And if my plans crash and burn, then I'll be right back here, on the same day I leave. With no one the wiser. Six years later.

Time travel is weird.

The only thing I did was wrap up my bottle of Chateau Latour in a box along with a note and dropped it off at FedEx to be delivered to Janice once I was gone.

Open this tonight and share it with Melissa. Yes, even if you're having re-heated lasagna for dinner, open it. Enjoy it. You never know what's going to happen tomorrow. I love you both.

I never did see her. I didn't want to. It would have been too hard.

That's another thing this whole experience had taught me. You can't have everything.

On August 12, 2010, I shut down my laptop. I was ready. There was a knock at my door two seconds later.

"You've thought about this?" Mr. Smith asked me.

"Yes. I have. I've made my decision."

"You've thought everything through? Carefully? Are you sure?"

"You're not going to change my mind."

"Very well then."

"Can I take something with me?"

"No."

Asshole.

I crumpled up the paper in my hand and let it tumble to the floor.

"I'm ready."

CHAPTER THIRTY-ONE

It's hot. It's so damned hot without air conditioning. And orange carpet? Why would anybody do that? It's hideous. But who cares? I raised the extra pillow beside me up to my nose and inhaled deeply. You just never know. She spent many nights sleeping with her head on that pillow at one time, what if there was a ghost of a scent there? Of her perfume? An echo?

There wasn't.

But there would be, soon.

I jumped out of bed, grabbed some paper and a pen and wrote down everything I'd need. Everything I'd committed to memory. Names, dates, times. Later I'd make four more copies. Just in case.

I watched him from the window this time, for a few minutes, before I stepped outside. Fifteen years old. In another life he wouldn't have much time to live. Five and a half years. Not in this one. Maybe this time he marries that cute redhead I'd seen him with around town before his number came up. In line at the theater, at the town fair, sharing a cone of cotton candy, smooshed into a booth together with a crowd of friends at Arnie's Diner. I might not be able to save any historical figures, that was beyond my reach, but his life is just as important, just as valuable as anyone else's.

With four younger sisters, college tuition, even as affordable as it is in this decade, was still out of reach for him last time around.

This time it won't be.

"Take the money, he earned it, how many times did he mow my lawn? Or, think of it as a loan if you want to, but take it, and get him to college."

His parents will protest, sure they will, but in the end they'll take it because college means a deferment. By then the media won't be sugarcoating the war anymore. They'll realize what a grinding machine Vietnam turns out to be.

"Thanks George, have anything else for me?" I asked him, as I took the paper from his hand.

"Ma'am?"

"In your back pocket?"

"Oh, yeah! How'd you know?"

"Lucky guess."

He handed me the small mirror and I looked into it. No shock, not this time, but there was a sense of sadness. I'd never see her again. Karen. No one would ever know she existed. There would be no pictures. She wouldn't be a part of anyone's memories. I'd be the only one who'd ever know that she was an actual person once upon a time.

"Ma said to tell you thanks, for letting her borrow it."

"You tell her I said she's welcome. And George?" I asked, as he started to turn back to his lawn mower. "Keep your grades up, in school, okay?"

"Sure Ms. Bryant, my dad would tan my hide if I didn't."

The minutes, one by one, dragged on for days.

The only breakup to the monotonous hours I had to wait

before I could see Judith again was Fran's call. And I was so happy to hear her voice I almost flubbed it all up.

"You're not sick." I could just see her squinting eyes, her tilted head and leaning tower of orange hair. "You don't sound sick. In fact you sound kind of...hey wait a minute, do you have a boy there? You do don't you? That's why you want to stay home! You sneaky-"

"She what?" Ralph's young muffled voice cut her off. "Give me-"

Thunking, scuffling, as the two of them wrestled with the phone and then she was back.

"No, Fran, I promise you, no boys. Cross my heart."

She finally let me off the hook even though she sounded unconvinced. Still, she was willing to take one for the team. A boring Saturday night in to let her friend have some alone time with whichever imaginary boy she was picturing.

Fine by me.

I know Mr. Smith said I'd meet Judith regardless, that I had the first time around. I have no memories of that. And even if I did, even if I was anxious to see Fran again, tonight, I wanted to be the same as I remembered it.

Why did I come all the way back to 1964? Why not just jump in right when I needed to, in 1969, my mother's eighteenth birthday? Because George needs to go to college, because Judith needs to be able to quit making records when she wants to, because my mother and William are going to need a little help getting started. Selling gloves and hats, no matter how high end they are, just isn't going to cut it. And because, haven't you heard? TVs cost seven hundred and fifty dollars! But beyond the money and needing time to accumulate it, the real reason...why not? If you had a chance to relive the days you fell in love with the person you'd be willing to give up an entire life for, wouldn't you?

Last time it was wonderful, this time it would be that much better. I wouldn't have the guilt that I'd felt before. Of taking over someone else's life. Of deceiving so many people. My parents. My actual parents, as it turns out. My friends. And of course, Judith.

I was even more anxious and nervous this time around when I pulled into the parking lot of the Saturn and Sun. This time I did actually clip the bumper of one of the parked cars. But have you seen the bumper of a 1960 Buick Electra? I would have had to hit it at forty miles an hour just to ding it.

The chain smoking woman at the window took my dollar without any questions. As far as she knew, she'd never seen or spoken to me before. I hadn't called to ask for any information this time. And I hadn't gotten lost. But I still showed up thirty minutes past eight. You can never be too careful.

I hadn't seen her in a month. The last time I'd seen her we'd been together, as a couple, for six years. The last thing she'd said to me was that she loved me. The last thing I'd said to her was that I was disappointed. And she'd had to live with that memory for a long time. I'd agonized over that for the last four weeks. When I saw her, sitting there, nineteen years old again, in her turquoise dress, her eyes fixed on the band, all I wanted to do was run up to her, wrap her up in my arms, and apologize over and over again.

And how would that look?

Instead I had to sit, just as before, and wait, twitching almost as much as the boy seated next to me. Come on! What's taking so long? Get up, ask her to dance, let's get this show on the road. I'd gotten there a few minutes earlier, I hadn't had to double back to get my purse, I hadn't wasted any time reading signs, or scanning the room. It was only a matter of thirteen or fourteen minutes difference but that's eight hundred and forty seconds. Just sit and count to two hundred, see how long that actually is, and then multiply that by four. It was excruciating. After what I was sure was an hour, the boy (and his thick cloud of aftershave) rose and made his way to her, past the still hopeful girls in their pastel dresses. The gears were in motion. Again that damned Buddy Holly trombone player pissed me off. Again I sat and heard her sing that disastrous song. And finally, again, I approached her.

"Hi. I just wanted to tell you that I think you did great up there."

She looked up from her shoes at me, with those eyes. Still the most beautiful thing I'd ever seen in my life.

Those three and a half hours flew by. Way too fast. Before I knew it we were in the parking lot, saying goodnight to each other.

I hadn't anticipated just how much patience I was going to need.

I hadn't seen her in a month and we'd been together for six years before that but that's it, goodnight. I was going to have to go home without her, to sleep in my hot muggy bed...alone.

Then I caught myself complaining. Not even a full day back and you're complaining. You're back in 1964. With her. She's alive. Suck it up.

I didn't follow her home afterward, I knew she'd make it home in one piece. I slept in my bed this time, not the rock hard couch with a stomach full of coffee. The next day I stayed home from church, just like before but this time I skipped the omelet and ordered two cheeseburgers and an order of fries when Betty took our order at Lou's. I smiled at Judith's wide-eyed reaction, but I knew she'd be too polite to comment on my gluttony.

"Just in case," I said.

She had no idea what I meant.

Remembering I wouldn't have too much time to eat, I skipped the soda talk and managed to eat a third of my burger before the future Texas state senator barged through the door looking like candy corn.

"Get off me, what are you doing?"

She gave me a half-frown half-smile as she flung her arm up, breaking my hug, and then elbowed my shoulder playfully.

"Look at that glorious hair, it's just so...big."

She tried not to look too flattered as she patted her pile of orange fluff. It didn't budge. Then she grabbed the untouched burger off my plate and took a bite out of it. Judith caught my eye and I shrugged. Lucky guess. I'd have a lot of those this go round.

The next one came just twenty minutes later when I tossed some money on the counter by the cash register, told Betty to keep the change, rushed outside, and managed to grab Fran by the waist and pulled her away so that instead of nearly breaking her foot she kicked at air and wriggled in my arms. Her small fists pounding at my wrists.

"How about a sundae? Huh? Let's go get some ice cream."

Some things changed, in a world with millions of variables and dozens of paths that you can take each and every single day, they'd have to wouldn't they? And I didn't remember every small choice or decision I'd made throughout the first six years. But they weren't large changes. Judith still performed at that concert, which I finally got to fully enjoy, she still had a singing career, her mother still can't stand me. Fran still chased after Dwight. That pained me, to see. Knowing it would be six wasted years that she could have been with someone else, but I had to stand by and let it play out. She marries Nelson and has two children with him. By 2010 they're grandparents to seven grandkids. I couldn't mess with that. But I did change some things.

In the summer of 1968 we'd attended a cookout at our friend Mary's house and the potato salad had been out in the sun just a touch too long. The two days afterward had been a miserable time for everyone who'd attended. Fran especially. As thin as she is, she can eat. This time I accidentally nudged the bowl off of the table and onto the grass before anyone had a chance to enjoy it. Top side down, then stepped in it...again, accidentally. I wouldn't put it past Fran to scoop off some from the top, calling it "salvageable".

"Boy, you know what would have gone really well with this chicken?"

"Jell-O?"

"Potato salad," Fran said, nodding her head, "yup, suuuuure wish I had some potato salad. Would have been nice."

Thirty minutes of that as she sat next to me, eating her chicken nibble by slow nibble and pretending to be having a hard time swallowing.

"Creamy mayonnaise would have helped."

And it would have sent you to the hospital.

We time travelers just can't catch a break sometimes.

CHAPTER THIRTY-TWO

December 1969. Plan A.

It didn't take a whole lot to convince Fran to come along with me on a visit to Alabama.

When I told her the circumstances, that two people were being kept apart just because of the differences in their skin color, she was in. She didn't even bother too much with the details.

"How do you know this Anne person?"

"She's a friend from school. She and her family moved to Alabama our junior year."

"Uh huh, but wouldn't that make her, what? Twenty-five? Twenty-six? Why would her father have any say in who she dates?"

"Why does that matter? We're going to right a wrong. Injustice, Fran. Injustice."

That was the magic word with Fran and it worked like a charm.

"Okay listen up Frannie, stop fidgeting with that, what are you doing?"

She finally snapped the clasps closed on her suitcase and tossed it, unceremoniously, into the trunk and slammed the top down.

"It's stuffed with sweaters."

"We're heading south you know, it isn't any colder there than it is here."

"Better to be too prepared than not," she said. Today she looked like a Christmas tree. Green coat with large red buttons, green knitted bobble hat, and, to match her buttons, a red tipped nose from the cold. With Christmas only a couple of weeks away, it was appropriate.

"You're right," I replied. "It is. Which is why we're not stopping. You hear me? Nine hours, we're driving nine hours, no stops to see a tic-tac-toe playing chicken or ostrich farm, no drum playing ducks, no fruit stands, and no demonstrations. If we see people marching or picketing we're not going to join them."

"Bu-"

"No. Afterward, once this is done, we can join all the protests and marches you want. Hell, I'll even spend time in jail with you if I have to. But not until after."

Fran's eyes lit up at that as she leaned against the trunk. Romanticizing sacrificing for a cause.

"You think we might get arrested?"

"I don't know what you think jail is like but I'm pretty sure it's not all warm fuzzy blankets and hot cocoa. And I'm probably better equipped to deal with what goes on in there than you are...or am I?"

She met my eyes and started to giggle.

In New York the year before, at the party, our conversation went a little differently this time.

"Evie, Evelyn! Some woman just asked me back to her hotel room."

"Really? Is she cute?"

She gave me a sly smile. "Yeah, actually, she is."

"Hey," I said, raising my drink, "your secret's safe with me, you're not married."

"Neither are you."

"Hey!" Judith shouted beside me, "that's only because we can't get married, don't go putting ideas in her head, go on, shoo, move it!" She turned Fran around by her shoulders and shoved her away.

Fran stumbled and then disappeared back into the haze of...let's call it cigarette smoke, and we'd lost track of her, just as before. But this time, when we entered her hotel room the following morning, she was sprawled across the bed, face down, on top of the covers instead of under them.

"Let's go Frannie, wake up, time to go, we have a plane to catch."

She twitched, then groaned, and then rolled over. Her shirt flapped open, all the buttons were undone, the last one was hanging by a thread.

"My head. Ugh...my head."

Judith lay down on the bed beside her and started rubbing at her temples while I started collecting socks, shoes, and shirts from the floor and stuffing them into her suitcase. Fran always did overdo it with the packing. I had to put my knee on it just to jam it closed. That's when I noticed a bra hidden in the folds of the bed cover.

"Since when do you wear red-"

Judith, one hand still rubbing at Fran's head, was waving at me with the other to catch my attention. When I looked up she had a childlike look of glee on her face and was pointing to Fran's neck.

"Is that a new trend you're starting up there Fran? Lipstick under the ear?"

"Huh? What?" Fran was still laying flat on her back, eyes closed.

"Along with wearing red hot lacy bras?"

Her eyes popped open.

"That's mine." (I didn't say it wasn't.) She jumped up from the bed, grabbed the bra from my hand, along with the suitcase, and started dragging it into the hallway. "Let's go!"

"You don't even have any shoes on! And who ripped your shirt open?"

"Shhhh! Ow!" She raised her hand and dug a finger into her temple, which made her shirt open wider.

Halfway down the hallway while clumsily trying to button her shirt, the overstuffed suitcase popped open and all her clothes tumbled out, a can of hairspray rolled to the stairway and started clunking down step by step.

"Damnit!"

"So what was she like?" Judith asked, chuckling, as she bent over to gather a pile of jeans.

"Shut up!"

"Come on, get in the car, you can tell me all about your little rendezvous on the way there."

I'm not saying it happened, I'm not saying it didn't, all I'm saying is that this time around Texas is going to have a senator with a slightly more interesting past.

"So why are we stopping in Montgomery and spending the night, when this place, what is it again?"

"Lynbrook."

"When this Lynbrook is only another hour and a half, or two hours away?" She slid into the passenger seat, while I sat behind the wheel.

I couldn't tell her the truth. That I didn't want to accidentally bump into my mother. Or who would eventually be my mother, or actually, who would never be my mother if things went according to plan. So I had to make something up.

"Because if Anne's father happens to see me there, he might get suspicious and then the whole plan falls apart, so we stay away until tomorrow morning. And we'll be leaving at four in the morning so no partying."

"Four?"

That was my plan. And I was feeling good about it. Because the whole thing seemed to be going exceptionally smoothly.

Sometimes we time travelers actually do catch a break.

Judith's last engagement before the end of the year had her skipping from Nag's Head in North Carolina, to Virginia Beach, and then two days in Atlantic City. Fran and I would be home without her even knowing we were gone. There would have been no way to explain to her my reason for wanting to go to Alabama. There would have been no way to explain to her the situation. How I knew this Anne girl. How I knew what was happening in her life, and how I knew what was going to happen on this specific date. I didn't like lying to her, but I really had no other choice.

The last time this same event, her being away and her mother wanting to tag along, which meant I had to stay home alone, had caused another argument. This time I could have kissed dear old Mom. I'm sure she would have loved that.

Getting Fran to come along was easy, but convincing her to keep it from Judith was a little harder.

She'd narrowed her eyes, looked at me sideways. "Why do I have to keep it from...hey, wait a minute. This doesn't have anything to do with another woman does it? Because if it does, you can count me out. And you bet your sweet bippy I'll be telling Judith about it too."

"Why the hell would I bring you along if that's what this was about?"

"Hm. Okay. You're right. But why the secrecy then?"

"Because. It might be a little dangerous. I don't want her worrying about it. And she might not let me go through with it if she knows."

Dangerous. (It wasn't.) But just like with the word injustice, that word intrigued Fran.

"So it's up to you, two people, being kept apart, just because-"

"I'm in."

"Yes, four in the morning and no complaints. We're already running late, we could have been halfway there by now if we'd left when I wanted to."

"Sorry, but I had to stop at Dwight's. He said he had something to ask me and I thought it might be something really important."

"And what did it turn out to be?"

"He wanted to borrow some Scotch tape to wrap presents with," she said, then slammed the car door shut harder than it needed to be.

Neither one of us was very talkative the first five or six hours of the drive. Which was unusual for Fran. But she seemed to be moping about Dwight and I had a lot on my mind as well.

This was it. Once I did this, that was it, there won't be any going back. I was going to be giving up an entire life and everything that went with it. Everyone I'd known, everyone I'd loved. I'd lived for thirty-eight years as Karen Stephens. Everything I'd done, every experience I'd had was now only going to exist entirely in my head. Leo the cat. My first kiss. The first time I successfully rode a bicycle without training wheels. Janice. Ericka Daniels was going to have her fumbling and awkward but sweet first time with someone else, not me. It had been the first time for both of us. Who's going to take my place? I felt a small stab of jealousy at the thought. Even though I hadn't thought about it, or her, for years, it didn't mean the memory wasn't special to me. Will I still be able to call them memories if the actual event never takes place?

When we stopped in Jackson, Mississippi for some burgers and fries and to switch seats, Fran seemed to be getting over her funk and tried to talk me into wandering around a bit but I shut that down. I couldn't let anything go wrong. Even though it was as simple a plan as they come. There really wasn't anything that could go wrong with it. Not that I could see. All I had to do was plant myself in front of the motel until William came along. If I had to ask everyone who came to the door what their name was, that's what I'd do. It didn't matter when my grandfather would be tipped off about him being back in town, I knew he'd checked into the motel and spent at least a little time there. That's all I needed, just a little time. And not even that much of it. All I needed to do was intercept him and tell him the situation. He could leave before being "roughed up", but not before telling me where he was headed so I knew where to send my mother afterward. Easy.

We arrived in Montgomery at ten o'clock at night and checked into a hotel. I didn't think I was going to be able to sleep but at least I could take a shower. That is if Frannie left me any hot water.

"Do you have the map?"

"What would I be doing with a map in the shower?" She emerged from the bathroom through a cloud of steam with one towel wrapped around her pink freckly body and one on top of her head. A white version of her old Marge Simpson hairstyle.

"I meant before, did you bring it with you? Put it in your purse? I can't find it."

She looked up at the ceiling, thinking. "No, when we stopped for gas the last time you stuffed it in the glove box."

"Great."

I pulled her pom-pom hat on over my hair, grabbed her coat, and headed out of the door and down the long corridor towards the stairs. Behind the last door I passed I could hear "Joy to the World" playing on the radio. That, along with the hallway, the orientation of the stairway, the Christmas wreath hung on the wall in front of me, gave me a sense of déjà vu. The dorm. Sophomore year in college. Only four of us had stayed over the holiday. Those of us who had no desire to go home, or who didn't really have a home. It sounds sad, but it really wasn't. We'd stayed up all night long, listening to carols playing on the radio, drinking heavily spiked eggnog, the four of us had even become "spit sisters" that night. No, not like that. None of us, even as inebriated as we were, wanted to slice open our fingers in the name of friendship so we'd just spit into our palms, and even then, it was just a small little "pttt", nothing disgusting, and then rubbed all of our palms together. I was still friends, or was, with two of those girls. Angela and Julie. It was one of my most treasured memories.

There was no question that I wasn't going to go through with it. I'd give up ten lifetimes to stay here, but giving something up is never easy.

I've heard it said that if you're unsure about a choice you're facing you should flip a coin. If you're happy with the result, then it's the right decision. If you're disappointed by it, it's not what you truly want to do. I didn't have a coin. But when I made it down the stairs, through the lobby and out into the parking lot, I knew the instant I saw him, that I was making the right choice. Because I was furious the choice was being taken away from me.

Mr. Smith was leaning against the hood of my car, just ten feet away from the stairs that led up to the lobby, arms crossed in front of his chest.

"I know what you're trying to do. And it's not going to work."

CHAPTER THIRTY-THREE

"Goddamnit! Don't you have anything better to do? There's a fucking war on, all these men are dying every fucking day, why don't you do something about that instead of this? Don't you think that's more important than keeping me from staying here?"

My yelling, my charging towards him, didn't seem to faze him at all. His posture remained the same. Calm. Aloof. Not a care in the world.

"I can't do anything about that," he said. He looked exactly the same, same age, same haircut, same non-expression on his face. Right down to the handkerchief in his suit jacket. Yet still blended in perfectly with his surroundings. The suit, short hair, black shiny shoes. He wore no coat, no gloves, and still his skin bore no signs that he was standing in forty degree weather. No red tipped nose or ears.

Less than a year. That's all I have left before I have to say goodbye. Again.

I take it back, I thought, I don't care about Ericka Daniels, I don't care about riding a bike or a kiss. I don't care about any of those memories, you can have them all. Please. Just let me stay here.

"This is a game to you isn't it? You knew all along and you waited until now to tell me. I could have stayed away from her. I could have stopped her from having to...God.

You knew that too didn't you? But you let me go on believing I could change it and now it's too late. Now she'll have to go through it all over again." No reaction. I shook my head in disgust, then walked past him. I opened my car door, found the map, slammed the door shut and started to walk away, back to the stairs that led up to the lobby.

"Where are you going?"

"I'm going back inside asshole, it's cold out here."

"Why do you need a map now?"

"What the hell do you care?" I started up the steps then stopped and turned back. "I can still do something, make someone's life a little better, even if it's not mine."

"No. You can't."

I should have stabbed him with a spork in that cafeteria.

"Fine, whatever," I said, and turned back around. Tomorrow morning I'd slip out of here before Fran woke up and head out to Lynbrook on my own. At this point I didn't care anymore. If he planned to plow a car into mine on my way there, so be it, at least there'd be a body and a reason for my leaving this time. She'd be able to grieve properly, then heal, and move on.

"She lied to you. And more importantly she got the date wrong."

I stopped on the third step and turned back. "Now what the hell are you talking about?"

"Your aunt. She lied to you. She's the one who told her father about William. Not one of his police friends or the desk clerk at the motel. He thought he could trust her. They got along fine before he left. Back when she thought it was just a harmless teenage crush. Before she knew they were seriously contemplating marriage."

Of course. Why did I not see that? How else would she have known the name of the motel and remember it after all these years? Because he'd told her the name of it. Because it had been eating away at her all those years. No wonder the story, retelling it, thinking about it agitated her so much. It was she who couldn't apologize to a dead person.

"I told you what you're trying to do won't work because it's over. He's been and gone. He arrived in Lynbrook this morning, found your aunt, told her where he'd be so she could relay the message. Only she told the wrong person. You know the rest. He's gone."

I sat on the step beneath me, feeling the cold of the concrete instantly penetrate through the fabric of my pants, but not caring. He'd known all along, what I had planned. Of course he did. It had been a doomed plan from the beginning. It always will be. I could come back twenty times, thirty, and I'd lose every single time. He would always know.

"But she said it was tomorrow, on my mother's birthday, she...why would she lie about that?"

"She lied about the betrayal, the date is just a faulty memory. She latched on to your mother's birthday because it was easier to remember. Forty years had passed by then. It happens."

"And you wait to tell me now, of course, once it's too late. It's not as if you could have told me a year ago could you? Because that wouldn't have been fun for you. Maybe you should have told me last night, you might have enjoyed that, seeing me race here to try to catch him and gotten your kicks when I arrived just a minute or two too late. Or gotten into a car wreck while speeding down the highway." I shook my head again then dropped it into my hands. If I didn't still have something to do, I'd tell him to take me back now. Just to get it over with, no use prolonging it. And maybe I should. What's the use of trying? If he won't let me change this, as insignificant as it is in the larger scheme of things, I could just forget about saving Judith's life.

Staying here was useless. I wouldn't be able to enjoy any of the time I had left. How could I wake up on Christmas morning and open presents with her and not break down? Eat

Christmas dinner with my parents? Celebrate another birthday? How? Knowing what was coming, for me, for her, for everyone. That my father will be dead in five years most likely because of me. That my mother will spend the rest of her life alone and with a broken heart.

There is nothing I can do about it.

I could hear the soles of Mr. Smith's shoes crunching the gravel beneath him as he made his way towards me.

"Do you remember what I told you? About not being able to break the rules?"

I didn't bother responding, didn't raise my head.

"Evelyn?"

"Yes! I do! Okay? I just figured...it doesn't matter. Nothing fucking matters now. Just. Leave me alone."

He didn't respond, and after a minute of silence, with my head still in my hands, I didn't even know if he was still standing in front of me. Maybe he'd done as I asked. Left me alone. I didn't hear him walk away but that meant nothing. I heard a couple of cars roll down the street. The lobby door opened behind me, I could feel the gust of warm air on my back. Two people, talking to each other. Their footsteps stopped, as did their voices, probably wondering what was wrong with me, sitting there in the cold, alone, my head buried in my hands against my bent knees. But not concerned enough to ask if I was okay. After a second or two their footsteps continued on down the steps and off into the parking lot. Merry Christmas to you too. I'm fine, thanks. When I felt tiny droplets of freezing rain start to fall onto the back of my neck I finally raised my head.

"About these rules."

"Oh, for...why are you still here? Can't you just leave me alone? Don't you have any compassion at all? Or is this part-"

"I said I couldn't break the rules. I never said you couldn't."

"What?"

"I can't influence your decisions, I can't make them for you, and I cannot directly change the course of your life. Only you can do that. You're here in Montgomery." He looked up at the sky, raised one arm to his side and spread his fingers out, catching a few raindrops in the palm of his hand. "So you've made your decision. A little information isn't going to hurt."

Looking back down, he pulled a card out of his jacket pocket from behind his handkerchief with two slender fingers and extended his arm toward me.

I took the card.

"Good luck."

For the first time since I'd met him, he smiled. Then he turned and walked away.

CHAPTER THIRTY-FOUR

"Frannie! Pack your junk! Let's go!"

The door banged open and slammed into the wall on the other side.

"What the heck! You scared the living- wait what? Pack?"

"Yes, or don't, I don't care. I'll buy you fifty outfits when we get home but right now we have to go."

"But we've only just got here, I thought-"

"There's been a change of plans, here." I took off her hat, smooshed it onto her head and then wrapped her coat around her over her pajamas. "You can change in the car."

She stood there for a few seconds, one eye covered by the knitted hat, then shrugged her shoulders and grabbed her suitcase.

Turns out I didn't need to be in such a rush. We arrived at the address Mr. Smith had provided within three hours, a little after three in the morning. But like Fran said, better to be too prepared. The house was dark, except for the twinkling multicolored lights running around the two front windows. The neighborhood was quiet. There was one lonely streetlight on at the end of the block. The rain had not followed us here, but the cold did. All the car windows were fogged up. I didn't want to run the engine, didn't want to attract any attention, so the heater was off. The last thing I needed was a wary neighbor calling the police. Fran was out, in the backseat, asleep, buried underneath a pile of clothes. I could see small puffs of vapor coming from one end of the pile with every breath she took.

The cold was enough to keep me from falling asleep as I sat there for four hours. I thought about Mr. Smith while I waited. He'd known all along. He'd known from the second I heard that song that day. He'd been trying to help. Should you make a decision like this right now? This rashly? You should think about things. Take a few days. Really think about things. But why did he have to go about it in such a roundabout way? Can't influence your decisions, can't make them for you...oh well. I'm not complaining. If all this works I'll never complain about anything ever again. Maybe I shouldn't have called him an asshole.

Finally, just when the sky started to turn from black to pale purple and then slowly to pink, a light went on in the house I'd been watching.

"Fran," I said, reaching behind me and nudging her. "Wake up, a light just came on, time to go."

"Right, right." Without complaint she threw the pants, jeans, and sweaters off of her and sat up, rubbing her eyes.

"You have all you need? The map, directions, address?"

"Mmm," she mumbled.

"Story?"

"Huh?"

"How are you going to get her here?"

"I don't know." She yawned, stretched her arms out.

"Frannie, come on, this is important."

"Are you doubting me? It's her birthday right?" She shrugged her shoulders. "I've got a present for her, just need to come with me, something like that."

I opened the door and got out, she hopped into the driver's seat and started the car.

"I won't let you down," she said, her voice and eyelids still heavy with sleep. She winked at me, shut the door, and pulled away from the curb.

The door at 5246 S. Lawrence Dr opened only a quarter of the way. The woman behind it, young looking, pretty, even this early in the morning and with not a stitch of make-up on and her hair in rollers, looked at me, then immediately raised her eyes over my shoulder toward the street.

"Can I help you?"

"I'm really sorry to bother you so early in the morning," I said, "I saw a light, I didn't want to knock until...may I please speak to William?"

She immediately looked suspicious. "You have the wrong house, I don't know any William."

"Please, there's no one with me," I said, before she could fully close the door. "I'm here on my own. I'll wait out here. Can you just please tell him I have something I need to tell him, about Anne? It's really important, ma'am, I wouldn't bother you otherwise."

She studied me for a few seconds, opened the door a little wider, then again, looked above my shoulder. This time she leaned forward and scanned the street, left and right. I instinctively turned to follow her eyes. There were several parked cars all along the curb but she must be familiar with them because she finally told me to wait where I was before closing the door. I could hear the click of a lock then her footsteps recede back into the house.

After only a minute or two she was back.

"Please, come in."

Compared to the frigid air I'd been sitting in all night, the small house felt almost too warm, like slipping into a bathtub when the water is just a tad too hot. Still, I welcomed the heat even though it immediately made me drowsy.

I followed behind the woman as she led me past the living room, into a darkened hallway and then to a door on the right of it. She nodded at me and walked back down the hall.

He was sitting up in a single bed with the curtains closed. A lamp shone from a nightstand beside him.

I'd been trying to picture him in my head now for years. The boy (or man, he'd be close to twenty-two now) who my mother could never get over. I'd pictured everything from a beautiful ethereal man, slender and tall with sculpted cheekbones, full lips, a sharp jawline and soft brown eyes the color of cognac, to a more rugged broad shouldered athletic type with muscular arms, deep set dark eyes and a scar running the length of his cheek. And everything in between.

And I was going to have to go on imagining. Because I couldn't tell what he looked like now, even standing in the same room with him. I could barely tell the color of his eyes. His left one was shut, the skin surrounding it shiny and puffy with a purple tint to it. His right iris was completely surrounded by a bright red, not even a hint of white. I could see raw pink flesh protruding from a gash on his swollen upper lip. There was a large knot on the side of his head above the black eye. Fresh blood was trickling down from one of his nostrils, which he dabbed at with a dark washcloth. And the way he was sitting, leaning slightly to the side above the waist, I knew he probably had many more bruises I couldn't see beneath his white t-shirt.

What an honorable and upstanding man my grandfather was.

"Is she okay?" he asked before I could even enter the room. I could tell he had an accent just like the woman who'd answered the door, but with his swollen mouth, it was hard to tell whether it was a true Alabama accent or not.

"Anne? Yes, she's fine," I said, even though I had no idea.

"Who are you? How do you know her?"

"I'm a friend. Look, I don't have much time before she gets here."

"She's coming here?" He jerked up straighter in bed, or

tried to. He grabbed at his ribs just underneath his left arm and winced, then winced again and touched his lip.

It made me grimace. "I'm sorry," I said, raising my hands. "I shouldn't have sprung that on you like that. But yes, she'll be here in however long it takes for my friend to drive there and back." I was only going to risk an hour. Lynbrook was only thirty minutes away. Or twenty, if you take into account the way Fran drives.

He put his hand back on his ribs and let out a deep breath.

"Maybe you should be at a hospital?"

"No, no ma'am, I'm okay."

"My name's Evelyn."

He shook his head. "She's not coming." He leaned his head back against the headboard. "He's not going to let her out of the house. Not after what just happened."

"You don't know my friend."

The sound of scraping wood on wood behind me made me turn my head. The woman was back, a chair in one hand, a cup of coffee in the other. She placed the chair next to me and handed me the cup.

"Thank you." Once again she nodded and left.

"My sister," William said, maybe seeing the question in my eyes.

I sat and sipped at the strong hot coffee.

"She'll be here. That is what you wanted isn't it? To be with her? She's not going to come all the way here only for you to tell her go back home are you?"

He stared me down.

"It's why I made the trip. Why else would I come all this way?"

Okay, stupid question.

"Where are you going to go?"

He took a long time to answer. Maybe sizing me up.

"How'd you know where to find me?"

I took a look at my watch.

"I don't mean to be rude, but that doesn't matter. I'm here now and I'm trying to help. So please, just listen."

He nodded, reluctantly, but he nodded.

"You don't have to tell me where you're planning on going, but I'm assuming it's not far from here. And thus, not far enough. He'll find you. Both of you, and when he does it'll be far worse than broken ribs you'll have to contend with. You know that. You are planning on marrying her?"

"As soon as I can."

"Then you're going to have to leave the country."

He tried to scoff but the pain in his ribs didn't allow it.

"He's a police officer, not an FBI agent."

I sighed. I didn't want to have to bring up anything that was going to make me sound unhinged but there was no getting around it.

"It's not just that. Your birthday is September 14th isn't it?"

He blinked the one eye he could. "How do you know that?"

I shook my head. Doesn't matter. "You drew lottery number one right? You need to get out of the country, go to Canada. Because you're going to Vietnam. And you're not coming back."

Again he took a good long while to stare at me, his chest going up and down, hitching with every breath. I took a look at my watch again. Forty minutes left. I had to hurry this up.

"Look, I know how it sounds-"

"My grandmother said the same thing," he said. "A month before the lottery. She, uh," he dabbed at his nose again, catching a fresh trickle of blood before it had a chance to reach his lip. The corner of his mouth twitched. "She has...dreams. Dreams that sometimes come true."

In another life I would have said grandma either had a few nuts and bolts coming loose or   that someone should mark the liquor bottles in her house, but not in this one. In this one I silently thanked her.

"Take this." I handed him an envelope from my purse. When he opened it and saw what was inside, he shook his head, and tried to shove it back into my hand.

"I can't take that."

"It's only money. I have plenty. I'm not boasting or anything, just, please, it won't be missed, take it. I also have a friend, her name is Peg, she lives in Canada, it's all set up. All the information you need is in that envelope. You and Anne can stay with her until you find a place of your own. This," I said, taking the envelope from his hand and shaking it, "should be plenty to get you started." I laid it on the bed beside him.

He left it there but still shook his head.

"I have friends," he said. "Two of them are over there right now. My brother went last year. He died over there. I'm not leaving the country."

"I'm sorry."

He nodded.

I did not know about his brother and I didn't feel right about pushing but I was running out of time.

"William, look, I know all about hard choices. I'm not making light of any of it and normally I would not advocate breaking the law or shirking duties but this is...if you've made up your mind about it, there's nothing I can do about that, but if you have, then you need to walk away. From her. You need to let her go."

"Why?"

"Because if you don't she'll follow you to wherever you want to go. You're going to take her away, away from everyone she knows, away from her home, and then you're going to go off to Vietnam and leave her alone. Even if you don't believe me, that I know...in fact, forget I even said that. You know. Your lottery number is one. You are going to be drafted, you know that. And you know that there's a real possibility you'll die over there. What then? What is she going to do if that happens? You think her family is going to welcome her back with open arms? What is she going to do all alone?"

He looked away and dabbed at his nose again.

"Look, I can't stop you from doing what you feel you need to do but please, for me, for your grandmother, and most of all for Anne, if you take her away, postpone it. Once you get your draft notice. Do anything to postpone it for a month, or two weeks. A month is better."

It's all I could do. I couldn't slap handcuffs on him, drive him to Canada and keep him locked up in a dark room until March of 1973 could I? If he postponed it, he wouldn't be in the same exact place at the exact same time. Maybe he dies anyway, but what can I do?

He turned back to me then placed one hand on the envelope and tapped at it with a finger.

"Will you please think about it?"

"My brother."

"Going there won't bring him back."

He nodded.

Fran did as I asked. She honked three times as she pulled my car up to the curb outside the house. I took my empty cup to the small kitchen connected to the living room, I thanked William's sister for her hospitality and then trained my eyes on the linoleum floor as she and Fran stepped into the house. It's why I'd asked Fran to come along with me on this trip. It was hard enough letting go. Seeing her would have made it even harder.

William, against his sister's wishes, got out of bed and made it to the end of the hallway.

Eighteen years old, younger than me by seven years.

Remarkable. And even more remarkable was hearing her gasp and begin to cry when she saw him. The only glimpse I got of her was of her back. Her dark brown hair in a ponytail, one of her hands was on his waist, the other gently placed on the side of his face.

Fran and I slipped out, got in the car, and drove away before any questions could be asked. She said she was your friend, no, the redhead, Fran, said she was a friend of yours.

Fran drove and never asked me a single question. She didn't ask the obvious. You said she was a friend from school. How could that be? She's too young. She didn't talk at all until we were well into Louisiana.

"Are you okay?"

I nodded silently.

A long while back, years and years ago, long before I'd walked into that cafeteria, I'd seen a show. One of those true crime ones. This one was about a grown woman who'd turned her mother in to the police. The crime her mother had committed had happened decades earlier when this woman and her younger sister were still only children but she remembered it, and all that preceded it with great detail. How both she and her sister had suffered extreme abuse at the hands of their mother. Essentially loaned out to strange men on many nights for money. They were no more than ten and eleven years old at the time. They were beaten and starved. Deprived of basic medical care. She bore scars from long ago knife slashes and cigarette burns. I noticed a silver line underneath her bottom lip as if her tooth had at one time cut right through the skin. She told the sad and almost incomprehensible story of how her mother eventually ended up killing her sister. Not intentionally, but cruelly nonetheless, by making her sit in a bathtub filled with cold water for three days straight in the middle of a Maine winter with the window cracked open, all because she'd accidentally dropped and broken a glass on the floor. And still, this woman admitted, even though she'd turned her mother in, even though she knew what a monster she was, she loved her. She still loved her, because she was her mother, wasn't she? No matter what, she was her mother. Compared to that woman, my mother, well...I only sat in my seat, wiped at my eyes a few times along the way, and Fran said nothing.

CHAPTER THIRTY-FIVE

It was a waiting game after that. Eleven months. I didn't know if it would work or not. Who's to say I don't end up with some other random couple as my parents? What if I wake up August 12, 2010 in Japan? Or in Switzerland? What if that happens and Mr. Smith never shows up again? How horrible would that be? Not that Japan and Switzerland aren't lovely but I think I've had more than enough to deal with to last for a lifetime. This lifetime. That's all I wanted.

One thing I was sure of, Karen Stephens wasn't going to be conceived on the night of November 14, 1970. I'd been in touch with Peg. William and Anne had arrived at her house three days after Fran and I left Alabama. Anne is still there, William is not. As of now, November 1970, he has been in Vietnam for a month. But he left for basic training three weeks after he would have had he not gone to Canada. I hope it's enough.

I'd prepared just in case. A trust and three trustees, can't be too careful. Four keys to four safety deposit boxes, all with a single envelope inside of them with the same message in each, to be delivered to Judith a week before that day in 1991. Fran has one. And even though she thought I was nuts she agreed to deliver it to Judith when the time came. "In twenty-one years? You want me to keep this thing for twenty-one years? Then give it to Judith. Is this some sort of scavenger hunt thing?"

"Yes. Yes, it is. Just hold on to it, and don't forget."

She'll probably forget. Or lose the key.

Or, more than likely, if I do disappear, she'll give the key to Judith long before the twenty-one years is up, thinking it might hold a clue as to where I'd gone, and that's okay. So long as she gets it. Even if she gets the message way too soon, it's not something that'll slip your mind is it? Someone mysteriously disappears but leaves behind a cryptic message about not getting on a plane on a specific day? That date will stay with you, no matter what. And if it didn't, she'd get three more keys closer to the actual date. Again, I'm not sure how that works, though I was told it would be fine so long as there was plenty of money in the trust to keep both the lawyer's fees and the boxes paid for, which it will, there's enough money to keep the rent up for fifty years. But what happens when I'm declared dead? Do the lawyers open them then? Again, so what? That date will stick. I was pretty confident that if I do wake up, this time in my living room in 2010, that there will be a sixty-five year old Judith Paige walking around when I do. And that'll be that. No more. I can't make her go through it all over again. I was done.

There was no argument this time. We never argued about her mother.

"Are you sure you don't want me to stay home? I have the feeling something's bothering you. You haven't been acting like yourself these past few days."

"I'm sure," I told her. How horrible would that be? If she were there when it happened, if it happened. Would I fade out? Or just pop! Disappear? No. She had to be gone.

"And my mother insisting she come along with me isn't what's upsetting you?"

"I'm not upset, I'm really not. You go, you and your mother have a great time. I'll be here…"

"Okay," she said, checking her watch. "I better get going."

She popped one more spoonful of ice cream into her mouth before she started to rise out of her seat. I pulled her back by her wrist and kissed her, never mind the couple heading to the door with their cones in hand.

She kissed me back, I could taste the peppermint on her lips, felt the cold of her tongue, before she pulled away and smiled. She turned towards the door but it was already closing behind the elderly man and woman, they didn't see anything. Maybell's son, on the other hand, I saw, quickly turned his head and started wiping away at the glass counter.

"It's only a quick trip, what are-"

"I love you Judith, I just want you to know that. These past six years have been incredible. I never thought I could love anyone as much as I love you. Whatever happens from here on out, you have to always remember that."

"What do you mean? What's going to happen?"

"Nothing." She was starting to look fearful so I tried my best to smile. It was tough. This whole week had been tough. How do you not just grab a hold of someone and not let them go?

"You're going to go to Illinois and have a great time, you're going to sing your songs, just like always, and then you're going to come home. That's all. I just don't tell you enough, how much I love you. How happy you've made me."

She didn't look convinced but she still followed me as I got up and walked with her to the door. I squeezed her hand one last time before she pushed the door open and walked out.

I watched her this time. I watched her get in her car, pull away from her parking spot, next to mine, then wave at me before she disappeared into traffic.

I remained at the door for a long time, staring at the now empty parking space, hoping that wasn't the last time I'd ever see her.

After calming Fran down on the phone, I thought of reminding her again about the key and the promise but that might raise suspicions, reminding her of it the night before I disappear, if I do. So instead I told her to remember that Dwight was only trying to protect himself, not hurt her, and said goodbye. Then, not wanting to prolong anything, I turned out the bedside lamp, leaned my head back on my pillow and closed my eyes.

Whatever's going to happen is going to happen. I no longer had any control over any of it.

CHAPTER THIRTY-SIX

A cold drop of water landed on my forehead. Then another on my cheek. Behind my eyelids, darkness. Dark clouds. Drizzle. Back to the cemetery.

How much time? How much time is it going to take me to get over her? How many years is it going to take for me to end up in a crumpled car on the highway? Will I ever be able to play one of her songs and enjoy it? Will I ever be able to watch that video and smile at the memories of that day? That morning? Or was it all going to turn into hateful bitterness? What was I going to name all of my twelve cats?

Another cold drop of rain landed on my lips, and stayed there for only a second before I felt it licked away and I opened my eyes.

"Judith."

She was leaning over the bed. The room was still dark, there was only a faint glow coming through the open doorway. She dipped the tips of her fingers into the glass of water she was holding and giggled as she flicked water at me again.

"What are you doing here? You didn't go? What time is it? Please say you didn't come back-"

"Yes, I did, I thought you'd be happy to see me."

"No, Judith, no," I said, beginning to panic. "You have

to...wait, five?" I rubbed at my eyes, checked the alarm clock again, ten after five.

"It's five in the morning? On Sunday? It's Sunday? November 15th?"

She set the glass of water down on the nightstand, next to the alarm clock, then put her hands on her hips.

"Yes, it is. Did you and Fran go out drinking last night? Is that it? You drank so much you can't remember what day it is?"

"It really is Sunday?" I asked, sitting up.

"Yes, Mom and I caught a ride with Harry, in his new plane. She thought it was a hoot but I was a nervous wreck the whole way. Those tiny propeller things are scary. Anyway, I was worried about you, but now I'm beginning to think I shouldn't-"

Many years ago it was she who held on to me the way I held her now. When she'd learned that being a star isn't all it's cracked up to be. When all she really wanted to do was to be with the people she loved, the people who really mattered to her. To be home.

CHAPTER THIRTY-SEVEN

February 2010, Leyfant

From my spot on the couch I could hear the sound of the door sweep sliding against the tile as she opened the back door and then back again as she shut it. The fire crackling in the fireplace wavered for a second as the cold air hit it, then settled back down.

I put my laptop to sleep, closed it, and set it down in front of me, on our coffee table.

It had been years since I checked up on them. Anne and William Blunt. An unremarkable but happy couple who live in Michigan, three grown kids, six grandkids. The latest picture, an old one one of the grandkids must have scanned and uploaded to her Facebook page. A family in the early eighties standing in front of a heavily decorated Christmas tree. Huge permed frizzy hair. A young boy holding a ColecoVision box and grinning widely, showing off his missing teeth. Anne with one hand on the shoulder of a little girl, the other arm wrapped around her husband's waist. She has her head tilted up at him, her mouth open in a smile or a laugh, as if he'd just told her a joke. His right arm is around her shoulders, his left is holding an infant dressed in a green and red striped onesie.

It must have been taken right around the time my father passed away, in 1982. I'd guessed that my mother would have had more time with him had I never disappeared and I was right. I wish it had been longer than eight years but I was content knowing that those years had been happy ones, not grief-stricken anxiety-ridden ones. She still passed three years ago, just as before, but not before enjoying a twenty-one year marriage to a wonderful man.

It was also right around that time that Sharon Sauer met her current partner. The woman she's been with now for twenty-seven years. Maybe it's time for me to stop feeling guilty about that.

"I found Fran's shoe." Judith put her hand on my shoulder and leaned over to kiss the top of my head. "It was caught up in one of the back hedges."

She's sixty-four now. Her once light brown hair is now entirely white, with a few grey highlights. But coupled with those amazing green translucent eyes, it makes me wonder why she didn't dye it that color twenty years ago.

She held the rhinestone-studded sandal out to me.

"What do you want me to do with it?"

"I don't know, mail it back to her?"

"It's a shoe. Big time senator, she can afford another shoe."

I stood, took the shoe from her hand and went to toss it into the coat closet.

"When is she coming back?" Judith asked as I made my way back down the entryway. She was still standing by the couch, running her hand along the back of it. "I miss her."

"September, I think, I'm not sure," I answered her as I stopped at the edge of the room and leaned against the wall. "Ask Dwight, he's the one who counts down the days until she's back in town."

She looked up from the couch and smiled. "You know the exact date she'll be back. Don't lie." She knew me well. Of course she did, after all, we'd been together for almost forty-six years now. Or fifty-two. Or fifty-eight. It all depends on how you look at it.

"September 9th," I admitted. I missed her too.

And Judith knew it.

"Maybe we should take a trip to Washington in a few weeks. It's been a while since we've been."

"Yeah, maybe." We both smiled at the thought, but only briefly. It never got any easier, going there. It was difficult for the both of us, for the same reason in ways, for a different reason in others. That wall. There were two names missing from it. William Blunt and George Kellem. But there were others that weren't. Plenty of others. Michael, Lewis, Andrew, Pete, and so on. Carl Paige, Judith's brother. I didn't know. It was five months after that morning in the middle of November that her parents got the news. I couldn't save him. I couldn't save them all.

"Well," Judith said, shaking her head, "anyway, we can decide...later..."

"Sure."

She walked around the couch and sat as I made my way over to the entertainment center. A record sleeve had fallen from one of the shelves onto the floor.

"Anyway, did I mention," she said, pointing towards the laptop on the coffee table, "I was contacted by someone yesterday, a representative from...I think it was a pharmaceutical company." She looked up towards the ceiling. "No, can't remember the name, but they want to use one of my songs for one of their commercials."

"Novmentis," I said, as I placed the sleeve on an empty shelf.

She turned towards me. "What?"

"That's the name of the drug isn't it?"

She gave me the same look she'd given me on the evening of October 18, 1991, when we heard about the crash. I tried everything to keep it on the ground, everything. But the pilot, young and fearless and brash, with that no-one-tells-me-what-to-do attitude only shook his head dismissively. Who's the pilot here? It's clear out. Perfect flying conditions. I did manage to talk two people out of the trip but I couldn't save the pilot. Or his one passenger. I'd never stop feeling guilty about that.

"Yes, I think that was it," she said, slowly. "But I told them no."

A large knot in one of the burning logs popped in the fireplace. It sounded almost like a tray hitting a hard tiled floor. I heard, all around me, the faint hum of murmuring, the sound of a roomful of people talking and eating. Forks and knives. My body went cold. "Karen?" A man's voice, or the ghost of one.

"What? Why?"

"Oh, you know what'll happen. Don't you remember, what was it, seven or eight years ago? When they used that one song, the one that only charted at number fifty-four in '67, for that movie. All those calls to perform it again. My stage days are over. I'm not getting back up there."

"Then turn them down. I'll take the calls, I'll tell them no. You have to say yes. You have to let them use it."

After all I'd been through, I still didn't know how it worked. Officially Karen Stephens does not exist. Believe me, I checked. But she did, at one time. And the only reason I was standing here in this room, at the age of sixty-five as Evelyn Bryant, was because she'd walked into a cafeteria one day in July of 2010 and heard that song. But what happens if it's not playing? What happens if, in some parallel universe, Karen Stephens walks into a cafeteria five months from now and instead of one of Judith's songs it's one of Lesley Gore's? What happens then?

She needs to hear it.

I lived thirty-eight years as Karen Stephens. I have now lived fifty-two years as Evelyn Bryant, if you count the six years I relived. (Not taking into account the twenty-six I have no recollection of.) That's a total of ninety years. I'm done.

Although, I thought, thinking of the Saturn and Sun. The parking lot, the chain smoking woman behind the window. That green and purple dress, twenty years old, walking in to see Judith, a sweet nineteen-year-old girl in a flip hairdo, the rest of her long life ahead of her. What would be so bad about that? Doing it all over again?

"Evelyn?" Judith had risen from the couch and was walking over to me.

"Yes. Tell them yes. Please." I wasn't going to mess with things I didn't understand.

"You'll take the calls? Are you sure? They badger, you know. You'll put up with all that for me?"

I took her hand in mine. "You have no idea what I'd be willing to do for you."

She was looking at me curiously.

"Does this have anything to do with the plane? With pocket phones?" It made me laugh. The name had stuck. Everyone teases her about it. She has never referred to them as cell phones.

"Yes," I told her.

"Will you ever tell me about it?"

"Maybe. When I'm ninety-eight and I won't have to sit in a mental institution for too long after you commit me."

She smiled and shook her head.

"Is there anything else?" she asked. "Will I have to avoid getting on a train in five years?" She was teasing, but not entirely.

"No, nothing. The future is as mysterious to me as it is to you," I answered truthfully if not just a little uneasily. I couldn't be sure, could I? Not until July 9th had come and gone. But she didn't need to know that.

She nodded then looked down towards the turntable beside us and the record sitting on it.

"Did you put that there?"

I looked.

"No."

"Is that an original?" She bent over to have a closer look. "It is. Didn't Ralph's granddaughter break the last one we had? Did you order that?"

"No, I didn't."

I took a look at the plain white record sleeve I'd just picked up from the floor. Stamped at the bottom of it, just on the edge, was "Mr. Smith's Vintage Records".

Cute.

"Then how-"

"Doesn't matter."

The turntable was new. I'd rather have the one we used to have, the one that used to sit in the living room of that tiny rental house so long ago, but you can't have everything.

I set the needle down on the record, pushed the power button, and the first few beats of the song came from the speakers. The same song that reached out to me and brought me back to her all those many years ago.

"One Day You'll Leave Me"

I took her hand and placed it on my waist and pulled her to me. She tilted her head and smiled as she slid her hand around to the small of my back and then rested her head on my shoulder. I slipped my own arms around her and we began to dance.

Yes, one day I would leave her. Or she would leave me.

But not just yet.

We still had plenty of time.

Printed in Great Britain
by Amazon